FICTION   Lutz, John,
LUTZ   1939-

          Dancing with the
          dead.

DANCING
WITH THE
DEAD

DANCING

WITH THE

DEAD

JOHN LUTZ

ST. MARTIN'S PRESS
NEW YORK

Design by Glen M. Edelstein

Library of Congress Cataloging-in-Publication Data

Lutz, John, 1939–
     Dancing with the dead / John Lutz.
        p. cm.
     "A Thomas Dunne book."
     ISBN 0-312-07693-2
     I. Title.
   PS3562.U854D34   1992
   813'.54—dc20   92-2997
                                                                    CIP

First Edition: June 1992

10 9 8 7 6 5 4 3 2 1

For Suzanne and David Nyemchek

The class of the ballroom dance world, on and off the floor

*In a sense the victim shapes and molds the criminal. . . . To know one
we must be acquainted with the complementary partner.*

—*Hans von Hentig,* The Criminal and His Victim

The author wishes to emphasize that the Romance Dance Studio and its instructors and students are purely fictitious, and to express gratitude to the many people who helped to make this novel possible. With very special thanks to:

Steve and Liz Brockman of Just Dancing
Stan and Nicole Collins of U Can Dance
Everyone at the Just Dancing and the St. Louis Arthur Murray studios

DANCING
WITH THE
DEAD

1

It had been a mad dance. He'd pressed his body against hers, backing her against the tall chain-link fence. Behind her the Mississippi ran like a black artery in the moonlight. Terror radiated through her body and drained it of strength, muddled and paralyzed her brain. She could hear him softly chanting her name: "Danielle, Danielle, Danielle . . ." With a breathless reverence, as if it were part of a religious ritual. She'd never dreamed he might be capable of this. Never!

She saw the glint of moonlight on the knife and struggled to speak. His body drew away from hers and the blade flashed sideways, leaving a cold trace of steel along her throat. Odd, she was sitting on the ground now, resting her back against the sagging fence. Something warm lay in her lap. He was smiling down at her, still holding the knife, and she understood that her throat was cut and he'd backed away from her before the flash of the knife so he wouldn't get blood on his clothes. She tried to plead with him but couldn't suck in air. Her mouth formed a rictus and she could feel the useless bellows action of her lungs. Her hands fluttered to her throat and she touched the horrible horizontal gap, and her heart exploded with panic. Yet a tiny cold part of her brain remained amazingly calm and objective. Music floated from inside the building as her heels beat wildly against the blacktop, out of time, she noticed inanely, feeling herself drifting, weakening.

She was aware of him pushing her the rest of the way down, then rolling her body on its side so her blood ran along a slight incline toward the river, away from him. Very efficient, he was, as if he'd done this many times before and had plenty of practice.

Her cheek pressed numbly against the hard ground, she watched the dark spreading flow with a sad detachment, letting its slow current draw her into greater darkness.

2

She heard a shriek and she was falling.

Two . . . three—*awake!*

Mary reached out a shaking hand, groping for the alarm clock. Its intermittent electronic scream was shredding her brain like jagged glass. Finally she found the clock, fumbled with its cool plastic case, and managed to silence it.

Reaching for it made her side ache where Jake had hit her last night. Pain zapped through her like high voltage, and she wondered if he'd cracked one of her ribs. It had happened once before, a year ago, and she was sure the doctors in emergency at Incarnate Word hadn't believed her story about slipping and falling on the ice. Not a lot of imagination in that one.

Well, it wasn't their business anyway. Her business. Hers and Jake's. Intimate as her dreams.

Mary Arlington had dreamed again she was flying. Soaring near the lovely domed ceiling of a limitless room, almost touching pure curved whiteness, one . . . two . . . three, to waltz time, two . . . three. . . . Floating in someone's arms. It wasn't clear whose. Far below, faces strained upward, pale ovals with dark, staring eyes and gaping mouths, watching her trace elegant patterns whose lines might extend into eternity.

But morning had arrived. She worked her way up so she was leaning back in bed, supported on her elbows, then she slowly swiveled her body and dropped her legs into space, struggling until she was sitting slumped on the edge of the mattress. More pain. She heard herself groan, but the rib didn't act up. Hey, the day was starting right.

Mary moved her hands slowly and gingerly beneath her nightgown, gliding fingertips over smooth flesh, seeking sources of pain.

They'd argued last night about the latest of Jake's unexplained absences. This one had lasted three days and two nights. He'd told her he'd spent the time at the big Victorian house three of his buddies leased in the suburb of Webster Groves, and she knew he did go there at times, paying rent for one of the upper bedrooms. What he had no explanation for was the long-term airport parking ticket stub she'd found in his pocket. This time maybe he'd left St. Louis, not just driven a few miles to Webster Groves.

Jake had worked himself to a high pitch of anger. Then he'd beaten her with the flat of his hand and then his fists.

This morning, early, he'd kissed her ear and whispered he was sorry, he loved her, he'd gotten carried away with the physical stuff. He'd make it up to her, he promised, he really would. Uh-huh.

"Don't come back," she'd told him, her voice hoarse from sleep. "Not this time!"

"Sure," he said, and kissed her again. "Whatever you say, Mary. Don't I usually try to make you happy?"

Only wanting him to leave, she hadn't answered. Finally she heard and felt him roll out of bed. The bedsprings moaned as if sharing her pain.

She'd lain awake listening to the roar of the shower, then to Jake thumping around her apartment getting dressed. He was supposed to meet some guys from work this morning. To go fishing, he'd said. Jake and his buddies; sometimes they were like a living beer commercial.

When she'd heard the door *snick!* close behind him, she'd fallen asleep again.

That was two hours ago, and here she sat with a numb mind and aching body.

Jake would be guilt-plagued, remorseful even in the way he moved. For days he'd loathe himself for what he'd done, an object of scathing self-pity. And, in Mary's eyes, a man pinned by his agony, writhing in pain as intense as hers even if it wasn't physical.

Others didn't understand, she knew, and wondered why she stayed with Jake. But the abuse had grown gradually, creeping up on her love, engulfing it and leaving it whole and somehow undamaged, like the tender walnut, safe within its confining yet protective shell.

That was the problem, she loved Jake.

And she had no one else.

But she knew she had to be strong. This time she meant it, he wasn't coming back. She wouldn't let him.

She drew a deep breath, without pain, and stood up, leaning with a hand on the headboard for a moment while her dizziness passed. She had to leave for work in half an hour, and she had a dance lesson right after supper.

She hoped like hell she could move okay. Tonight was tango.

3

They knew Jonas Morrisy in the parish. The honest merchants, the con artists, the whores, the gays, the blues and Cajun musicians, and the grifters; they knew him and played straight with him, because he played straight with them. If he said he'd crack skull if they didn't cooperate, he meant it, always. He'd been a beat patrolman there for twelve years before making sergeant, ridden in a two-man patrol car for five more years before becoming plainclothes. Now, at fifty, he was a New Orleans P.D. homicide lieutenant. The cop everyone had known twenty years ago hadn't changed: He was tough, shrewd, and persistent. And still honest.

He sat now behind his wide, cluttered desk in his office in Homicide, a sloppily dressed, shambling man sucking on a meerschaum pipe he never lit. His gray eyes were as bright and calculating as when he was a rookie, even if now there were crow's feet at their corners. His hair was almost completely gray but still thick and unruly, and his lower lip still jutted determinedly. Perched on an off-center nose, the no-nonsense black-framed glasses suggested he was a man of decisiveness and violence. Thick and scarred knuckles added to the impression.

In his big hands he was holding a copy of the medical examiner's report on the Verlane woman. Detective Sergeant Waxman, who'd just handed him the report, was standing in front of Morrisy's desk, neatly dressed as usual, his tie knot the size of a pea, his suitcoat buttoned despite the river delta heat and humidity that the air-conditioner wasn't quite coping with today.

"Something, eh, Lieutenant?" Waxman said. He was a lean, handsome man with sleekly combed red hair, built for the expensive clothes he wore. Sometimes Morrisy wondered where he got the money to dress so well, but he never asked.

Morrisy grunted and read on. Something, all right. There'd been so much blood at the crime scene he hadn't realized the extent or nature of the injuries. Except for the horrendous slash across the victim's throat.

"Weird, huh?" Waxman asked, still searching for a reaction.

Morrisy laid the file folder on his desk and looked out the window at the buildings across the street. Fat gray clouds were building up. Rain clouds. Rain this time of year wouldn't do a thing to break the heat, only add steam to the recipe for misery. He said, "We don't tell the husband the worst part, or the media."

"I'm assuming hubby might already know," Waxman said. "A certain bell doesn't ring with that guy."

"Maybe. But we need to keep this from him just in case, and keep the media in the dark on it, 'specially those TV jerkoffs. That way it'll be our card to play when we bring in a suspect."

Waxman's heavily lidded eyes flicked to the folder on the desk, back to Morrisy. "I been in Homicide a long time, Lieutenant, and I never seen that kinda thing."

"That's why it's such a good hole card." It was standard procedure in a homicide investigation to hold back a few pieces of crucial or defining evidence that only the police and the killer would know. It made it easier to obtain accurate statements and helped nail down convictions.

"The media'd love it," Waxman said.

Morrisy nodded. "Wouldn't they?"

"They already like the fact she was out doing the light fantastic with men she barely knew, dressed the way she was, maybe asking for it, you know?"

"It doesn't hurt that they like it," Morrisy said. This was still the deep South, and a prime piece like Danielle Verlane out slutting it up even though she was married, then paying for her transgressions with her life, made especially juicy copy. Straight out of the Old Testament, far as the news media were concerned. They could moralize their guts out over this one. And if they knew the rest, the nightmare part, it would really play like crazy. Morrisy prided himself on being adept when it came to dealing with news people, using *them* instead of the other way around. He was determined that would be the way it went on this case. "Any word on the prints?"

"Too smudged to mean anything, lab report says."

Morrisy leaned back in his chair and sucked air through his dead pipe, making a soft whistling sound. Though he hadn't fired up the old meerschaum since his doctor had warned him to stop smoking six months ago, he could still smell and taste tobacco when he breathed through the tooth-dented stem. And in his mind he could still smell, and even taste, the thick coppery stench of blood at the Verlane murder site. The nicotine smell helped to make that less repellent, had allowed him to eat a big breakfast of eggs and grits this morning.

He thought about the husband, Rene. Maybe Waxman was right and the guy was good for the murder. Important guy, but not so important he was too big for Morrisy to go after. Just the right size, in fact. Plenty of publicity, but not much career liability. If the press could be played right. Used.

Which it could be. Oh, yeah, it could be, all right.

"Bring me the statements of the customers in the lounge," he said to Waxman, "then we're gonna go talk to some people."

Waxman flashed his handsome smile and strode out the door into the squad room. Morrisy knew he'd order the unmarked car brought around on his way to get the computer printouts of the witness statements. He could count on Waxman. They made an efficient team because they thought a lot alike.

That's what it would take to nail the bastard that did the Verlane bitch, Morrisy thought, teamwork. This was no ordinary murder.

But then, he was no ordinary cop. He'd proved that over and over.

He could prove it again.

4

Nose follows toes.

Her instructor, Mel Holt, had told Mary to think of that when she danced in promenade position. Mel was leading her through tango promenade turns now, gliding over the smooth wood floor. Her back was straight, pelvis thrust forward, knees slightly bent; she was tight up against Mel, and her body responded to his every move as he drove forward with long, stalking steps: slow, slow, quick, quick, and sloooow. She closed her frame, spinning neatly to face him on the second slow count and trailing a leg, her skirt swinging gracefully. She loved to dance, but she especially loved to tango.

Her left side had ached at first, where Jake hit her too hard, even though she'd stood for almost half an hour under a hot shower before coming to the studio. But after warming up with swing and fox-trot before the lesson, the pain went away and she was moving loosely and in time to the music. Dead on the beat.

At work, Victor the realist had noticed the darkness beneath her left eye this morning. He shook his head, causing his round, wire-rimmed glasses to slip down on the bridge of his nose and give him his nerdy Ben Franklin look. He knew Jake must have been at her again. Victor should mind his own business.

As Mel led her through a series of turns, she glanced in the mirrors lining the studio walls. In Mel's arms was a medium-height, dark-haired woman with narrow, symmetrical features, delicate yet not without strength. She was still attractive though with a gauntness she feared might soon take on a pinched, hard quality. Her lean body moved elegantly (if she did say so herself), bending back gracefully now in a *corte.* Mel closed the step and swept her toward the center of the floor. If he'd noticed the bluish circle beneath her eye, caked now with disguising makeup, he hadn't said anything.

But Mel wouldn't. No one at Romance Dance Studio would. That sort of comment wasn't meant to be part of this world.

Among other things, what students bought here was a carefully controlled alternate reality.

Promenade turn again. She snapped her head around. The head was so important in tango.

For an instant she was again staring at herself in the mirror, but this time caught by surprise, as if she were a stranger noticed gazing through a window. Her mouth was set in a grim slash of concentration, her dark eyes burning. Then she composed her features, the way people do before mirrors. Mel—tall, loose-jointed Mel—was smiling absently as he drew her even closer and whirled her into another turn, then a flare.

When she was dancing she forgot about Jake, about everything but music and motion. And Mel. They'd been dancing together for almost two years, and she sensed his leads sometimes even before he began them. The world outside the studio was chaotic and threatening, but here, inside, were design and beauty and the ages-old marriage of pattern and grace.

The Latin music came to an abrupt stop. Something with a loud, simple four-four beat began to play. Kevin, another instructor, and his student June, began doing triple-time swing over by the stereo tape deck.

"Oh well, time's up anyway," Mel said, stepping away from Mary.

She knew he was right. The wall clock indicated her hour lesson actually should have ended five minutes ago.

As she walked off the dance floor with Mel she noticed Kevin leading June, who was a fifty-year-old widow, through a series of underarm turns. June had regained her figure with a liquid diet and looked like a slender teenager spinning out to the end of Kevin's reach, then rock-stepping back into dance position. Mary figured June had signed up for lessons so she could meet men. Well, nothing wrong with that.

"We got a lesson booked for Thursday?" Mel asked, as they stepped onto soft carpet.

Mary nodded. "Seven o'clock."

He grinned, handsome and easy and so at home in the world. "See you then."

As he started to walk away, he turned; he even did that as if he were dancing. "By the way, you planning on competing in Miami next month? We could still pencil you in for extra lessons and get you ready."

"No, not Miami," Mary said. She had a well-paying job, but it was formidably costly to compete. "Maybe Ohio in November," she told Mel, who was standing there looking as boyishly hopeful as if he'd just asked her to the prom.

He seemed so crushed. "Aw, I'm sorry you can't make the Dancerama in Miami—" he suddenly brightened—"but we'll start working to get ready for Ohio. Can I consider you committed to go?"

Mary shook her head no, a little flustered. She had to build her savings if she was going to the Ohio Star Ball in Columbus, the most prestigious of the competitions held around the country. "I'll let you know, Mel. I've gotta look at my finances."

"Hey, that I understand." He grinned and squeezed her arm. "See you next time, Mary."

Still smiling, he turned away from her.

As Mary sat down on the upholstered bench to remove her dance shoes, the door swished open and Helen James entered, carrying her plastic "Showtime" bag. Helen was a mildly overweight woman in her late thirties, with a flesh-padded, sweet face and an overdeveloped bust. She was beautiful in a way more dependent on attitude than appearance, like one of those full-figure fashion models flaunting their oversize clothes.

Nodding to Mary, she sat down next to her to change shoes. "Coming or going?" she asked.

"Going," Mary said. "I just finished a private lesson."

"Why don't you stay for group?" Helen asked. "It's gonna be merengue."

"I've gotta get over to visit my mother, or I would stay. I could use work in the merengue."

"Couldn't we all." Helen slipped into her black practice shoes, stood up, then stared down at Mary. She narrowed her eyes. Women who were close acquaintances somehow knew, if they paid attention. And Helen was the sort to pay attention. "You okay, Mary Mary?" It was her habit to make Mary's name into an affectionate nickname.

"Sure, fine."

"Looks like somebody took a poke at you."

"No," Mary said, "that's not what happened."

"My daughter, Ann," Helen said, "her ex-hubby used to pound on her all the time."

"Why?" Mary asked. "What'd she do?"

"Do? Why, she didn't do a thing to deserve it. He'd beat on her just for the pure hell of it. Make up a reason, if she asked him. Finally he put her in the hospital and she got smart and left him. It took Ann three years in therapy before she realized none of it was her fault. Sounds odd, but that's the way it seems to work. It's a power play, really, something that's just in some men, like it's hormonal."

"They should help themselves, get that kinda thing outa the way they think. Or get professional help."

"They don't change, Mary Mary. Not ever. They'll lie their ass off to you, but they won't change."

"None of that's got anything to do with me," Mary said. And it didn't. Not anymore. Finally and forever, she'd cut Jake out of her life.

" 'Course not. Hey, you see this?" Helen picked up a folded newspaper that was lying on the table near the bench. "That girl got her throat cut in New Orleans was in a dance competition I went up to Chicago to see. I remember her 'cause of the hot pink dress she had on when she won first place in cha-cha."

Mary glanced at the brief news item about a woman who'd been found murdered in a vacant lot. Her photograph appeared above the simple caption, "Victim." She was a pretty, dark-haired woman, about thirty. Danielle Verlane was her name. The newspaper mentioned nothing about her being a dancer.

"You sure it's the same woman?" Mary asked.

"Oh, yeah. I remember her name 'cause it's kinda unusual. Her, all right. Did a helluva tango, too. You never know what's gonna happen, huh? I mean, maybe her husband did that to her. Started out beating her, love taps or some such shit, then it led to that. It happens."

"God, no!" Mary exclaimed. "That's silly. And if that's how it was, the police'll find out."

"Won't do her much good now, though, will it?" Helen did a practice rumba step and grinned.

Air stirred around Mary's ankles as three other students, two men and a woman, pushed through the door. The men were Curt and Willis. Curt was a two-hundred-pounder who'd been taking lessons about six months and was constantly apologizing for stepping on his partners' toes or giving them the wrong lead. Willis was a wiry little gray-haired man who danced almost well enough to be an instructor. He was going to Miami with his instructor Brenda and would probably return with a trophy. The third student was Lisa Burrows, a twentyish woman who was tall and bony and reminded Mary of a beautiful thoroughbred racehorse. Lisa had been dancing for several years but had only been coming to this studio for about a month. Mary didn't know her very well.

Hellos were exchanged, and Lisa and Willis sat down to change shoes. Curt danced in leather street shoes, which was part of his problem. Lisa began brushing the suede soles of her shoes vigorously with a wire brush, to raise the nap and decrease friction so her steps would glide. The muscles in her lean arms were corded like a man's.

"Remember a girl named Danielle who competed in Chicago?" Helen asked Willis.

He shook his head no, watching Lisa brush her soles, or maybe studying her improbably long legs. *Shoosh! Shoosh!* went the brush, sending flecks of suede flying. She seemed genuinely unaware of his scrutiny, which appeared to intrigue him all the more.

"Well, she was murdered in New Orleans," Helen said.

Lisa handed her brush to Willis to use on his shoes and said, "So what was she doing in New Orleans?"

"She lives—lived—there."

"I was there once, for Mardi Gras."

Shoosh! Shoosh! "Murdered how?" Willis asked.

"Helen thinks her husband did it," Mary said.

Willis shrugged. "Well, that's usually the guilty party, the victim's spouse." *Shoosh!* "That oughta do it." He handed the brush back to Lisa.

"Or boyfriend," Helen said, looking at Mary.

"Same thing."

Lisa snorted, somehow making even that seem sensual.

Two more students, Jean and Marci, who took turns driving

each other to the studio, came in from outside, talking and laughing. Suddenly silent, they nodded, then glanced around for a place to sit down and change shoes. Mary stood up and moved away, leaving space on the bench.

Larry, another instructor, bustled out of the office smiling. "Everybody ready for merengue?" he asked, clapping his hands. Enthusiasm was his long suit.

"Ready for anything," Lisa said. Willis stared at her.

"All right, onto the floor, folks. Staying, Mary?"

"No, I gotta be somewhere."

"Aw, *nooo* you don't! Come on and stay!"

"Sorry, Larry, gotta run."

"Awww!" Then he seemed to shake off his acute disappointment; life would go on for him after all. "Okay, whoever's coming, let's go!" Swaying his hips in Cuban motion, he merengued over to the far side of the dance floor. The students followed.

"Take care, Mary Mary," Helen called over her shoulder, then got in line with the other students.

Carrying her dance shoes in their nylon bag, Mary walked to the door, subtly swaying to the rhythm of the Latin music now pulsating from the speakers. "Weight over the *bent* leg!" Larry was yelling. "Atta girl, Helen! Beauuutiful!"

Mary pushed the door open and stepped outside into a cool, light drizzle, the real and indifferent world greeting her with a slap in the face.

Before climbing into her yellow Honda Civic, she held the door open so the dome light stayed on and looked in the back of the little car. A woman alone had to take precautions. She'd heard on the news, or somewhere, about women being attacked by men who'd hidden crouched behind their cars' seats and then made themselves known by an arm around the neck along some desolate stretch of road. A knife against the throat.

No knife-wielding maniac tonight. But then she hadn't really expected one. Stories like that were mostly rumor grown to become urban legend.

As she drove away she glanced in the rearview mirror and thought she saw a shadowy form pass behind the car, very near. Though startled, she felt no fear. She simply stepped on the accelerator and instantly was away from any danger, real or imagined.

Imagined, she was sure, as she turned left from the parking lot onto the brightly lighted avenue.

Imagined.

Urban legend.

She switched on the radio and found music.

5

Mary's mother, Angie, lived alone in a one-bedroom flat on Shenandoah Avenue in South St. Louis. It was only a fifteen-minute drive from Mary's apartment on Utah, but Mary didn't go home before stopping at a White Castle drive-through and picking up hamburgers, french fries, and Pepsi for supper. Home wasn't a place she deliberately avoided, but also not one she yearned to experience. No home of Mary's had ever been that to her.

Even the aromatic hamburgers couldn't overcome the pungent, mingled cooking and cleaning scents of the flat as Mary shoved open the door with her hip and trudged up the wooden steps to the second floor. The upstairs hall smelled as if it had recently been fogged with perfumed insecticide.

Angie had heard her coming and was standing with the door open, waiting. She was barefoot and wearing her beige terrycloth robe, as if she'd just taken a shower, but her hair was dry. Her feet were old, with prominent tendons, yellowed nails, and talons for toes.

Angie was an older version of Mary, with red hair. Her features were haggard, with flesh as delicate and crinkled as worn folding money surrounding her eyes, and dark lines swooping from her nose to the corners of her thin, set lips. She'd borne Mary when she was thirty. She was sixty-five now; the skin beneath her jaw had become mottled, and fine veins had ruptured in her nose. Pain had moved into her eyes to live permanently.

Mary nodded a hello and edged past her into the apartment. The place was cheaply furnished but clean. A sofa draped with a pale green slipcover squatted against one wall on the imitation oriental rug. K mart sheer curtains softened the illumination from the evening sun as it angled through the slanted venetian blinds. The walls were bare except for a dime store print of two men playing cards at a table—a segment of a Rembrandt painting, Mary thought, but wasn't sure—and a square, plastic frame containing a collage of black-and-white snapshots, some of which were of Mary as a child. Though the evening was cool, the window air-conditioner was humming away, blowing only neutral air. Angie had forgotten to turn it off after the heat of early afternoon. Angie often forgot things.

She closed the door and followed Mary into the tiny kitchen. "Been dancing?"

"Had a lesson," Mary said, placing the White Castle bags on the Formica-topped table. She carefully drew the waxy, damp Pepsi cups out of their bag and poked straws through their rigid lids. The straws squealed on the plastic as they penetrated.

Angie said, "I dunno why you spend so much on that kinda thing. You got a good job, but it's still too expensive. Go to work every day so you can learn how to put one foot in front of the other on the dance floor. Don't make sense."

They'd had this discussion before. "There's a lot more to it than that, Angie." Mary hadn't called her mother anything other than 'Angie' for years. She glanced around the apartment. No bottle in view. No indication that Angie drank. And drank. Good. Though Mary knew about Angie's ingenuity in hiding bottles, it was still nice not to see the trappings of alcoholism lying around. Their presence suggested a certain laxity, a hopelessness that was contagious.

Angie claimed not to have touched a drop of liquor before Duke Arlington, her husband and Mary's father, died drunk in an auto accident speeding the wrong way on a Highway 70 exit ramp. Mary knew that wasn't true. She remembered lying in bed as a child, listening to her mother and father in drunken, senseless arguments. She'd heard the slurred insults, heard Duke use his open hands on Angie, then his fists, his belt. She'd seen the welts and bruises on Angie. Angie occasionally talked about Duke abusing her. Her alcoholism, and Duke's other familial indiscretions, she wouldn't acknowledge at all, despite two stays in detoxification centers, despite the gin bottles tucked in the backs of the kitchen cabinets or in the bedroom closet.

Angie lived now on her Social Security checks, a small pension, and the interest from Duke's insurance policy.

And she drank.

"I sure like these little bastards," Angie said, dropping into a chair and picking up one of the greasy cardboard folders that held the aromatic hamburgers. White Castle hamburgers were inexpensive, small squares of beef and chopped onions on square little buns. They tasted like no other hamburgers and, for South St. Louisans, were addictive. Sometimes they were affectionately called Belly Bombers. Sometimes not affectionately.

Mary sat down opposite her mother and took a sip of Pepsi, began munching her crisp and salty french fries.

"Arlington women don't have to worry none about their weight," Angie said. "We can eat what the fuck we want."

Mary thought, I dance it off, you drink it off. But she said nothing and chewed. Boris, Angie's tiger-striped gray cat, padded silently into the kitchen, attracted by the scent of food. He glanced at Mary, then away, and passed out of sight. Mary could hear him purring as he rubbed against one of Angie's legs. Or maybe he was licking her bare feet; Mary had seen him do that. Angie tore off a portion of hamburger and her hand disappeared beneath the table, an automatic, lonely offering to companionship. The purring stopped.

"Boris is scared of something," Angie said.

"How do you know?"

"He got quiet, and I can feel him trembling up against my foot."

"Maybe he heard a dog bark."

"This cat ain't scared of dogs."

"I had a good lesson tonight," Mary said, trying to change the subject. "Tango."

"I read somewhere the instructors at them studios try to get the students sweet on 'em, so they'll keep coming in and paying."

"Some studios are that way, not this one. You're getting cynical in your old age, Angie."

"I been cynical quite some time, honey."

Angie had to smile.

"That studio's conning you outa your money," Angie said. "Selling you an illusion."

"I know it's an illusion, but I like it. I *need* it."

"You want illusion," Angie said, "buy one of them lava lamps that throw dancing shadows on the walls."

Mary gave up. She knew Angie wouldn't understand, but now and then she tried to reach her mother anyway. Angie's illusion was inside the bottle, but it was one she denied. Life was all about illusion, delusion; Mary had learned that. Reality was nothing more than how people saw things, and there were as many realities as there were people. And didn't that explain everything? Wasn't that the *only* explanation?

Angie was on her second hamburger. Her appetite was good, Mary noted. She must be exercising at least *some* control over the booze.

Staring at her with bloodshot blue eyes, Angie suddenly said, "Jake popped you one again, didn't he." Not a question, a statement. One combat veteran to another. Angie knew the signs.

"No, it was an accident. He was talking and flung his elbow out and caught me in the eye."

"Bullshit, Mary." Now Angie was grinning. "I know how it is. Oh, *just* how it is. We both know your late father sometimes lost his temper with me."

"And with me," Mary said, remembering the flushed face, the huge hands that trembled before they flew out of control and struck. She recalled most of all her father's hands, the crescents of grit beneath the fingernails. Duke had driven a truck and was always tinkering with it, or adjusting something under the hood of the family's old Dodge in the driveway, as if he might somehow fine-tune the mechanical trappings of his life and so make everything else perfect.

"Every time Duke spanked you, it was because you had it coming," Angie said defensively. "That was childhood discipline." After all these years, she still stood up for him. Her wifely duty.

"He broke my nose once, Angie." Not to mention more intimate and serious transgressions.

"That was an accident."

"Like my eye."

Angie was quiet. She sipped Pepsi through her straw, staring down at the cup. Its dark level of liquid was visible as a curved shadow.

"Jake staying with you?" she asked after a while.

"He was," Mary said. "He won't be there tonight. I'll get phone calls from him, maybe even flowers, but I won't see him for three or four days. That's the way it always is afterward."

"Sure. He's sorry about the eye?"

"Yeah." And the ribs. For a second Mary thought of Mel Holt, elegant and gentle Mel. She couldn't imagine him striking anyone.

"I don't give a shit how sorry or ashamed he is," Angie said, "he won't change."

"I know. This time I'm not letting him come back."

"That's good, Mary, because there's something about Jake. Something that goes beyond how Duke could be sometimes."

"Well, it doesn't matter now. It's over."

"That's how it has to be. They won't seek help, Mary. And even if they do, it don't work." Angie took another bite of hamburger and chewed very methodically, as if there might be a tiny hard object hidden in her food.

Mary said, "Fred doesn't always treat you so well." Fred was Fred Wellinger, the semiretired bricklayer who sometimes spent time with Angie. He'd been a friend of Duke's and known her for years.

"Fred never in his life hit a woman."

"Maybe not, but he talks to you like you were his dog."

"Only sometimes, and not very often. The Lord never made a perfect man, Mary. Nor a woman. Fred's got his points." Angie dropped her half-eaten hamburger onto the table.

"So what's the matter?" Mary asked.

"I ain't hungry, that's all." She finished her Pepsi, making a slurping sound with the straw, then absently pushed the cup away.

Mary sighed. "Okay, let's not fight. God knows I've had enough of that for a while."

She wasn't hungry anymore, either. She stood up and cleared the table, stuffing everything back into its white paper sack and cramming it noisily into the wastebasket. Angie wiped crumbs off the table with a damp red dishrag, then rinsed and wrung out the rag at the old white porcelain sink. She folded it over the edge of the sink to dry, letting the tap water run and flicking a wall switch. The Disposall went *chunka! chunka! chunka!* and whined and gurgled busily until she flicked the switch again and turned off the water.

Mary stood watching her mother's kitchen ritual; the familiarity was there no matter what kitchen Angie was in, the same posture as she moved toward the sink, the same outthrust hip and elbow as she leaned forward and wrung out the dishrag, the same air of finality as she stopped the flow of water and turned away from the sink. Rhythms and images of childhood that would never leave Mary. The child always lived somewhere in the adult.

She smiled at her mother, but Angie didn't notice.

Mary followed her into the living room, where Angie switched on the table model TV and they watched yet another "Let's Make a Deal" rerun, dreams bearing fruit between commercials. Afterward they talked of everything and nothing until Mary was ready to leave.

As she stood up, she noticed on the floor alongside the sofa the newspaper Helen had shown her at the studio. It was folded so the item about the New Orleans murder, with the photo of the dead woman, happened to be visible. The victim, dark hair, sparkling eyes, vividly alive in two dimensions, was smiling up from the floor with an expression that seemed to strike some sort of chord in Mary now, though the woman herself still didn't look familiar.

Mary said, "I didn't think you took the paper."

"I don't," Angie told her, still slouched in the threadbare wing chair. She wriggled her toes. "Don't usually buy one, neither. Fred brought that one by earlier."

"Well," Mary said, "I'm gonna get going. I'll call you later."

Angie braced with her brown-spotted hands on the chair arms and levered herself to her feet. "You take care of yourself, Mary. I mean, with Jake and all."

"Sure, Angie."

As she moved toward the door, Mary found herself glancing back at the folded newspaper. It pulled at her gaze, making it an effort to look away.

She was oddly drawn to it and wasn't sure why, intrigued by the photo of the woman who had danced and was now dead.

18

6

Mary's apartment was on Utah, an upscale street in a part of town that changed personality block by block. Though her building was one of a row of rehabbed prewar apartments, some of them boasting ornamental stonework too expensive to create now, just a few blocks away the brick apartment buildings were crumbling with decay and peeling paint.

Her building was a slate-roofed brick structure with green wood trim and with regal stone lions flanking the front steps. The smell in the vestibule was exactly like that in the building where Angie lived, though the floor was veined marble and the mailboxes polished brass.

The stairway, however, was wooden. Mary trudged up the creaking steps to her second-floor unit, noticing that the bulb on the landing was burned out again. She'd have to call the landlord, or have Jake (*Jake?*) replace it.

Then she saw the flowers. They were lying like a cat's offering on the black rubber welcome mat in front of her door. Roses again, this time with the delicate flower known as baby's breath setting off their deep red blossoms. She bent and picked them up, then squinted to read the square white card in the faint light: "Sorry, sorry, sorry! Love, Jake."

Cradling the tissue-wrapped bouquet as if it were an infant, Mary keyed the lock to let herself in.

That was when she noticed the marks on the doorjamb near the knob. They were slashes, and shallow notches that appeared to have been made by a large knife as someone butchered the wood while trying to pry open the door enough to force the lock.

The marks on the wood were apparently ineffectual; if someone had tried to get in, they didn't seem to have succeeded.

Not daring to look around her in the dim hall, she entered the apartment quickly. After closing the door, she stood motionless for a moment. The air was still and stale, but it felt like home. Security. She was alone here, sheltered for a while.

She pictured someone working on her door with a knife and shivered. Jake? Maybe he'd forgotten his key and was angry, used the knife out of spite.

And then left roses? Not likely.

She turned around and set the deadbolt and chain-lock. Then she carried the roses into the kitchen and found a tall vase, ran some water into it, and stuffed the stems of the flowers down inside it. Roses and Jake, Jake and roses. How many times had he sent her roses? She took the vase into the living room and placed it on the low table that held the phone. The splash of bright red was vivid as an open wound.

Only the beige-shaded lamp by the sofa—the one she always left on when she wasn't home at night—was glowing, and the living room was dim and shadowed. She switched on the brass floor lamp and illuminated the tasteful contemporary furniture that was mixed with older things given to her by Angie. Angie had explained there were certain possessions she didn't want around anymore because they reminded her too much of Duke, so Mary was the recipient of a wing chair, the oak curio shelf that had held Duke's bowling trophies, the floor lamp, and various odds and ends that felt like 1963 and childhood.

Mary slipped out of her shoes but didn't sit down. Instead she wandered through the apartment to put her mind entirely at ease, even opening closet doors. The faith she'd placed in the heavy-duty locks the landlord had installed last summer seemed justified.

She went into the black-and-gray tiled bathroom and got a large Rubbermaid pan out from beneath the washbasin, ran hot water into it, then carried it and a folded white towel into the living room. She placed the pan on the floor, settled in a corner of the sofa and lowered her feet into the hot water.

Heaven! Dancing sure took a toll on the feet, but it was worth it.

Letting the hot moisture penetrate and loosen her stiff muscles, she wriggled her toes underwater and wondered if she should call the police about the door. That kind of thing happened in this neighborhood, so she was sure nothing would come of it, but she pulled the phone over to her anyway and punched out Information.

*   *   *

They were there sooner than Mary would have guessed. A young patrolman and an old one with a gray mustache. They studied the damaged doorjamb, made sure the lock was in order, and questioned Mary about potential enemies. She said she had none, glancing at the roses and not mentioning Jake.

Possibly it was the work of kids looking for drugs, the mustached cop speculated, as if that were in a league with playing hopscotch. His partner pointed out that there'd been a lot of that the past few months, frustrated addicts committing vandalism and random attempted break-ins because of a recent police crackdown on local dealers. They'd run extra patrols by her building, they assured her, and if she noticed anything suspicious she was to phone them.

Fifteen minutes after their arrival she was seated again on the sofa with her feet submerged in hot water, and they were no doubt a few blocks away looking into crimes actually committed. Probably they were right about the marks on her door. Frustrated vandalism. Not likely to be repeated.

She withdrew her bare feet from the water and patted them dry with the towel, then carried the pan into the bathroom and refilled it so the water was steaming.

When she'd placed the pan before the sofa again, she didn't sit down. She was going to play the Ohio Star Ball video she'd taped from the Public Broadcast System presentation of last year's finals. It showed only the highest levels of competition on the last night, when Juliet Prowse acted as hostess. But the same glitter and motion would be there during the earlier Novice and Intermediate Bronze pro-amateur competition, the categories in which Mary would dance with Mel.

As she stood up to pad over to the TV and slip the cassette into her VCR, the phone jangled.

She picked up the receiver and pressed cool plastic to her ear, standing gracefully with her feet in fifth position, waiting.

"Mary? It's me, Jake."

She wasn't surprised. The old pattern was developing, the dance of contrition and forgiveness.

"You get the flowers?" There was music in the background. And voices. A woman laughed hysterically. Good times rolling. He was probably speaking from Skittles, the bar near where he worked. He'd go there often after his afternoon shift's ten-thirty quitting time and stay until well past midnight, drinking with his warehouse buddies. "Hey, Mary? Babe?"

"Yeah, I got them, Jake."

He was quiet for a moment. She wondered if he was drunk. Probably at least halfway.

"Jesus, Mary, I'm sorry!"

"It said that on the card that came with the flowers," she told him.

He gave a short, sad laugh. "Yeah, I guess it did."

"Jake, did you do something to my door?"

"Your door? What's that mean?"

"Just what I asked."

"Why would I do something to your door?"

"I thought you mighta forgot your key and tried to get in."

"I always got my keys with me." When she didn't say anything right away, he said, "Mary?"

"You hurt me pretty bad, Jake."

"How bad?"

"Bruised some ribs."

"Christ! I'm sorry, babe, you know I am."

"Do I?"

"Well, I hope you know."

"You been drinking, Jake?"

"Some. I needed to get a little bit drunk so I'd have the guts to call. Last night—damn! I don't know what the fuck came over me, Mary."

"You never do."

"I know it sounds dumb of me to promise it won't happen again. But I *can* promise you this, and I swear it on all I hold holy: I'll try my damndest not to ever let it happen again. I never meant to hurt you that way; I'd kill anybody that'd hurt you. I mean *really* hurt you. You know that, don't you?"

"I know it, Jake." And she did know it; she believed him.

"I guess you don't wanna see me again."

"Would *you,* if you were me?"

"No, I gotta admit I wouldn't. Tell you the honest truth, I don't know why you put up with the shit I hand out."

"I don't put up with it. I've quit. You and I are over, Jake."

"I hear it but I can't believe it, Mary."

She said nothing, letting him squirm while she listened to the faint hollow hiss of the connection. She was pressing the receiver so hard to the side of her head that her ear was beginning to ache as if he'd hit her there.

"Lemme come over," Jake pleaded. "We can talk about it, huh?"

"No, Jake, and don't call me back."

"Mary! Don't hang up! Please! Give another shot, huh, babe? You know I mean well. It's just that I got this . . . ."

"Sickness?"

"If you wanna call it that. This sickness in me. I hurt people, and not just with my hands, then I'm sorry as hell. I been doing it all my life. Christ, I hate myself right now, Mary."

"I've gotta hang up now, Jake."

"Mary, lemme see you again, okay?"

"I don't think so, Jake."

"Mary! Don't hang up, Mary. Mary?"

She slowly replaced the receiver.

Absently, she switched on the TV, then slid the tape of the Ohio Star Ball into the VCR and punched Play.

But when she'd sat back down on the sofa and resubmerged her tired feet, she didn't watch the dancers whirling on the flickering screen. She thought about Jake, how he could control her with his love, his violence, and his self-pity. Bondage wasn't too strong a word. But now it was bondage broken. She wasn't sure if she'd really been in love with Jake, because no one had ever given her a reliable definition of love. Jake could be violent, but he could also be as gentle as a kind father, and as approving and encouraging. Yet always the other half of him was there, a lurking ugliness of soul, a beast leering out from beneath the surface and somehow holding her in thrall.

And at the studio there was Mel. There was no violence in Mel, she was sure. He was so young, only in his twenties, and professionally solicitous and handsome. Mary suspected that if her money ran out, so would Mel's affection. But did it matter? Mel was, in his fashion, no less a real love object than Jake. She saw both men in her own way, mentally shaping them to her intimate yearnings, as if they were romantic figures in a novel she was reading and wanted to continue and conclude at the same time. She was nurtured not by the present, but by what might grow from their relationships someday.

That was her problem, she thought. She lived for Someday.

But she'd been abused for the last time. Now it would be a someday without Jake.

Familiar music blared and her eyes focused on the TV screen. The tango finals had begun.

In the searing water, her feet moved.

He stood staring into the freezer. Before the repairman had arrived, he'd wrapped everything in white butcher paper. Even the knife. The knife had to be kept in the freezer to keep it pure and free of the disease. It wouldn't have done for the repairman to see what was in the freezer.

Somewhere he'd read that near the South Pole tiny animals that had lived and been frozen alive before the birth of Christ had been thawed out and were still alive today. So there was no reason time couldn't be made to stand still in a small freezer that was just as cold.

Anyway, the repairman had finished and said the freezer was as good as new and would last for years. Years would be fine; a new freezer could be bought soon, one that would last a lifetime. Some of them even had lifetime guarantees.

He unwrapped the knife and looked at it, looked at what else was in the freezer, and smiled.

There was no way to guarantee a lifetime.

7

Helen James said, "The police don't think it's significant that she danced."

"That who danced?" Mary asked, working her feet into her Latin shoes. Leaning down from where she was seated on the vinyl bench, she fastened their straps in the last hole, so the shoes would stay tight; tonight's lesson was going to cover cha-cha and mambo, which meant lots of pressure against the floor.

"Danielle Verlane." Helen had her shoes on and was waiting for her seven-thirty private lesson with her instructor, Nick. She stood with her weight on one foot and was avidly reading this morning's *Post*. "She's the woman who was killed in New Orleans, remember?"

Mary said she remembered. She didn't feel like talking about Danielle Verlane. Or listening. Work today at Summers Realty, where she was a closing woman, one of two brokers who handled final transfers of titles, had been a blur, an exercise she'd gone through automatically merely so she could reach this evening as soon as possible. She'd been so mindless she'd made mistakes she'd have to rectify tomorrow. But she wouldn't think about them until morning.

The flowers had arrived at work at eight-thirty, and she'd had to shyly acknowledge they were from Jake, all the while avoiding Victor's knowing gaze. What the hell had *he* been staring at?—the bruised tissue under her eye was no longer noticeable beneath her makeup. She'd become adroit at applying cosmetics to disguise injury.

She rummaged in her dance bag and found her wire brush, then began working its stiff bristles across the soles of her shoes, forward toward the toes. Satisfying work.

"The husband's name's Rene," Helen said, still with her nose in the paper. "It turns out Danielle was seen dancing in a couple of French Quarter hot spots. Doing some fancy jive, was the way one witness put it. Another place she was tangoing with some guy, and that was the last time she was seen alive."

Mary suspected that Victor, who was a fifty-year-old widower with male pattern baldness, had a crush on her. Well, the hell with him. He was too old for her, and he wore way too much perfumed deodorant, probably something male models dressed as cowboys splashed on in TV commercials. Why was that sort of man always interested in her? Did she send out some kind of goddamn vibes that attracted them, like smart bombs?

"The husband wants the police to check out dance studios to find the guys she was dancing with, but they don't see it as all that significant that she was dancing. Hubby thinks it *is* significant. The cop in charge disagrees and says she happened to be in places where there was dancing, so she danced. Cops for you."

"The cops might be right," Mary said, standing up and shifting her weight from leg to leg, loosening her hips. She'd recently trimmed her toenails and one of them was digging into the side of the adjacent toe, but it was only a minor discomfort she could ignore. Once she began dancing she wouldn't feel it.

"No, no, Mary, she was a *dancer*. Like us. So I say right on, Rene, don't listen to the fuzz."

"Nobody calls the police fuzz anymore," Mary said, smiling.

"They do if you hang around the right places."

"Where do you hang around?" Mary asked.

"Here," Helen said. A subtle sadness had edged into her voice. "This is what's left of my social life now that George is gone. And I guess you're right, nobody here calls the cops fuzz. They're all too refined. Or they pretend to be."

Murder in New Orleans was bad enough. Mary really didn't want to talk about Helen's dead husband. Or the one she'd divorced last year after a disastrous two-month marriage.

"Ladies! We ready to dance and learn?"

Mel and Nick had come out of the office and were standing side by side behind them. Mel was much the taller of the two, smiling along with Nick, who winked at Helen. Nick looked Greek or Italian and was slightly overweight, but when he moved on the dance floor he seemed to weigh only two or three pounds.

"*I'm* ready to dance, anyway," Helen said. Her voice suggested she was still thinking about George and the past. The past was sticky. It never really let go of anyone.

"Don't be pessimistic, dear," Nick said, gliding over to her and gently gripping her elbow. "Not here. Here's where we learn and have *fun.*" He steered her out onto the floor, beneath twisted white ribbons of crepe paper and clusters of red and white balloons that had been strung for tomorrow night's practice party. "Mambo tonight, dear," Nick was saying. "We'll practice arm checks, then I'll show you how to do flicks."

"You okay, Mary?" Mel asked quietly, still smiling at her.

She had to smile back. "Sure. I was just listening to Helen tell me about some woman who got herself killed down in New Orleans." She nodded toward the folded paper Helen had dropped onto the bench before being escorted out onto the dance floor.

Mel's gaze followed the motion of her head, then he did a double take. He walked over and picked up the paper. "Hey, she looks familiar."

"Her name's Danielle, I think. She did ballroom dancing. That's why Helen's interested in the case."

"I remember her now!" Mel said, gazing wide-eyed at Mary. Death wasn't part of his world, yet here it had dared to turn up, right here in the studio where even the slightest unpleasantness wasn't supposed to intrude. It was as if the Antichrist had arrived in suede-soled shoes. "I remember her from about five years ago when I taught at a studio in New Orleans. God, she was my student!"

Mel seemed so stricken by surprise at the proximity of death that Mary didn't know what to say. "Well, she's dead," she muttered stupidly.

"You say she was murdered?" Mel asked, not bothering to read the words that accompanied Danielle Verlane's photograph.

"That's what the paper says. Her husband wants the police to start questioning people who went to the same dance studio."

"Huh? They don't think a dancer had anything to do with her death, do they?"

"That's what the husband thinks, according to Helen. What it says in this morning's paper."

"Well, that's really weird."

Mel dropped the paper back onto the bench and stretched his lean frame. He grinned, tossing off the news of his former student's murder with an ease that astounded Mary, considering his previous apparent shock. What could it have to do with him?

With smiles and balloons? With youth and life and promenade pivots?

"Time to dance, Mary." He extended his arm for her.

"Keep your weight on the inner edge of your feet, dear," Nick was gently admonishing Helen as Mel and Mary passed them. Helen was frowning in concentration, trying to shift her weight and rock her wide hips in the Cuban motion that was necessary for Latin dancing.

"We'll work on mambo first," Mel said. "That way we can use their music, if you don't mind." He moved close to Mary in dance position, tucked a hand around behind her back, then lifted her right hand and leaned slightly toward her.

Dancing to someone else's tune, Mary thought, tightening her body and waiting for the beat. "I don't mind," she told Mel. What would it matter even if there were no music, as long as she was dancing and forgetting her boring job, her struggle to be competitive in Ohio, Angie getting older and more cunning at hiding bottles. And Jake and his fists and flowers. Jake.

What was it Angie had said about Jake being somehow beyond what Duke had been?

"Freeze completely on the one count," Mel reminded her, rhythmically flexing his knees in time to the music. ". . . two, three, four, *one*. That's it—*freeze!*"

Then the music took them and they danced.

That night she dreamed she was dancing the tango, but not with Mel. They were in a vast, airy place and she couldn't see the man's face, but he was a beautiful dancer, leading her through steps she'd seen only Silver-ranked dancers do. She slipped into perfect tango rhythm, feeling it pulsate through her entire body, through her soul. The man was whispering something to her she couldn't understand. What he said didn't interest her anyway; only the way he danced, and how it made her feel. Her body was young and strong and supple, and she knew it was acting out flawlessly the patterns and elegant lines of her imagination. Her feet knew where to go and when. She held her counts when she was supposed to, snapped her head around with precision, whirled with perfect grace and poise.

Then suddenly she was aware of another couple on the floor, dancing with the same grace and precision. They whirled into sight. Jake dancing with Danielle Verlane. He was smiling over her shoulder at Mary.

When she awoke she lay silently in the dark. She was perspiring heavily and her heart was beating very fast. The whine of truck tires drifted all the way from Kingshighway into her bedroom. In the distance a dog was barking frantically and forlornly. Night sounds.

Wondering what her dream had meant, she lay awake till daylight.

8

Friday night Mary drove to Casa Loma. It was where several of the Romance dancers met occasionally outside the studio, fledglings venturing from the nest and testing their wings.

Casa Loma was a vast, art deco ballroom on the corner of Cherokee and Iowa in South St. Louis, and it had existed as long as Mary could remember. She could recall Angie and Duke going there at least once, long ago. Though it had recently been refurbished, the dance hall was little changed from those days. The spacious floor was worn but gleaming waxed wood, its perimeter surrounded by blue-clothed rectangular tables. At opposite corners were small bars that sold bowls of popcorn as well as drinks. The floor was encircled above by a balcony along which lights twinkled in sequence. The upper floor also contained tables, and Mary liked to sit alone up there sometimes and look down from the balcony at the dancers swirling in kaleidoscope patterns.

She could hear the band as she paused on the landing of the steps leading to the ballroom and paid her five-dollar admission to an elderly woman behind a cashier's window. A drum pounded out a frantic, syncopated rhythm, then a trumpet's wail rose like a melancholy sob as the rest of the band joined in.

Dangling her dance shoes in their drawstring bag, she climbed the rest of the steps, handed her ticket to an attendant, then passed through a small seating area and entered the ballroom itself.

The music was suddenly much louder, a waltz now. Beyond the tables, dancers were whirling about the floor in elegant rise-and-fall motion, their movements exaggerated as they swirled through the dappled light cast by a glittering mirrored chandelier. The band played their gleaming instruments in front of an elegantly draped royal blue curtain patterned with stars and a crescent moon. There was an unreal quality to all of it; or perhaps it seemed that way because it was so vividly real. Mary couldn't decide which.

Casa Loma was crowded tonight, as it usually was on Fridays. Many of the dancers were older and had been regulars for decades, but there were also a lot of younger people, some of them in their twenties and even a few who looked like teenagers. Mary saw Helen dancing with Willis from the studio. He was slightly shorter than his partner, but the waltz was one of the wiry little man's best dances, and they made a graceful pair.

Mary scanned the tables and spotted June sitting with big Curt, who was sipping a beer and gazing out at the dancers, no doubt wishing he'd taken lessons long enough to learn their moves. Most of the dancers at Casa Loma were at least somewhat skilled, which made it one of the few places where there was a proper counter-clockwise line of dance, and a couple could do a waltz or fox-trot and not expect a collision.

As Mary moved toward the table she noticed equine Lisa, the fashion model, dancing with a dark-haired man. Mary didn't recognize him, but he was holding Lisa close and rubbing up to her in a more than friendly way. Fridays brought out the hunters at Casa Loma; Mary made a mental note to refuse politely if the man asked her to dance. There were no instructors from Romance Studio dancing at Casa Loma. The no-fraternization rule applied. Mary understood why it should. One *paid* to dance with an instructor. Business did play a part in this; there had to be more to count than beats and measures.

"Over here, Mary!" June, smiling and waving, didn't realize Mary had seen the Romance Studio table.

Mary squeezed between chair backs and the occupants of the next table. She nodded to Curt, who tore his gaze from the whirling dancers and grinned at her. "Band good tonight?" she asked.

"They sound fine to me," Curt said, "for whatever that's worth." He hadn't been taking lessons long enough to lose his self-effacing attitude. Give him another six months, Mary thought, and he'll probably be telling all the women how to dance. Too many men were like that. Male-pattern boldness, she decided, and almost giggled at the thought.

As soon as Mary had slipped into her dance shoes, a tall, gaunt man named Jim, who used to be a student at an Arthur Murray studio, asked her to dance. He was wearing dark slacks, a gray sportcoat, and a red tie with a fresh stain on it. His long, pale face was somber, but she knew it often broke into slow smiles that suggested wisdom but possibly meant nothing.

She stood up and he led her out to the floor. They'd met at a Romance Studio guest party when he'd been invited by a former student, and she'd later seen him at Casa Loma. There was a kind of ballroom dancing subculture in St. Louis, as there was in most big cities. After a few years, the people who did this kind of dancing knew each other as those who communicated in a special language of the body.

"So how you been?" he asked, as he gathered her in for a fox-trot.

"Okay. You?"

"Same as always." He assumed a rigid dance frame, waited for the one beat, then stepped forward. "I haven't been taking lessons for a while, but I'm gonna go back soon as things slow down at work."

"I'd never know you laid out."

"Thanks." He smiled. "Now I better not trip and fall."

"I'm still out at Romance," Mary told him, following his lead through a neat promenade pivot.

A couple in their twenties was doing swing near the edge of the floor, instead of toward the center where they'd be out of the way of the other dancers. The man led the woman through multiple underarm turns. Jim did a neat contrabody turn and guided Mary around them. He was smooth and had a confident lead, and he didn't try to show off by taking her into intricate steps she might not know. Mary enjoyed dancing with Jim.

He opened her into promenade position just as the music died, so he merely did a neat check, extending his right leg forward, then drawing it, and Mary, briskly back.

They stood somewhat awkwardly for a moment in the vacuum left by the suddenly silent band, then he thanked her for the dance.

"Gonna do any competition dancing?" he asked, as he escorted her back to her table.

"I'm sorta planning on Ohio in November."

"The Ohio Star Ball?" He seemed surprised.

"Sure, why not?"

He shrugged and grinned. "I can't think of any reason why you shouldn't. Hell, you're good enough, Mary."

"I'll have to train."

"Everybody trains hard for that one. It means a lot to dancers all over the country."

"The world," Mary corrected him. "Some of the top Canadians and Europeans compete there, too."

"Okay," Jim said, laughing, "the world." He squeezed her arm gently. "Take it easy, Mary. If you compete and lose, life won't punish you."

She sat down thinking that was an odd thing for him to say. Maybe he'd glimpsed some intensity in her she didn't suspect was that obvious, a desire to compete and win. A desire that, burning bright enough, could be visible in people, like madness. She got up, and went to the bar for a diet Pepsi.

When she returned, Helen and Willis had joined June and Curt at the table.

"Saw you dancing with Jim," Helen said, her smile made sly by violet eyeliner.

"Well, that's why I came here," Mary told her, "to dance." She pried up the tab on her soda can, fizzing some of the cold liquid onto her knuckles, and poured Pepsi over the ice in her plastic cup. Helen could be irritating; she sounded like a teenager at times, every school's overweight, gossipy sophomore.

The bandleader said something into the microphone that, where the Romance Studio people were seated, sounded like an echoing, indecipherable announcement at a bus terminal. Then the band began playing a rumba. Big Curt thought he could handle that one, so he stood up and asked Mary to dance.

She followed him out to the edge of the floor.

Curt had improved in the last few months, but he still couldn't stay on the beat. Mary listened to him muttering under the music, "Slow, quick-quick; slow, quick-quick," as he guided her through a series of simple box steps. She began back-leading to make it easier for him, and he grinned in appreciation. Affable Curt. "Not one of my better dances," he said apologetically. He told her that about every dance, every time they danced.

About halfway through the rumba, Mary glanced beyond Curt's hulking shoulder and saw something that surprised her. She back-led skillfully so she was facing the right direction, and made sure her eyes hadn't tricked her.

They hadn't. There was old Fred Wellinger, dancing with a woman about forty who was wearing a tight red dress that belonged on a woman about twenty. He had his gray hair plastered sideways over his bald spot and was grinning down at her, and she smiled and said something, then rested her head against his chest. Fred's right hand slid down to the swell of her buttock, his fingers gently stroking the taut red material of the dress as she swayed her rear in Latin rhythm.

Fred, you bastard! Mary thought. What would Angie say if she knew?

Fred happened to glance her way. A shock of recognition played over his features. Seen a ghost, Fred? He quickly danced his partner out of sight on the opposite side of the crowded floor.

Well, at least he hadn't dragged the woman over and introduced her as a platonic relationship.

Curt stepped on the very tip of Mary's toe, pinching the nail and causing a jolt of pain that made her temporarily break rhythm. Immediately he faltered, shaking his huge shaggy head and apologizing as fervently as if he'd just insulted her and all her ancestors.

Mary told him not to worry, he hadn't hurt her, it was her fault, really. One of the first things dancers learned was that it was always the woman's fault if she got stepped on, some flaw in her technique.

Reassured, he danced on, and she concentrated on following.

After the evening's last dance, a waltz Mary did with Jim, she changed her shoes, said her good-byes, and left the dance hall to cross the street to the lot where her car was parked.

The night was dark, and Mary was almost at the car when she noticed something odd. It took several seconds for her mind to accept it. Something, a bird, seemed to have alighted on the car's antenna. At first she was amused, until she realized the bird was motionless and in an awkward position with its wings drooping, and she could see the antenna protruding a few inches *above* it.

Her stomach tensed and moved with revulsion as she stepped closer and saw that someone had broken off the antenna to a sharp point and then impaled a sparrow on it.

She moved along the car and slumped against the rear fender, nauseated and trembling.

Something touched her shoulder and she jumped, almost shrieked.

"Mary?"

It was Jim.

"What's wrong, Mary? You sick?"

She nodded toward the dead bird, frozen in its macabre imitation of flight. Heard Jim say, "What the hell?"

He walked closer to the bird, shook his head, then returned to her. "Don't worry, I'll get rid of it for you, Mary."

She said nothing as he went to his car and returned with a wad of Kleenex in his hand. She turned away, and when she looked back, the bird was on the ground.

"Kids, I guess," he said, dropping the Kleenex near the bird. "Probably saw a dead bird in the street and thought they'd give somebody a scare. Guess they managed."

She knew that was what the police would say. No crime had been committed here. There was no victim other than a sparrow. There was no proof someone was trying to terrorize Mary and had sent her a sick and frightening message. Even she couldn't be sure. Maybe the marks on her door and the dead bird were in no way connected. Maybe.

"Want me to follow you home, Mary?"

She told him no, she'd be okay. He moved close and strapped his arm around her.

"I'll be all right," she said. "Thanks, Jim." She squirmed. Right now she didn't want a man hugging her.

He sighed and removed his arm, smiled his slow smile. "Okay.

Go home, have a drink, and try to forget this. Can you do that?"

She nodded, thinking a drink was the last thing she wanted.

Avoiding the dead bird, she climbed into her car and started the engine.

Jim stood watching as she drove away.

9

Morrisy was to meet Waxman at a Cajun restaurant a block off Bourbon Street to talk before Waxman went off duty. Morrisy loved Cajun food, had loved it even before it became a fad. He was eating blackened redfish when Waxman slid into the seat opposite him in the booth.

Waxman was wearing a neat gray sportcoat, paisley tie, blue slacks. He looked fresh, not as if he'd been slogging around all day in the heat. "How can you get to sleep after eating that stuff so late at night?" he asked.

Morrisy finished chewing a bite of fish and swallowed, took a slug of Dixie beer. "Helps me doze off," he said. "How'd you make out with Verlane today?"

"He gave me the same answers, wanted to know why I was asking the same questions. He's getting plenty testy. Keeps trying to make a big deal of the fact his wife did ballroom dancing."

"I used to dance myself," Morrisy said. "Used to do the twist."

"No shit? Hard to imagine."

"Means nothing about nothing," Morrisy said. "Just 'cause a witness said the victim was dancing at that lounge don't mean any more'n me getting down and screwing up my knees when I was young and dumb. People dance, people play golf, tennis, then they go out and get themselves killed anyway and so what?"

"Think maybe hubby wants us to go off in some direction other'n him?" Waxman asked.

"What do you think?"

"My thought is he's extremely tense. I told him lots of people besides his wife were dancing at the lounge that night, and they're still alive. Thought he was gonna poke me. He's that tightly wrapped."

"Good. You want one of these peppers?"

"God, no."

Morrisy smiled. He got to why he'd wanted to meet Waxman. "I talked with Schutz today."

Waxman nodded. Schutz was a police psychiatrist. The young blond waitress who'd waited on Morrisy sashayed over and Waxman ordered a cup of decaf.

"What he told me dovetailed with some of our conclusions," Morrisy went on. "Autopsy report shows the perpetrator was skillful with the murder weapon, a very sharp knife, used in a way that suggests the perp knew exactly how much pressure to apply and at what angle. Way we reconstruct the crime, he almost certainly took precautions not to get any of the victim's blood on him, as if he knew about arterial blood spurting. Schutz looked over the evidence and said the killer did the Verlane woman with a deliberateness that indicated detachment and planning. Work of a bona fide sociopath."

"I coulda told you that," Waxman said, sipping steaming black decaf.

"And our guy has a pathological hatred of women."

"Coulda told you that, too."

"But not using all that psychology jargon like Schutz," Morrisy said. "Upshot of it is, Schutz sees psychological signs, we see physical signs, that the killer's done his thing before. Us and Schutz together, we're seldom wrong about something like that."

"Computer check showed no similar killings in this or any other parish," Waxman reminded him.

Morrisy relished the last bite of redfish. "Still, my feeling is our boy's had practice. Experience. Another thing Schutz said: The killer himself might not know he's committed the murders. He might be blanking out the experiences in his mind, his way of coping so he can live with his conscience. Schutz says that happens."

"Happens a lot in court," Waxman said, "when guilty parties are trying for insanity pleas and light sentences."

"Hmph. Go ahead, try one of these banana peppers."

He made it sound so much like an order that Waxman took a cautious bite from the tip of one of the tiny green peppers that had rested in hot sauce on Morrisy's plate. Morrisy watched as Waxman scalded his tongue gulping coffee to squelch the greater fire.

"Jesus!" Waxman gasped. He was pale.

"Everybody's agreed the guy's killed before," Morrisy said, "so naturally the next question is—"

"Will he do it again?" Waxman finished.

He waved the waitress over and breathlessly asked for some water. She smiled, apparently used to the request, and hurried away. Morrisy watched her, noticing she had a pretty good ass.

"Actually," Morrisy said, "there's not much doubt in my mind. He'll do it again."

"So we need to collar him before he does," Waxman said, sort of wheezing. He was still having difficulty talking and breathing at the same time, and the waitress was nowhere in sight with the water.

Morrisy slid his half-full stein over to Waxman, said, "Wash down that pepper with some cold brew, why doncha?"

Waxman did. His breathing smoothed out, but his eyes were still watering.

Morrisy said, "Starting tomorrow, let's find out *every* goddamn thing about the husband, and I mean all the way back to when the bastard was potty trained." He stared hard at Waxman when he said this, making it plain it was something to bear down on, a career maker or breaker.

"Gotcha," Waxman said.

The waitress arrived with a glass of water with ice in it. Waxman drank that, too.

10

The next morning was hot. Mary awoke eager to climb out of the perspiration-damp bed. She slapped the alarm clock button down, and in thick silence padded to the air-conditioner and switched it on, twisting the thermostat dial all the way to Coolest. The air-conditioner hummed and gurgled impotently for a few seconds, then the compressor *thunk*ed on and the blower's tone became deeper and more powerful.

Mary stooped low so the flow of cool, chemical-smelling air flowing through the brown plastic grill washed over her face and evaporated perspiration. Then she straightened up, stretched her back, and went into the living room and switched on that window unit so the rest of the apartment would be cool when she emerged from the bathroom.

After showering, she dressed methodically, taking care to avoid snagging her pantyhose with a fingernail, choosing from her closet a lightweight gray skirt and blazer and matching medium-heeled shoes. Checked out Ms. Businesswoman in the full-length mirror and was reasonably satisfied.

When she went into the kitchen, she found it was too warm in there, almost as if there were something baking in the oven. Sunlight slanted in golden, syrupy rays that traversed the kitchen and lay in glimmering warm pools on the linoleum. The heat stifled what appetite she had, so she stuffed a filter into Mr. Coffee, spooned in some decaf, and ran water through it. Then she poured herself a glass of grapefruit juice and carried it and a cup of black coffee into the living room, where it was cooler.

She sat down on the sofa, set the glass and cup on the coffee table, and used the remote to switch on the TV and tune to the weather channel.

Eighty-five degrees at the airport, and it wasn't even eight o'clock. No wonder the apartment hadn't cooled down during the night. The temperature was expected to reach the high nineties today, the forecaster said, with what seemed to be barely disguised sadistic satisfaction. God, St. Louis in the summer was a city something like hell. She thumbed the remote to tune in CNN, downed the glass of sour grapefruit juice abruptly, as if it were medicine, then settled back on the sofa with her steaming coffee.

Trouble in the Middle East, said the anchorman. Tape showed a horde of raggedly dressed youths hurling rocks at some kind of armored vehicle. Doors sprang open in the side of the thing and soldiers poured out, carrying their weapons low and running in a cautious crouch. The stone-throwing youths scattered, and the tape ended. Mary sipped her coffee while another tape showed a drug bust in Washington, screaming cops battering down the front door of a shoddy house and shoving the startled occupants up against a wall and frisking them. Was it a real world out there? she wondered. Had all this actually happened? Somehow she couldn't relate to any of it, any more than she could grasp the true meaning of the federal deficit or the trade imbalance. Did any of it really mean anything, or was it all floating around in her life in the abstract, like astrology or Einstein's mathematical theories, so that it touched her only indirectly, if at all?

She sat forward suddenly, sloshing hot coffee over her thumb.

Danielle Verlane's photograph was on the TV screen, the one that had been in the newspaper. Mary's interest quickened. Maybe, she thought, she was fascinated by the murder because of the victim's connection with Mel. The same Mel Mary danced with, the Mel who held her close as he must have held Danielle Verlane. Mel and ballroom dancing were two things Mary and the dead woman had in common, and Mary couldn't put that out of her mind. The anchorman was talking about the murder in New Orleans. The victim had been mutilated with a knife. Police said there were no leads in the case, but the investigation was continuing.

The scene shifted to a sprawling, cream-colored stucco house with a red tile roof, red awnings, and decorative black wrought-iron railings. A shiny gray convertible was parked in the driveway. After the exterior shot of the large house with its lush green shrubbery and lawn, the camera moved inside, where a TV journalist was interviewing the victim's husband.

The camera showed only the back of the interviewer's blow-dried hair. The husband, Rene Verlane, was seated on a gray and white striped sofa. Behind him was an arched window with flowing white sheer curtains.

He was a slender, crudely handsome man about forty, wearing a well-tailored pale suit. His black hair looked wet and was slicked back. His eyes were a very light blue that matched his shirt, and he had thin lips and a deep cleft in his chin. He seemed angry yet composed.

"What I object to," he was saying with a hint-of-molasses Southern accent, "is the way the authorities are implying my wife was doing something immoral simply because she was seen dancing with several men the night she was murdered."

"Do you care to name anyone specifically who's implying that?" the interviewer asked hopefully.

"I won't name names at this point," Verlane said, "but what people don't understand is that Danielle was an avid ballroom dancer. She competed and won trophies. Dancing was very, very important to her. A sport. An art. Not simply a social skill. Or a . . ."

"Means to meet men?" the interviewer helpfully suggested.

"That's what the police seem to be implying," Verlane said, his accent suddenly thicker. A quick, bright anger came and went in his pale eyes. Something about him; he was watchable as a film star.

"So Danielle danced to keep her skills honed," the interviewer said, backing off a bit.

"Exactly. That's not uncommon in the world of people who take ballroom dancing seriously. There are competitions held all over the country, and many of the same dancers attend them, thousands of people. It's a subculture that isn't widely understood, or even known about, but my wife was part of it, and that's important. To imply that since she danced often and with different partners meant she was somehow less than a perfect wife is misguided, judgmental, and a hindrance to the investigation into her death. It's the world of ballroom dancing the police oughta be delving into, not snooping around as if my wife were somehow unfaithful—which she definitely wasn't."

A frontal shot of the interviewer, a perfectly groomed mannequin from third floor Menswear, looking intelligent and interested. "So you're unhappy with the police work in your wife's case?"

"Yes. And with the way the media have treated this." Verlane squirmed on the sofa and knitted his fingers together, squeezing. "As if Danielle did something wrong. As if somehow what happened was *her* fault and she *deserved* it."

Exterior shot again. The newsman was standing before the big stucco house with its arched windows. An elaborate black iron fence was visible now. He was leaning against it casually, loosely holding a microphone a few inches from his lips. "So Rene Verlane, whose wife Danielle was brutally murdered two days ago, is unhappy with the way local authorities have handled this case, and especially with how he feels the victim has been portrayed. This is—"

Someone was knocking on the door.

Mary placed her cup on a magazine so it wouldn't leave a ring on the table, then got up and crossed the living room. She stood close to the door and peered through the fish-eye peephole at the distorted figure standing in the hall.

Jake.

11

A single red rose this time, held like something injured in his huge rough hand and backed by an embarrassed smile. He said, "I heard someplace a rose by itself meant I love you."

She could meet his rage easier than his shame. Looking at him obliquely, she said, "It takes more'n a rose, Jake."

"Don't you think I know it, Mary?"

"No."

"So, can I at least come in?" He glanced from side to side; he didn't want any of the neighbors seeing him standing there like a schoolboy with a peace offering.

"Come on," she sighed, and stepped back to let him pass. He hadn't been home, wherever he was staying, after getting off work last night; he smelled faintly of old dust, old sweat, and stale beer. She closed the door behind him, suddenly thinking, God, he's in now! A few nights ago I swore this would never happen.

"Cool in here," he said, looking around as if the place were strange to him.

"What'd you expect?"

He smiled. "Naw, I mean the air's cool. But sure, I expected you to be cool to me. You got a right."

"I sure as hell do." She tried to muster anger, but it rose and then fell back in her, unable to sustain itself. It found the level of irritation, aimed more at herself, for letting him in, than at Jake.

She looked at him, still looming awkwardly with the rose in his hand. He was a tall man, and hefty. Handsome when he dressed up in jacket and tie, which was seldom. Wavy black hair going thin on top; permanently arched black eyebrows above narrowed and seeking gray eyes; a drooping dark mustache that gave him a somber expression despite his habitual half-smile. Today he was wearing khaki slacks, smudged from the warehouse and with a pair of leather work gloves protruding like limp severed hands from a back pocket. He had on scuffed brown loafers, a blue pullover shirt with an alligator sewn over the pocket. *See you later,* she felt like saying.

"You thought about our phone conversation?" he asked.

"There was nothing to think about; it was a conversation we've had lots of times. I don't believe I wanna see you again, Jake."

He waved the rose helplessly and with desperate meaning, as if it were a signal light on a black night. "Hey, Mary, you can't mean that!"

And maybe she couldn't mean it. Maybe she was simply acting out a charade because the alternative might be some crueler truth. But she had to try. She studied the dark pouches beneath his eyes. "You look like shit, Jake."

"Well, I stopped off for a couple drinks and some socializing after work. I been up all night." He extended the rose toward her, along with the boyish half-smile. "Be nice to me, Mary. A thorn's digging into my hand. You got a place to put this flower, or should I drop it so you can stomp on it?"

She went into the kitchen and rooted through the cabinet over the sink. All she could find that might accommodate the long-stemmed rose was a tall beer glass with "Busch" stenciled on it in dishwasher-faded blue letters. She ran three fingers of water into it and carried it into the living room.

Jake hadn't moved. She took the rose from him and inserted it in the tall glass, then set the glass on top of a *TV Guide* on the television set. A jackhammer chattered outside, off in the distance. Something being built, or torn down.

"What happened to your door?" Jake asked.

"I don't know. It looks like somebody tried to get in while I was gone."

He shot her a concerned look. "You call the police?"

"Yeah. Not much they can do." She considered telling him about last night outside Casa Loma, then decided she didn't want to confide in him and give the impression she needed him.

"So," Jake said, "you leaning toward forgiving me?"

"You know which way I'm leaning."

He started to cross his arms, but he changed his mind and absently scratched a bulging bicep. Then he let his hands dangle at his sides, like lifeless appendages made obsolete through evolution. "Listen, you sure you're . . . okay?"

"I'm about healed, if that's what you mean."

"Goddamnit, Mary, I hate to hurt you . . . to have hurt you. You know that, don't you? It's important to me that you realize it. I wouldn't admit this to anybody else, but I get scared sometimes, Mary. I just lose it and lash out. It's fear, that's what it is—fear. You understand what I'm trying to say?"

"What kinda fear?"

"Hell, I'm not sure, or I could do something about it, you know? Sometimes I can't figure out why I do things, Mary."

She felt the familiar pity trying to coil itself like snakes around her heart. *Not this time, not this time!* "Jake, Jake . . . I could have you arrested."

"Yeah, you could." He stared at the carpet. "I wouldn't blame you. Maybe you should."

"It won't be necessary," Mary said, "if we stop seeing each other. Or if you go get some professional help."

His mustache arced down and his eyes flashed anger. He drew a deep breath, containing his aggravation. "It's nothing I can't handle myself!"

"You haven't so far."

"That's *so far,* right?"

She sighed. "Right, Jake." How he wanted to be tough, to kill the parts of himself that felt.

The weekend early news had gone full circle and was rerunning on TV. Mary had been barely conscious of it, but now a name snagged her attention: "Danielle Verlane."

A severe woman in a tailored suit was co-anchoring the news this morning. She led into a repetition of the tape Mary had watched earlier, Rene Verlane being interviewed in his New Orleans home, seated on his sofa and looking handsome and suave and deeply touched by tragedy, wearing his grief like a true Southern gentleman. He again expressed his opinion that his wife's murder might have had something to do with the world of ballroom dancing, since on the night of her death she'd been last seen doing a tango with a man in a New Orleans night spot. Not many men, he pointed out, knew how to tango. This tape ran several seconds longer than the last version Mary had seen. She watched as Verlane barely repressed his outrage at how the police and some of the media were suggesting Danielle was somehow to blame for her own murder.

"See what your dancing can get you?" Jake said, his injured gray eyes fixed on the screen.

Mary knew he was only partly joking. They'd talked about her dancing before. Jake thought it was a stupid pastime and refused to join her in it, but he accepted her absences when she spent time at the studio. She'd tried to explain why she danced, but either he couldn't understand or she couldn't find the right words. It was her fault, she supposed, because she'd never completely explained even to herself why she so desperately needed to dance.

"None of my business, Mary, but I know how much those lessons cost."

"Cost doesn't have anything to do with—"

"So whadda we have here? Art?" For some reason he was angry. "You're no twenty-year-old Ginger Rogers. You're a thirty-five-year-old yuppie career woman, am I right?"

"You're right if you wanna be, Jake. You get outa bed right every morning, and you go to bed that way at night."

He grinned and shook his head hopelessly. "Hey, I went and got you mad again. Got myself mad. I'm sorry, babe, I really am."

She knew he was, but she didn't want to acknowledge it. "I have to leave for work, Jake."

"Huh? It's Saturday."

"I'm working extra hours. Besides, weekends are the biggest days in real estate."

"You're really serious? You're going to work?"

"That's why I'm up and dressed, Jake."

"You never worked before on Saturday."

"Sure I have."

"Not very often."

"Well, I need the money."

"For what? Something to do with dancing, I bet."

"You'd win that bet."

He thought about that, then shrugged. "Well, if it makes you happy it's okay with me."

"That's indulgent of you, Jake."

He glanced again at the TV; a commercial for dog food now, edited so beagle pups appeared to be dancing in unison. The New Orleans murder hadn't been a big story, so it had played toward the end of the broadcast.

"You oughta remember what happened to that guy's wife, Mary. I mean, in a way it was *her* fault, out dancing with strange characters. You take a big chance, doing something crazy like that."

"She didn't murder herself, Jake." The pups began to sing.

"You wanna play games and run back and forth across the street blindfolded, eventually you're gonna get hit by a car. It'll be the driver's fault, but then again it won't be. It'll be your fault for tempting fate. That was the game she was playing, tempting fate."

"She went where men knew how to dance," Mary said. "That's not tempting fate, it's wanting to tango."

"Her husband shouldn't have let her go. So in a way it's kinda his fault, too."

"He obviously didn't know where she was. Or maybe he knew and didn't care. I mean, for God's sake, she was only dancing."

"And now she's only dead."

Mary picked up her purse. "I gotta get outa here, Jake."

He put on his hurt-little-boy expression, ludicrous on such a big man. "Mary, I worked till past midnight, and I been up all night."

"So go home and go to bed. I've gotta leave."

"Hey, I'm exhausted. Why can't I catch some winks here?" Hint of a smile. "I mean, it's not like I'm a stranger to the bed."

"Jake—"

"I'll be gone way before you get home, Mary. I promise. So what'll it hurt? If I try to drive now, I'm so beat I'm liable to fall asleep at the wheel and plow into some kid on his way to school."

"Not on Saturday, Jake."

"So maybe he's going to school to earn extra credit, the way you're going to work to earn an extra couple of bucks."

It was impossible to argue with him. And he looked immovable, all 220 pounds of him. But she didn't want him here, in her bed again. Didn't want to make that concession, turn that corner.

Then she saw again the horrible thing on her car last night, and the knife marks on her door. There might be some advantages to having Jake in the apartment while she was away. Anyone watching the place might assume he was still living there, or that he might turn up at any time. She thought, Better than a doberman.

She said, "All right, Jake. Just this once. I'm only working till one o'clock, and I expect you to be gone when I get back."

"Hey, Mary, didn't I promise?"

"You've promised before and broken your word."

"I know," he said miserably. He peeled off his shirt and turned his broad back on her, swaggering toward the bedroom. The shirt had been plastered to his flesh. He was sweating heavily despite the coolness of the apartment. He raked his fingers through his dark hair. "Don't work too hard, Mary," he called over his shoulder.

She wouldn't. The office was only her first stop, and she planned on spending a little over an hour there to get her desk in order. Then it was on to Romance Studio for an extra lesson with Mel.

She said, "Thanks for the rose," and closed the door behind her.

12

After her lesson with Mel, Mary had gone window shopping, then had lunch at one of the mall's food courts. She'd wandered around and killed time until three o'clock before returning home.

There was no sound in the apartment; the air was thick and still. She placed her dance shoes on the coffee table, then removed her street shoes, leaving them lying on their sides like casualties on the carpet. In her stockinged feet, she crept down the hall and peered into her bedroom.

The bed was empty. Jake was gone.

Mary puffed out her cheeks and exhaled in relief. Or at least she told herself she was relieved. She walked to the bed and smoothed the sheet, fluffed the pillow, and brushed a dark hair away.

Standing back with her fists on her hips, she looked around. There were Jake's socks wadded on the floor near her dresser, as if he needed to leave something of himself behind to mark his territory. Mary went to the socks and picked them up gingerly with her thumb and forefinger. She carried them into the kitchen, where she deposited them in the wastebasket. After washing her hands at the sink, she dried them on a paper towel, then stuffed the towel down through the lid of the wastebasket, on top of the socks. She wouldn't have to think about Jake now.

Sunday morning Angie was drunk.

As soon as Mary walked in the door, she could smell gin on her mother's breath. "Oh, damn, Angie!"

Angie appeared mystified. "Something wrong?" Her enunciation was precise. *Too* precise. Her hair was combed neatly on the right side of her head but stuck out in wild red tufts on the left. She looked like a child's worn-out doll, left too long at the bottom of the toy chest.

"It's only ten o'clock," Mary said.

"That's true, Mary. You're late." Mary and her mother had a

standing date to have Sunday morning breakfasts at Uncle Bill's Pancake House.

"And you've been drinking."

Angie was wearing her good navy blue dress, but it was buttoned crookedly so it bunched around her waist. "Oh, that. It was just a nip of an eye-opener. Nothing to cause concern, daughter."

"Bullshit, Angie. I know you and alcohol. It's all or nothing with you two."

"Like a couple of lovers, huh?" Angie said. She turned away from Mary, bowing her head. Was she crying? She didn't sound like it when she said, "Just who the fuck in this world can you depend on? Will somebody tell me that? Will they?"

Mary touched her shoulder. "Me. You can depend on me, Angie."

Angie shivered as if cold and walked out from under her touch. "Yeah, I s'pose I can."

Mary strode the rest of the way into the living room and sat down on the sofa. Angie hadn't switched on the air-conditioner. The apartment was hot. The smell of gin was strong, like sweet medicine.

"You spill some liquor?" Mary asked.

Still looking away, Angie said, "I got a little upset and a bottle broke."

"You dropped it?"

"Threw it against the wall over there." A vague wave in the direction of the front wall.

Mary saw a stain on the wall, just beneath the windowsill. Broken glass in the carpet glinted in the morning sun. Angie had been pissed off, all right. Desperate. Mary said, "This about Fred?"

"Yeah, fickle Fred."

"Who told you about him?"

Angie snorted, wiped her nose, and turned to face Mary. There was a bead of mucus on her upper lip, and her eyes were rimmed in pink. She looked very tired and very old, and, for a frightening instant, not like anyone Mary knew. "Fred told me about Fred."

"What'd he say exactly?"

"Said you was bound to tell me about him dancing with a woman at Casa Loma Friday night, so he mize well tell me first."

"Well," Mary said, "he was only dancing with her." Wasn't

that all Danielle Verlane was doing the night of her death? Wasn't that how Mary had defended her against Jake's accusations yesterday? Now she was defending Fred, but not meaning it.

"Fred's sure as hell no dancer," Angie said. "The knees he's got, he's lucky he can walk across a room without falling on his ass."

Mary had to smile. "Yeah, the truth is he didn't look all that smooth."

Angie pulled a wadded Kleenex out of her pocket and wiped her nose as if trying to tear it from her face. Maybe she'd hurt herself, because she dabbed delicately at her eyes. "Fred said not to make anything outa that Casa Loma thing. Said the woman you saw him with was just somebody he knows from his part-time job, and they're friends is all. You believe that shit?"

"I dunno. So what'd you tell him?"

"Didn't tell him anything—I hung up."

"When was all this?"

" 'Bout an hour ago. Phone's rung several times since then."

"It's possible Fred was telling the truth," Mary said.

"We had a date Friday night. He called and broke it. Said something about an emergency on the job. Bastard threw in a lotta details to make me believe him. I know that game. You do, too."

"What's that mean, Angie?"

"You and Jake." Her nose was dripping again, mucus catching the light like the broken glass in the carpet. "I know about men like Jake, Mary. You and him back together?"

"No."

"Good. The sick bastards don't change. Your father—"

"Angie!"

"Okay. Duke had his good points; I get dru—Sometimes I forget that, but you shouldn't. I don't wanna say anything I'm sorry for. But Jake, I mean, I see Duke in Jake. Maybe that was to be expected, that you'd go for a guy reminded you of Duke."

"Jesus, Angie, Jake's nothing like Duke was!"

" 'Cept in a dangerous way."

Mary remembered the marred doorjamb, the message of the dead bird. Jake wasn't the only one who was dangerous; in fact, having him back in her apartment would provide a certain degree of protection. But this wasn't the time to tell Angie that.

"If Fred called an hour ago," Mary said, wanting off this subject, "you can't have been at the gin very long."

"Sometimes it don't take long."

"What about this morning?"

Angie breathed in deeply and stood very still, her arms extended straight out to the sides at shoulder height. "I'm okay this fine morning. Really, I am. I only had a couple of hits off the bottle, then the phone rang and I knew it was Fred calling back, so I lost my temper just listening to the goddamn phone, and that's when I made that mess over there on the wall." She grinned. "Felt great, even if it was a waste of good booze."

"There's no such thing as good booze for you."

"Oh, you're right, Mary. I know you're right." She dropped her arms suddenly so her hands slapped against her thighs, as if abruptly giving up on a momentary notion of flying.

"You think you're okay to go get some breakfast?" Mary asked. "You need food in you, and I think we need to get outa here."

"I can make it," Angie assured her. "Least I'll be fine by the time we reach Uncle Bill's. You better drive, though."

"I'd intended on it. Button your dress straight, all right?"

"Ain't that the style?"

"Like feather boas," Mary said, and waited patiently while Angie fumbled with the buttons.

She watched Angie take the stairs to the street door. She seemed to be moving okay, had her balance, even though she had a death grip on the banister.

In the car, Mary gave her a cinnamon Life Saver from the roll she kept in the glove compartment to freshen her breath before dance lessons. "You gonna forgive Fred?" she asked.

"To forgive's divine," Angie said, chomping on her Life Saver so hard Mary feared she might break a tooth. "It's in the Bible."

"I don't remember the nuns at Saint Elizabeth's telling me that."

"You done really well in school, Mary, right through college. I mean, truly applied yourself."

"Is Fred gonna be the recipient of divine forgiveness?"

Angie stared out the window at the sparse Sunday morning traffic. "Fred's all I got, such as he is."

"Could be worse, I guess," Mary said.

"We tell ourselves that, don't we?"

"Yeah, we do."

"You're a good daughter."

"I know, I know."

"Gimme another one of them mints, will you? Women like us, we gotta stick together."

13

They sat in a window booth, gazing out at the traffic swishing past on Kingshighway, while they ate Uncle Bill's pancakes and sipped coffee. The restaurant was crowded as always on Sunday mornings; many of the customers were dressed up, on their way to or from church. Waitresses scurried between the tables, balancing trays of hotcakes, eggs, and steaming coffee, refilling cups and smiling and dealing out checks signed with a scrawled "Thank you" above their names. In the air was the faint smell of hot cooking grease and frying bacon. The murmur of conversation flowed over the clinking of flatware and china.

Angie had ordered wheat cakes and saturated them with butter and syrup. She didn't say much while she ate, but Mary could see she was feeling better, and the three cups of strong black coffee she'd downed had to have gone a long way toward sobering her completely.

After her last bite of pancake, Angie fumbled in her purse for a cigarette, then leaned back and fired it up with a disposable lighter. An elderly couple at a nearby table glared as a finger of smoke found them, but Angie paid no attention. This was the smoking section, and Mary knew her mother would defend with nail and fang her constitutional right to foul the air. Her life was pulled this way and that by forces she didn't understand, but what territory she was sure of, she would fight for with tenacity beyond reason. Mary was glad the people at the nearby table were almost finished eating. She'd seen militant nonsmokers and Angie clash before, and didn't want to see it again. She wondered as she often did how a woman so fierce in public could have been such a punching bag for Duke.

As if reading her mind, Angie exhaled a glob of smoke thick as cream and said, "It's a pattern that's sometimes impossible to break, a relationship like yours and Jake's."

Well, she hadn't been reading her mind quite accurately. "I was thinking about you and Duke," Mary said. She could defend her territory in public, too.

Angie's mouth smiled beneath weary eyes, her teeth stained by years of nicotine. "Okay, just so there's some way I can get you to understand. Duke, Jake, they're all alike; put 'em in a bag and shake it and it don't matter which drops out. That's the point. It's like they're born with the need and the cruelty, and early on they learn what buttons to press and strings to pull so they can control people. Some men are like that. They move knowing how it'll make *us* move. It's like a dance we do and we got no choice in. You oughta understand that."

Mary stared out the window. "That's not my idea of dancing."

"Okay, so it was a bad whatchamacallit—an analergy."

"Analogy," Mary corrected. "An allergy's something that makes you sneeze."

"So I see why you was a whiz in school." Angie flicked ashes onto her plate. "I phoned your apartment yesterday morning. Jake answered."

"He didn't spend the night," Mary said, irritated that she felt she owed her mother an explanation. Maybe the reference to school had put her in that frame of mind; lonely hours of study, trying to make everything perfect. Buttons. Strings. Duke. Her professors at the University of Missouri. The past was gone, no longer existed, yet it seemed to illuminate and shadow her life like time-delayed light from a dead star.

"Some things have been happening to me," Mary said, trying to get Angie's mind off Jake. She told her about the knife marks on her apartment door, but not about the Casa Loma incident with the dead bird. She didn't want Angie to worry *too* much.

Angie waggled her cigarette and said, "Jake."

"Jake isn't into that kinda thing, Angie, believe me!"

"Maybe he's got reasons you don't know about."

"Not likely. I understand Jake."

"Nobody understands anybody."

The couple who'd been bothered by the smoke stood up to leave. The man laid a dollar bill on the table for a tip and shook his head at Angie before walking away, as if to say it would be hopeless to try reasoning with her. A woman and a young man with a dark beard were shown to the table and sat down. They wore jeans and matching turquoise sweatshirts. The man was carrying a fat Sunday paper. Mary found herself peering at it to see if there was anything about the Danielle Verlane murder case, then decided she shouldn't be so interested. It was something that had happened in New Orleans, not here in St. Louis. It was coincidental and irrelevant that the victim had been a ballroom dancer like Mary, and, like Mary, Mel's student.

But suddenly it occurred to her why she might be intrigued by the story. She and Danielle Verlane were somewhat the same type. Not only did they both dance, but both had the same general facial shape, approximate hair color, and there was something in common about their individual features, especially the eyes. That was how Mary saw it, anyway, insofar as anyone actually *knew* what they really looked like to other people. But it did seem Danielle Verlane was a slightly younger version of Mary. It gave Mary an eerie feeling, as if someone had tapped her on the shoulder, and when she turned around, no one was there.

"More coffee, hon?"

The waitress was hovering above her with a bulbous glass pot. It reminded Mary of a detached eye with the brown orb of its iris rolling sightlessly at the bottom. She nodded, then moved her hand off the table and out of the way while the waitress topped off her cup. Angie waved the pot away with her cigarette hand, leaving a tracer of gray hanging over the breakfast debris like smoke over a bombed city.

"You always had a kinda pluck," Angie said. "I'm counting on that to overcome the family weakness for the wrong men. Don't take Jake back this time." The waitress glided away and veered toward another table with the coffee pot. "Don't do it. Can you promise?"

Mary thought, Promise, hell! "Didn't you tell me on the drive over here you were gonna forgive Fred?"

"But Fred never hit me, not once."

"There's other kinds of abuse, Angie. Some of them worse."

Angie sat back and smoked. Said nothing.

Mary didn't feel like sitting and letting the awkwardness and pall of tobacco smoke build. She touched the puddle of maple syrup in her plate and licked her finger. "That's tasty."

Angie didn't answer.

"You think there really is an Uncle Bill?"

"Sure," Angie said. "We just ate his pancakes. You gotta believe."

That night Mary awoke just before midnight, and there was Jake in the shadows of her bedroom, poised like a stork on one leg and calmly taking off his pants. Her first thought was that she was dreaming. But she lay flat on her back with her head raised, her eyes wide and staring. The room with its subtle noises and smells, the slow-motion turning and bending of the quiet figure now laying the folded pants on the chair, the soft night sounds of distant traffic, the summer breeze drifting in through the window with its gently swaying curtains—it was all real.

Jake was real.

Here in her bedroom.

She sat straight up as if yanked by a string. "Jake, goddamn you!"

He wheeled, startled. "Whew!" His shoulders drooped as his hulking form relaxed. She couldn't see his face in the shadows. He made a half-joking grab at his heart, fingers splayed across his bare chest. "You scared holy shit outa me, Mary."

"What're you doing here, Jake?"

"Doing? Well, I forgot some stuff yesterday, and I figured I'd come get it, but the lights were all out and I knew you'd already gone to bed. Then I said to myself, what the hell, Jake, whyn't you just let yourself in with your key and look around. But I couldn't find what I left, so I thought, well, hell, no point waking Mary up, I'll just sack out here and ask her in the morning if she knows where my stuff's at."

"A pair of socks?" Mary said with disbelief. "You came back for a dirty pair of socks?"

He laughed. "Them? Hell, no. It's my wallet I can't find. It's gotta be here, though. Probably in this room. You wouldn't want me to turn on the light so's I can search for it, would you?"

"I'll look for it in the morning, Jake. I'll call you if it's here, which I doubt. I wanna go back to sleep. Now go home."

"Mary! . . ."

"Go home, Jake! Please!"

He walked over to the bed, wearing only his socks and jockey shorts. "Mary, lemme be totally honest. I miss you like crazy and I don't wanna be alone tonight. You don't wanna be all alone either. I know it."

She tried to will him away, but he kept coming and sat on the edge of the bed. The springs groaned and the mattress gave, tilting her toward him. She didn't want to slide in his direction, so she dug her fingertips into the softness of the bed.

Gently, he touched her hair, stroked it. "Ah, Christ, I'm lonely. I miss you so damned much. You miss me at all? The truth, now, Mary, okay?"

He sounded like a schoolboy playing a guessing game.

When she wouldn't answer, he said, "Mary? Babe?" Then he stopped stroking and sat very still. He bowed his head as if in church.

Something shifted in her, some rigid structure beginning to crack. He'd know it somehow; he'd be able to sense the weakness in her. She resisted. "Jake, dammit. Go! Please! You got no right to do this! No damned right!"

"Yeah, I wouldn't claim any kinda rights where you're concerned. Wouldn't force you into nothing you were dead-set against." But he didn't budge.

"Oh God, Jake, what is it you want?"

"Not sex."

"I know that." And somehow she did.

"I wanna lay down next to you is all. So I feel home. So the need and emptiness goes away and I can live through till morning. Don't you ever feel that way? Like you're all hollow inside except for something pulling you in on yourself, like one of those black holes in space that'll suck anything into nothingness."

In the faint light filtering through the curtains, she was astounded to see tears gleaming on his cheeks. The agony written on his face wrenched her insides.

"Lemme just lay down near you till morning, then I'll leave first thing. Will you do that for me, Mary? I won't even touch you, I promise. Not sex, only sleep. I haven't slept more'n half the night since we fought. I'm asking for your help."

"I know you are." She lay very still, listening to the night sounds beyond the walls, and the steady breathing of the man she'd so often lain beside. In the kitchen, the refrigerator clicked on and hummed.

"Mary?"

She was tired, so tired of arguing. She arched her back slightly, dug in her heels, and slid over to the cool side of the sheet.

The mattress tilted, then leveled as he stretched out alongside her and his weight was evenly distributed. She could feel his nearness and the heat emanating from his body. A tremor ran through the bed. She turned her head and saw that he was quietly sobbing, afraid of something but not knowing quite what, ashamed of his vulnerability.

"Not sex," he said again. "Only sleep . . ."

She cradled his head against her breasts while he cried. A warm breeze pushed in through the window and explored the room. Faraway sounds took on a lazy, reassuring rhythm, the city dreaming and softly stirring in its sleep.

Eventually, Jake dozed off before she did.

When the alarm woke her in the morning, she was startled to find herself alone.

14

"So what's it gonna be, Mary?" Mel asked. Grinning, he absently did a complete and perfect spin, casually as another man might unconsciously tug at his earlobe, while waiting for her answer. The blur of action made his sparkling grin seem to linger in the air. Like the Cheshire cat's, Mary thought.

She didn't need much time to decide what dance to concentrate on for the Ohio competition. "Tango," she said.

"It's a good choice," Mel said thoughtfully. "You're strong in tango. We can do that in the Bronze category. And I think you oughta enter Novice class and do some of the other dances. Swing, rumba, fox-trot. Really, you're strong enough in those dances."

They'd stopped dancing beneath one of the many clusters of red and white balloons strung from the ceiling from the last studio party. The one wall that wasn't mirrored was decorated with a series of colorful cut-out dancers, life-size and in perfect dramatic or joyous postures. The festive atmosphere never entirely left Romance Studio. The momentum of each day's dancing seemed to carry to the next.

Ray Huggins, who owned and managed the Romance Studio franchise, ambled out of his office and saw that Mel and Mary had stopped dancing in the middle of the floor and were talking instead. He smiled at Mary and walked toward them. Huggins deftly sidestepped Willie and his instructor Marlene as they wheeled into fifth-position rumba breaks.

Huggins was forty-six and at least twenty pounds overweight. He wore youthful clothes and a tight perm to disguise those facts, and he still moved with the ease and grace of a much lighter and younger man. Ten years ago he was winning trophies in international competition with his rhythm dances, and he could still compete in the smooth dances if he had time to train. But the studio, and the students, demanded most of his time.

"You two cooking up a conspiracy?" he asked with a bright grin. He had perfect teeth.

"Talking about the Ohio Star Ball," Mel said.

Huggins's grin generated even more candle power. "Hey, you're gonna enter. That's great, Mary! You'll knock 'em dead."

"*Maybe* I'm going to enter," Mary said, feeling herself blush.

Huggins gave a loose backhand wave. "What dances you gonna compete in?"

"We thought the tango," Mel said. "I been telling her she's super-strong in tango."

Huggins pressed the tip of his forefinger to his chin, as if trying to form a dimple there, thinking. "Yep, I've noticed Mary's tango. Good choice." He clapped his hands, touched Mary's arm, and said, "Well, I better leave you two alone to practice."

But after he took a few strides he turned around, making it look like a dance maneuver. "Listen, Mary, I shouldn't be telling you this, but the cost of the trip to Ohio for the competition is gonna go up ten percent next month. If you could pay now, it'd save you some money."

Mary had just sent in for new dance shoes, anticipating going to Ohio, telling herself she needed the expensive shoes anyway, even though it wasn't true. "Let me think about it, okay?"

Huggins touched his chin again, rotating his finger this time; there was a lot going on beneath those curls. "Listen, just for you, if you can put a few dollars down, make a commitment, I think I can hold the price for you."

"Like how much down?"

"Oh, just a small percentage."

"Why not ten percent?" Mel said.

Huggins glared at him as if he'd just screwed up nuclear arms negotiations, then he shrugged and grinned. "Your instructor's taking good care of you," he said. "Since Mel made the offer, okay, I'll live with it. Ten percent down, and you're locked into the present price for the Ohio Star Ball. My promise to you."

Mel was smiling, pleased he'd helped work this out in her favor.

"Tell you what," Huggins said. "You decide you can't compete, you get half the down payment back. That's about the best I can do. But for God's sake don't tell anybody I'm sticking my neck out this way for you."

"I won't," Mary said.

"You better keep a lid on it, too, okay, Mel."

"You betcha, Boss." Mel casually did another spin.

"See me in the office when your lesson's over, okay, Mary? You can write a check, and I'll type you out a receipt."

"Fine," Mary said. She and Mel watched Huggins walk back across the dance floor, cross the short stretch of carpet, and enter his office. He left the door open.

"Tango!" Mel said, smiling and stamping his foot. He didn't shout "Olé!" but it was in the air. The quick-quick-slow rumba beat Willie and Marlene had been dancing to was ended. Mel made a good-natured show of beating Marlene to the tape deck, and tango music began. He returned and moved close to Mary into dance position, his young body lean and hard against her. For some reason she thought about him dancing with Danielle Verlane in New Orleans. She hadn't known Mel had taught at a New Orleans studio before coming to Romance. "Nobody really knows anyone," Angie had said, but she'd been talking about Jake.

During the rest of the lesson she forgot about her problems with Jake, about her day at work that went by in a disorienting blur, about Victor hanging around her desk and trying to make small talk. Victor was such a schmuck. And there was more to it than that, really. Sometimes, for reasons she couldn't quite understand, he gave her the absolute creeps.

Mel led her through some *cortes,* then some fans. Mary felt the beat coursing like fever in her blood. She knew she was dancing beautifully.

"Wonderful move, hon," Mel told her, drawing her close again after a series of fans. She smiled, determined to concentrate on her posture, to trace a line even more elegant. Being on the gaunt side could be an advantage in dancing; with the right dress she could seem exquisitely graceful if only she made no glaring mistakes.

After going into Ray Huggins's office and writing a money-market check for five hundred dollars, Mary felt even better. In fact, as she left the studio and walked toward her car, she felt absolutely exhilarated. Only a tango step away from Columbus in November.

She approached the car with some trepidation, almost expecting another grisly symbolic message.

But she'd deliberately parked directly beneath one of the bright lights, and the little yellow Honda was exactly as she'd left it. She climbed in and drove away fast, not looking at her rearview mirror.

Her phone was jangling when she let herself into her apartment.

She expected to hear Jake's voice when she said hello, but instead a woman asked if she was the daughter of Angela Arlington. Something about the voice; the impersonal tone of officialdom. News of tax audits and deaths came in voices like that.

Mary stood still for a moment, a chill on the back of her neck.

"Miss Arlington, is it?"

"Yes."

Silence except for muffled voices, as if a hand had been cupped over the receiver for temporary privacy.

"Has something happened?" Mary finally asked through the lump of apprehension in her throat. She was having difficulty breathing; something heavy seemed to be resting on her chest.

"Your mother Angela was checked into the detoxification center earlier this evening here at Saint Sebastian Hospital. We found your name and phone number among the possessions she left at the desk."

"My God! Is she all right?"

"We think so," the woman said, "but her alcohol level was dangerously high when she was brought here. It's still at an unacceptable level, and there's some possibility of alcohol poisoning."

"Who brought her there?"

A pause. "He didn't leave a name."

"I see."

"I think it'd be a good idea if you came down here, Miss Arlington. So you can see your mother and then speak to the doctor yourself."

"I'll come right now," Mary said.

She hung up the phone, dropped her dance shoes on the sofa, and hurried to the door.

During the drive to Saint Sebastian, her fear for Angie's life clashed with anger at her mother for doing this to herself again. And yes, doing it to her, Mary. She felt a stab of guilt for seeing herself as a victim. *Angie, Angie, don't you know the pain you cause?*

But she was sure Angie did know, only she lost sight of the fact from time to time. It wasn't something you could put in a bottle and look at, like gin.

15

Morrisy bit down hard on the stem of his unlit pipe. He'd been thinking about his former wife, Bonita. About the time he'd discovered her in bed with—

Hell with that! Better not to remember it.

He removed the pipe from his mouth and focused his mind on the Verlane mess. He'd decided to turn the screws tighter on the husband. The asshole kept shooting off his mouth to the media, and it was having its cumulative effect. Subtle and not so subtle pressure, from the media and from higher-ups in the department, was being applied to Morrisy to bring the case to a conclusion. They were beginning to squeeze, and Morrisy didn't like it.

The loose tail kept on Verlane had been stepped up to almost constant surveillance, and in a way calculated to let Verlane know he was being observed. So far there'd been no results, but Morrisy knew these things could take time. Then, when there *were* results, they could be sudden and decisive.

He was leaning back in his desk chair, staring at the dark patterns the gentle salvos of beginning rain were making on the building across the street, when he heard a perfunctory knock and Waxman walked into his office.

Morrisy's swivel chair squealed as he turned away from the window and the view of outside gloom. He liked the expression on Waxman's smooth, handsome face; it suggested he'd found out something he was eager to share.

"Verlane's called the airport," Waxman said, standing close to Morrisy's desk.

They had a tracer on Verlane's home phone, but not a wiretap. Pansy-ass judges needed more than Morrisy could give them right now for a wiretap warrant. A cop's intuition didn't count for as much as it used to, as it should still. "Which airline?" Morrisy asked, nonetheless liking this development.

"I'm supposed to find out any minute now. We can ask some questions when we know, get Verlane's destination." Waxman adjusted his tie's strangulation-tight knot. His sleekly combed hair looked a little wet from the rain. "Think it's cut-and-run time?"

"We'll know more when we discover the destination," Morrisy said, "assuming Verlane made a reservation. Could be just a business trip, but if he's got a seat on a flight to South America or someplace like that, we can figure he's broken enough to confess, providing we pick him up and work him right."

Actually Morrisy didn't think Verlane had reached the point where he'd flee, even if he was guilty. He'd so far demonstrated more anger than fear, shown he had some balls. But you could never tell, so Morrisy allowed himself to hope.

"What if it's South America?" Waxman asked.

"We let him almost make the flight, then we collar him at the airport." Maximum psychological effect; Dr. Schutz would approve.

"And if it's Atlanta, someplace like that?"

"We let him fly, but we keep tabs on him. We wouldn't want him to make a connecting flight in some other city."

"He runs anywhere," Waxman said, "and it doesn't gel with Schutz's theory that the killer might be blanking out the crimes and not know he's guilty."

"I never put a lot of stock in that one anyway," Morrisy said. Yet a part of him knew it was unwise to dismiss completely anything Schutz told him. But this theory made him unaccountably uneasy. "I don't even want to hear about that nonsense," he said to Waxman.

"Fine by me." Waxman carefully brushed raindrops from his hair without mussing it. An oddly feminine gesture. "Verlane hasn't been back to work since Danielle died," Waxman said. "They told me at the brokerage firm he'd taken some vacation time. We got the usual story there, how he loved his wife and they seemed happy together, all that stuff."

"You'd have heard the same thing about Bluebeard's wives," Morrisy said. He meticulously placed the pipe in an ashtray, as if it were actually lit.

"Guess that's true."

"Stay tight on him," Morrisy said. "Wherever he's booked a flight to, when he leaves home, I wanna know how much luggage he's carrying."

Waxman nodded and turned to leave.

"When I say tight," Morrisy said, "you know what I mean?"

"You mean tight," Waxman said. He smiled and left the office.

Morrisy turned back to the window and watched the rain, falling much harder now. It had been raining when Bonita—

He picked up the pipe and clamped it between his teeth again. Stared harder at the grayness beyond the glass.

Squeeze anything tight enough, he thought, and something's sure to break.

16

An overweight nurse with a blotchy complexion and too much perfume sat down with Mary and confirmed Angie's Blue Cross status, then she told Mary to wait and someone else would talk to her shortly. She stood up and walked behind a long, curved desk, where she sat down again. The woman apparently wasn't the one who'd talked to her on the phone, so Mary asked again, "Who was it checked my mother in here?"

The nurse squinted at her computer's glowing green screen. She tapped a few keys and caused the tiny printed information to scroll slowly while she peered at it, then she swiveled in her chair to face Mary. "Sorry. Whoever brought her here didn't leave a name."

A very tall man in a wrinkled white uniform came in and laid some yellow forms on the desk, and the nurse turned her attention to them. She began methodically stapling blue forms to the yellow ones.

Mary walked across the hall and sat down in one of a dozen molded plastic chairs in a drab green waiting room with a low table cluttered with tattered copies of *Time* and *Newsweek.* High in a corner, a TV mounted on an elbowed steel bracket was silently showing a rerun of "Wheel of Fortune." Vanna White was waving her arms gracefully above an expensive-looking stereo outfit, as if trying to cast a spell and make it play without benefit of electricity. She was smiling broadly, even though Angie might be dying. Mary picked up a *Newsweek* with a photo of Mikhail Gorbachev on the cover. He was smiling like Vanna White. Mary tried to read the magazine but couldn't concentrate. She tossed it back onto the table, crinkling the cover and causing Gorbachev to frown.

A woman who looked as if she was from India pushed through wide swinging doors and stopped to talk to the nurse behind the admissions desk. She was tiny and attractive, and wearing a pale green gown and cap. She had on white shoes with clear plastic wrappings over them, so that even her dainty feet were sterile for wherever she'd been or was going.

The nurse pointed to Mary, and the Indian woman walked over to her, very precise and delicate in the way she moved, and with an exotic, somber face. Mary's imagination superimposed a sari over the surgical outfit, and a jewel on her forehead.

"I am Doctor Keshna," the woman said in a high and musical voice, smiling faintly now and offering her hand to Mary.

Mary shook the hand, also delicate, and very limp and dry. "How's my mother?"

"Not well, of course, though she will be better as soon as the alcohol is out of her system. But naturally that won't solve her problem. Our records show she was a patient here in Detoxification before."

"Yes, about three years ago."

"So, your mother has an ongoing problem with alcohol?"

"Yes. But off and on."

"I see. Has she been dealing with it through a support group?"

"She's been to a few AA meetings, if that's what you mean."

"That's what I mean." The tall man in the wrinkled white uniform shuffled past with another handful of forms. Dr. Keshna glanced somberly at him and nodded. Farther down the hall, he began to whistle "Chattanooga Choo Choo." "Do you think you can persuade her to resume attending AA meetings?"

"It's difficult to persuade Angie to do anything."

Dr. Keshna smiled again. "You and your mother live separately, I believe."

"Yes, we have for years."

"When she leaves here, I think you should make sure she has no alcohol in her place of residence, and that she understands it's extremely dangerous for her health if she resumes drinking."

"I think she already understands that, though she doesn't admit it. Can I see her now?"

"Briefly. She's about to undergo some tests. Preliminary examination indicates she's been imbibing heavily for a very long time. Is that true?"

"I'm afraid so."

"We need to know what damage has been done."

"Damage? What's that mean? She only got drunk, didn't she?"

Dr. Keshna shook her head sadly. "Alcohol ravages the body

slowly, then suddenly the damage makes itself evident. Your mother seems disoriented beyond what is normal for her present alcohol-to-blood ratio. I want to make sure there is no permanent mental impairment."

"My God!"

"I'm sorry. I don't mean to scare you."

But Mary *was* scared. She wanted her mother to remain Angie, not some mentally enfeebled victim of alcoholism. She remembered the inane ravings of her grandmother, Angie's mother, who'd secretly and silently drunk herself to death long before her withered body had surrendered to time in an Illinois nursing home. Mary didn't want to lose Angie, to be alone, to be lonely. *Thinking of myself again.* "Is she conscious?"

"Yes, but not totally coherent, and not feeling very well, I'm afraid. We want to keep her overnight."

"If you think that's best."

Dr. Keshna smiled and nodded. "The nurse at the desk will tell you your mother's room number. You can have about ten minutes with her."

"Thank you."

Dr. Keshna nodded rather shyly, then turned and walked back through the swinging doors.

The nurse behind the desk directed Mary to Room 242 on the second floor, cautioning her which elevator to take.

The room smelled like iodine. Angie was propped up in bed, looking ancient and dazed. Her pale lips arced down tightly, and her eyes gazed dully out from shadowed hollows with the bewilderment of the suddenly and inexplicably old. She seemed to be wondering how she'd gotten here, to this room and this point in time and space. At first she didn't seem to recognize Mary.

"How you feeling, Angie?" Mary asked. She perched on the edge of the high bed and barely touched Angie's arm, surprised by the coolness of the flesh. "You warm enough? I can pull the sheet up around you."

"S'okay the way it is."

"Why'd you go off and get stinking drunk like this?" Mary asked. She was afraid of the answer, because she knew it might in some measure be her fault for noticing Fred Wellinger with the woman at Casa Loma, then letting herself be noticed. That might have started something that had unraveled and led to this.

65

Angie merely shrugged and looked away.

Mary couldn't let it rest. "Because of what Fred did?"

"Guess so," Angie said, still facing away from Mary. Her voice was flat and seemed to be coming from somewhere beyond the wall. "I really tried to forget it, but it kept gnawing on me. Kept a grip on my mind like a pit bull. Know what I mean?"

"I know."

"So I gnawed back, at Fred. We got in a hell of an argument."

"That's happened before."

"It was quieter this time, and it hurt more. I'm sure he's been seeing that woman."

"He gonna keep seeing her?"

"He says no."

"Well, there you are."

"Yeah, here I am with alcohol poisoning. At least that's what they call it in this place."

"You're alive."

"Am I? It don't feel that way." Her scrawny chest heaved and she exhaled loudly. "I don't know if I can believe Fred. I can't believe what men say. Nobody can, not even other men."

For the first time Mary glanced around the room. It was the same drab green as the waiting room, only the paint was fresher. There was a black vinyl chair by the bed, and a nightstand with a green pitcher of water and a box of Kleenex on it. Near the head of the bed, a device for checking blood pressure was mounted on the wall, along with some sort of equipment with dials all over it. Mary suddenly noticed something was taped to Angie's chest beneath her white hospital gown; a coiled black wire extended over the edge of the bed and was probably attached to the machine with the dials. Mary saw glowing digital numbers blinking over and over on the machine but had no idea what they signified.

"Who brought you here?" she asked.

"Guy named Jeffrey, or Jerome, or sump'n like that."

"Hm. Where'd you meet Jeffrey or Jerome?"

"Place on Cherokee."

"A bar?"

"Where'd you think I'd go to drink, a church?"

"Some of those bars on Cherokee are rough, Angie."

"I was feeling rough. Like life had shit all over me. And know what?—It had."

"Angie!"

"Anyways, Jeffrey or Jerome was a decent sort, and he sweet-talked me outa the dump and drove me here instead of to his place or my place."

"You weren't going to—"

"I'm an old woman, Mary. And don't forget I'm your mother."

"Yeah, I won't. I can't."

Dr. Keshna pushed open the door, glanced pointedly at her wristwatch, then withdrew without speaking.

"I've gotta leave soon," Mary said. "They wanna run some tests on you, keep you here overnight."

Angie didn't respond.

"You need anything?"

"Besides a drink?"

"C'mon, Angie. What about clothes?"

"I can't much care right now, Mary, about anything. Can't even cry. I'm sorry."

Mary leaned over and kissed Angie's cool forehead. "I'll bring you some fresh clothes to wear home tomorrow morning, okay?"

"Sure, thanks."

Mary started to walk to the door, then she paused and looked at Angie, who was still staring at the closed blinds masking the room's one window. She hadn't really looked at Mary since the first few seconds after Mary had walked into the room. Mary said, "Fred's not worth what you did, Angie. Nobody is."

Angie slowly swiveled her head to stare directly at her. "Just who the fuck is this talking to me?"

"It's me. Mary. Your daughter."

For an instant Angie looked terrified. "My daughter, all right. It's in the genes."

"What's in the genes?"

The door opened again, allowing a draft from the hall. Mary assumed it was Dr. Keshna, but when she turned she saw a young blond nurse carrying flowers. "For you," she said, smiling at Angie. "Where would you like them?"

"The windowsill," Mary said, when Angie didn't answer.

The nurse placed the flowers—azaleas, in a small pot wrapped in red tinfoil—on the sill, then bustled out. Her rubber-soled shoes squealed like mice on the tile floor.

"There's a card," Mary said. "Want me to read it?"

"I know who they're from," Angie said listlessly. "And I ain't astounded he somehow found out I was here. He's got his ways."

Mary stepped over and turned the white card so she could read it. " 'Love, Fred.' That's all it says."

Without emotion, Angie said, "Surprise, surprise."

"Better'n nothing," Mary said.

"That's what I'm s'pose to think."

"I'll see you in the morning, Angie."

"Mary?"

"Yeah?"

"Don't take the bastard back. Don't do the same stupid dance."

"Let's worry about you for a change," Mary said.

"There's a fresh bottle in the hall closet, behind the vacuum sweeper."

"Why tell me?"

"Aren't you gonna drive over to my apartment and clean it of anything with alcohol in it, like last time this happened?"

"That's where I was going," Mary admitted.

"Just trying to make it easier for you," Angie said.

"Thanks."

"Anyways, you'd've found that one right off."

"Want me to feed Boris?"

"No, he's a cat that makes out for hisself. Just leave the kitchen window open a crack so he can come and go as he pleases."

Mary walked from the room. Dr. Keshna was far down the hall, coming toward her with tiny, mincing steps. As she passed, she nodded and smiled warmly, as if Mary were an old and dear friend, but she didn't speak.

As Mary was leaving the hospital, she saw Fred slumped in one of the beige plastic chairs in the waiting room. He spotted her, dropped his *Newsweek*—the one with Gorbachev on the cover— and hurried over to stand nervously in front of her. "You seen Angie?"

He looked as if he'd dressed in a hurry, and his breath smelled like bourbon. Great.

"How'd you know she was here?" Mary asked.

"Buddy of mine name of Jerome brought her in. After he

dropped her off, he realized who she was and gave me a call to let me know what happened."

"They're gonna run some tests," Mary said, "then release her in the morning."

"But how is she?"

"Not good." Let the bastard worry.

"That nurse behind the desk don't know elbow from asshole. She told me nobody could see Angie."

"She's right. That's why I had to leave."

"I can be here tomorrow morning to check her outa this place," Fred said.

"I'll do that," Mary said. "She's expecting me."

Fred gave a bourbony sigh and wiped the side of his neck. "Listen, I don't blame you for not liking me so much, Mary."

She didn't answer. Started walking toward the door.

"I tried to get in touch with you soon as I heard," Fred said behind her. She felt his closeness as he followed. "There was no answer at your apartment, so I called Jake at work to see if he knew where you might be. He clocked out right away and went looking for you but couldn't find you neither. He's the one drove me down here."

Mary stopped. "Where is he?"

"Still parking the car, I guess."

Leaving Fred standing there, she walked quickly out the door and strode across the parking lot toward her car. She didn't want to see Jake. Not now. Please.

She made it into the car and scooted down low behind the steering wheel. She was afraid. She didn't like the vague, dispirited way her mother had talked, as if there were nothing left behind the weariness and defeat in Angie's eyes. Angie was someone she'd always taken for granted, but if something happened to her, Mary would be alone. How alone she was now beginning to realize. Yet she'd see more and more of Angie—the Angie up there in the hospital bed—each morning when she looked in the mirror. There was no way to get more alone. That was how she felt right now, anyway. Her future lay like a trap before her.

"How's Angie?" she heard Jake ask. God, he'd noticed her even slouched in her car parked among hundreds of other cars.

He'd opened the passenger-side door and was scooting in to sit next to her.

"I don't know," Mary said. "They're not allowing anyone to see her till tomorrow."

"Christ! She that bad from guzzling nothing but booze? Hey, you positive she's not into serious drugs?"

Mary hadn't thought of that, but she was sure nothing could come between Angie and gin. "Alcohol's her drug of choice. She doesn't need anything else."

"Hell of a way to be, huh?"

"They wanna run some tests."

"Hospitals love to run tests," Jake said. "Keeps them in business. And that's all they are these days, believe me, nothing but businesses." He must have cleaned up before driving to get Fred; Mary could smell his deodorant, which was not unlike the admitting nurse's perfume. It was making her nauseated in the car's stifling interior. Panic was circling her like a vulture, eager to exploit any sign of weakness.

"I gotta go," she said. She twisted the ignition key and the engine kicked and sputtered to life.

"Mary, you said nobody can see Angie now anyway. No sense staying here."

"That's exactly why I'm leaving."

"I meant there's no sense in *me* staying. So let me come with you, Mary. Please. For you. You need somebody."

The future, like a trap. Either future. Some world. She was glad Fred was waiting inside. Fred, good for something.

"No," she told him. "Anyway, you've gotta drive Fred home."

"I can phone and tell him where my car's parked, and where I got an extra key taped behind the license plate. Let him drive it to his place and we'll pick it up later. This is no time for you to be by yourself, babe."

He was right. They both knew he was right, so why fight it? Why pretend?

Reluctantly she embraced something deep in her. Then the trap, the cold future, seemed to recede. A person had what and whom they had, and she might as well own up to that fact.

She wished right now she were somewhere else, a place where there was music and dancing, a secure, predictable corner of her life that wasn't threatening or ugly.

But she was here, in the hot parking lot of Saint Sebastian Hospital, talking to Jake in the sickly glare of the overhead lights. Like it or not, this was her reality.

He placed his hand on top of hers on the steering wheel and gave it a gentle squeeze that hurt slightly and pressured her heart. "Please, Mary?"

"Let's go," she said. "You can help me search for bottles."

17

Mary clenched her eyes shut and felt what he was doing take her over. She was helpless, shameless and defenseless, and in a way it was a relief to relinquish control to someone, something, beyond her. No control, no responsibility, no fear.

She couldn't have stopped herself even if that was what she wanted. Her stomach tensed and her upper body levitated off the mattress as she groaned and reached orgasm. She was someone else and she was no one at all. For an instant she felt as if she were soaring toward the ceiling. Then she was aware of Jake's heavy hand beween her breasts, pushing her back down on the bed.

He knew her so well, knew how to move in her and what to say, and when not to say anything. Within a few minutes she twined her legs around his thrusting buttocks and reached orgasm again, though this time not so violently.

Seconds later he moaned. She thought she heard his teeth gnash. Then his body arched trembling against hers and she felt him release inside her.

Energy went out of him as he exhaled against her cheek in a long, hot sigh.

"You okay, babe?" he asked. Despite the fact that he was supporting himself on his elbows, his perspiring body was a crushing weight.

"Yeah, I think so," she said hoarsely. "Just get off, please."

After he rolled off her they lay silently, listening to the hum of the air-conditioner and feeling a cool draft flow across their damp nakedness. It had all been so systematic, by now almost a ritual.

About half an hour passed before Jake kissed the side of her neck and moved his hand down between her legs.

"No, not again," she said, and pushed the hand away. It lingered like a predator only temporarily discouraged. "Not so soon."

"Aw, it's not soon at all."

"It is, Jake. Listen to me, please? Will you?"

"Shit!" The voice of a disappointed boy denied a toy.

"Jake . . ."

"Okay, I'm sorry, Mary. I missed you, is all. Hey, you oughta be glad I want you so much." Deliberately rustling the sheets, he settled down noisily on his side of the bed, not touching her. "Maybe when we're old and gray it won't be like that, and you'll be sorry."

"No way I'll get old and gray if you kill me first."

He laughed, his vanity tickled. Mary could manipulate a little herself. No way to live with Jake and not learn something about it.

She said, "I've gotta get up early tomorrow so I can call into work and tell them I won't be there till afternoon."

"I'll drive you down to the hospital to get Angie."

"I don't think that'd be a good idea."

"Yeah, guess you're right. I gotta say your mother's not crazy about me."

"She doesn't have to be," Mary said, and rolled over and kissed Jake on the mouth. What if Angie stayed uncaring and distant from everyone, including Mary? Not like the old Angie? A lifetime of alcohol could do that; Mary had seen it happen. She scrunched closer to Jake and clung desperately to him.

"Hey," he said, "I thought you were the gal that wanted to sleep."

"Changed my mind."

His hand slid between her thighs again and closed possessively on what he sought. Fingers began to massage. She wished he'd move them higher, and he did. Then he pressed his mouth close to her ear and whispered, "I own you, babe, you know that?"

She said she knew.

*   *   *

When Mary stumbled into the kitchen the next morning to put Mr. Coffee to work, the first thing she saw was the line of gin bottles on the table. Five of them, all taken from Angie's apartment. Three less than half full, two unopened. They drew the morning light and recast it as a rainbow of color over the table, reality bent and filtered through a prism and made beautiful. Temporarily.

Mary sometimes wondered how she'd escaped the compulsion to drink. The illness that was so often hereditary. Angie was—let's face it—an alcoholic. And Duke had probably been one. Mary told herself she could take or leave alcohol, yet she seldom drank anything stronger than wine. Maybe that was because she'd seen what hard liquor could do. What it had already done to her life, even though she hadn't been the one who'd drunk it. She tapped one of the opened bottles lightly with her fingernail. The clear tone it emitted was bell-like and beautiful.

Angie had been ingenious in hiding her stash of booze. One half-full bottle had been in the kitchen cabinet, like a decoy. It had turned out to contain water instead of gin. The other bottles had been buried in a flour canister, submerged in the toilet tank, stuck inside the bottom of the sofa through a rip in the upholstery. And of course there was the bottle behind the vacuum sweeper in the closet, the one Angie had told Mary about. Only it had actually been tucked inside the sweeper's zippered bag, lying there like something waiting to be born.

Mary and Jake had searched the apartment for over an hour; she was reasonably sure Angie would return to an alcohol-free home. Of course, nothing was stopping her from phoning out and having a bottle delivered from the corner liquor store, but at least there wouldn't be alcohol already in the apartment, tempting her.

Mr. Coffee had begun gurgling. Mary padded barefoot back into the bedroom.

Jake was still asleep, lying on his stomach with one arm draped over the side of the bed so his hand lay palm up on the floor. Mary looked at the clock. Quarter to eight. She'd be able to call someone at Summers Realty soon.

She didn't feel like going back to bed, so she decided to take a shower and get dressed. After calling the office, she'd phone Saint Sebastian Hospital and find out what time she should pick up

Angie. She thought that past ten o'clock or thereabouts, and Angie'd be charged for another day in the room. Blue Cross might bitch about that. Nobody wanted trouble with Blue Cross.

Mary went into the bathroom and douched, then turned on the shower. She let her nightgown puddle to the floor and stepped out of it, naked and cool.

When the water was warm enough, she climbed into the shower and washed away some of what Jake had done to her, soaping her genitals and rubbing gently, feeling some of last night happening to her again.

Jackie Foxx, one of the more aggressive salespeople at Summers Realty, answered on the second ring. Mary explained that her mother was ill and had to be checked out of the hospital, and she wouldn't be able to get to work until that afternoon. She'd go directly to the title company for the scheduled closing on a piece of commercial property out in Chesterfield. Jackie Foxx asked if there was anything anyone could do to help, but Mary assured her everything was under control. "Everybody's mother gets sick sooner or later," Jackie said in a sympathetic voice, then hung up and left Mary trying not to think about where that line of logic ultimately led.

Mary called Saint Sebastian and was told her mother would be ready to leave anytime between nine and ten o'clock. Past ten, and the room rate for that day kicked in. Like a motel, Mary thought glumly, only there were two ways to check out.

She didn't have to leave for at least half an hour, so she used the remote and switched on the TV. She tuned in "Good Morning America" at low volume, so it wouldn't wake Jake, then sat back and sipped her coffee.

When her cup was half empty, there was a TV journalist standing in front of the Verlane house in New Orleans again. Network news shows had now fallen in love with this case. And why not? It had everything: murder, anger, mystery, the victim's husband at odds with the authorities.

Mary's thumb eased down on the remote's volume button. ". . . perhaps a new development," the bland-featured journalist was saying. Wind was gusting in New Orleans, riffling his hair and causing a strand of it to keep getting stuck in the corner of his earnest eye.

A tape of Rene Verlane was shown again, this time soundlessly, while the journalist talked about how police were now speculating that the murder of a woman a month ago in Seattle, Washington, might somehow be linked to Danielle Verlane's death. The similarities of the two murders were more than what the police called obvious *modus operandi.* Though both women's throats had been slit, there apparently was something more, a mysterious and grotesque something the police were keeping to themselves, that connected the two homicides. The journalist also said that for the first time Rene Verlane himself might be considered a suspect in the eyes of the police.

Fade to an interior shot of the handsome Verlane seated on his white sofa with his legs crossed. He was wearing a cream-colored suit with a white shirt and flowered tie. Behind him the pale sheer drapes undulated in the breeze like the gowns of dancing angels; at least that was how Mary saw them.

Verlane was explaining that he, too, thought his wife and the woman in Seattle were probably murdered by the same person. The Seattle woman, Martha Roundner, had been a dark-haired, 35-year-old aerobics instructor who'd also been taking ballroom dancing lessons. The police, it seemed, were making light of that correlation and concentrating instead on whatever pertinent fact they were keeping secret.

As Verlane talked, Mary studied his face, searching for some flicker of guilt, but there was none. She hadn't considered before that she might be looking at the killer of a woman, or women, who'd borne a superficial resemblance to her, who'd been "her type" and who'd danced. There was about Verlane a smooth kind of brutality that strangely intrigued her. Merely watching the man on television, Mary could feel his magnetism.

"It isn't fair," he was saying in his syrupy accent, "that the New Orleans police, and now the Seattle police, are keeping some key piece of evidence from the husband of one of the victims. Sure, I understand they want a trump card to play on the suspected killer—if the investigation ever reaches the point where they have a suspect—but a husband has the right to know everything possible about his wife's death."

The interviewer, now with his hair neatly combed, was professionally noncommittal about that, and tactful enough not to point out that the spouse was traditionally the prime suspect in a murder case. Was Verlane putting up a front? Talking like a guilty man? Let the viewers draw their own conclusions.

"What, if anything, do you intend doing about it, Mr. Verlane?" he asked smoothly.

The camera zoomed in for a tight close-up. Verlane's strong dark features were set (Mary wondered how he shaved the deep cleft in his chin without cutting himself; it was a ravine), and his lips barely moved as he spoke. "Since I can't get anywhere with the New Orleans police, I plan to travel to Seattle and find out what I can about the Roundner woman's murder."

"Do you intend to conduct your own investigation?"

"Why not? The police don't seem to be making progress, either on my wife's case or on that of the murdered woman in Seattle. There's certainly no law against my trying to learn what they won't tell me. I'll go wherever necessary, and I'll do whatever's necessary, to find my wife's killer, and the police be damned!"

Somewhat unnerved by the vehemence of Verlane's response, the interviewer thanked him and turned to face the camera squarely, addressing the New Orleans station whose tape was being used on the network news.

Mary found herself sitting on the edge of the sofa, leaning forward and staring at Rene Verlane, who was still visible behind the reporter. She sat fascinated by him until the picture faded and a commercial came on the screen, an aerial view of cars speeding in formation across the desert.

She decided to buy a *Post-Dispatch* on the way to the hospital, not only to read more about the Seattle murder, but to see if there was an accompanying photo of Martha Roundner. She wondered how strongly the Seattle victim, like Danielle Verlane, resembled her. And might there be some other connection? Had Mel also instructed this woman?

It was strange, this powerful compulsion to satisfy her curiosity about the deceased, almost as if she hungered to learn about a sister she'd never met.

She sat for a while longer with the TV turned off, sipping coffee and listening to Jake's snores drifting like muted thunder from the bedroom.

When her cup was empty, she left the apartment, still thinking about the dead woman in Seattle.

18

There was no photograph of the victim, in fact nothing about the Seattle murder, in the newspaper Mary bought in the hospital gift shop.

She managed to check Angie out of Saint Sebastian without incident, though Angie had to agree to see the gently persistent Dr. Keshna the next week. In the interim, the doctor would phone with the results of Angie's tests. A young volunteer in a candy-striped uniform brought Angie down to the lobby in a gleaming chrome wheelchair while Mary got the car. Angie didn't need the wheelchair, but she didn't object; she had been here before and knew it was standard check-out precedure.

During the drive home, she sat subdued and staring straight ahead, as she had after her previous stays in Detox. There was no way to know how much or often she'd been secretly drinking during the last few years; this might be her first really dry time in months.

While Mary was stopped for a red light, Angie said, "You sweep my apartment clean of bottles?" Her words carried little emotion, the voice of a pull-string doll.

"Got 'em all," Mary said. She felt the idling car's vibration running along her buttocks, up her back.

"Bet you didn't."

Mary glanced at her. "Five gin bottles, including the one with water in it."

Angie, still looking older and wearier than Mary could ever remember seeing her, stared over at her and raised her eyebrows in mild surprise. "Well, I guess you did find 'em all."

Accelerating away from the now-green light, Mary wondered if that was true. Alcoholics were like any other kind of drug addict; though they might be naive in other areas, when it came to their addictions they were incredibly savvy and conniving. Lying to themselves and others was the necessary evil in their lives.

"Still feel okay?" Mary asked, turning a corner.

77

"Sure." The same flat tone. Angie screwed up her eyes against the harsh sunlight and gazed intently out at the traffic, as if she'd never before seen a car. "Gets a little tougher each time this happens," she said. "Or maybe that's 'cause I'm getting older." She flipped down the sunvisor.

"Getting older's better than the alternative," Mary said, concentrating on her driving.

"That's what they say. Used to say the earth was flat, too."

"Don't talk that way, Angie."

"Well, why not?"

"For one thing, Fred sure as hell isn't worth it."

"Such a wise daughter about other people's lives. You search my apartment by yourself?"

"Jake helped me."

"Uh-huh. And I guess he's home in your bed right now."

"That's right, Angie." Irritation swelled in Mary and became full-blown anger. She stomped down on the accelerator and roared around a bus whose diesel fumes found their way into the car. The lumbering vehicle had a liquor advertisement on its side, a young and gorgeously healthy couple toasting each other by candlelight. "Seems to me you've got enough to worry about without concerning yourself with me and Jake."

Angie said nothing, but she pursed her lips in a way that made them look withered. The mouth of an old, old woman. Mary felt her anger plunge and become pity. She shouldn't have talked that way to her mother.

She said, "How'd you know Jake and I were back together?"

"Fred told me. He phoned this morning."

Mary saw her knuckles whiten as she squeezed the steering wheel. Why didn't Fred mind his own business? Why didn't they all?

"I'll drop in on some AA meetings, like I was told," Angie said. "I won't drink any booze for a long while, anyways. You know I never do after a hard bender."

Mary did know. That was a common pattern with alcoholics after a stay at a detox center. It was as if they were immune from their desires for a while. But there were exceptions, and things could become unbearably ugly. Something else might set off Angie again, sending her bouncing from bottle to bottle and bar to bar.

Mary didn't want that to happen. Didn't even want to think about it.

"I need you to drop by the apartment so's I can get my mail," Angie said, "then I gotta go to the bank and cash my pension check. You mind the driving?"

"No."

"I know you gotta get to work."

"It's okay." Too much snap in her voice. Take it easy, Mary; go with the rhythm and follow the lead, like dancing. *Will the new Latin shoes fit when they arrive?*

"I know I'm a pain in the ass in my old age," Angie said, playing the martyr now.

"I said it was okay!"

Silence except for the clattering hum of the motor. At least Angie was making sense, even if she was grating on exposed nerves. Her mind seemed to be working normally. Enough brain cells had somehow survived the years of alcohol.

"Mary, I appreciate what you're doing."

"It's no trouble. I don't have to be anywhere until a one o'clock closing." Mary let herself relax into the car's upholstery. She'd been sitting with her back muscles tense and her shoulders were sore. It was a strain, fighting Angie and the ghosts of childhood and the spirit of a dark future. There was no point to it, no way to win, like jousting with windmills that continued grinding out the same slow diet of agony no matter what.

"Want me to stay with you this morning after we come back from the bank?" Mary asked.

"It's not necessary," Angie said. "Fred's coming over."

When Mary got back to her apartment to change clothes and go to work, Jake was up. He was wearing only baggy Jockey shorts and a white T-shirt, standing in the breeze from the kitchen air-conditioner and building himself a sandwich. An open can of Busch beer was before him on the counter, a puddle around it.

As Mary sat down at the table, he stopped spreading mayonnaise and looked at her and smiled. "How's Angie?"

"Good as can be expected."

"She gonna be okay at home by herself?"

"Fred'll be there. Probably is already."

He placed the top piece of bread squarely on his sandwich, as if precise alignment were crucial to taste. "That's good; she needs somebody right now."

"Not Fred."

"Aw, the old fucker's not such a bad dude."

"Angie'd agree with you, but that's because she's not thinking straight."

Jake took a big bite of sandwich, chewed rapidly with his mouth open, then washed down the half-masticated bread and pastrami with a swig of beer. Mary waited for him to belch, but he didn't. Point for Jake. He said, "You gonna eat lunch, babe?"

"I'm not hungry. Stopped for doughnuts on the way to the hospital." She was lying; she simply didn't want to eat with Jake. A hamburger to go, consumed at her desk between phone calls, was more appetizing.

Had she really enjoyed sex with this man last night, or was he a stranger come to repair the dishwasher? Sometimes Mary felt that way about Jake, as if there were nothing between them and never had been. He kept a part of himself intensely private, came and went at odd hours, disappeared for days at a time, going out of town, she was sure. He was as much an unknown to her, as much an alien, as someone she'd happened to glance at on the street and then seen again. Of course, sometimes she felt that way about her entire life, as if it were somebody else's and she'd somehow become trapped in it. Everything was happening of its own momentum or lack of it, and she had no control. At times Mary thought people's lives progressed like billiard balls across a pool table—once stroked to travel in a certain direction, all the deflections, spins, hard angles, and collisions were unavoidable. And so was the waiting pocket.

The murder victims who'd danced, had they felt that way in their final moments? Or before? Had they sensed their destinies propelling them?

She realized that at this moment she'd genuinely rather die than lie down again with Jake. Dying couldn't be worse, and probably not so different. Wasn't sex—orgasm—much like death only not permanent? A pinnacle of emotion and then a slipping away of self? Death might be like nothing so much as the final, profound orgasm.

Jake said, "You better drive me over to get my car from Fred.

I need to go help some guy change his brake linings before I go into the warehouse."

Mary had forgotten about Fred still having Jake's car. She'd have to drive back to Angie's apartment and drop off Jake before going to the title company. "How about getting dressed, then?" she said. "I need to get going." She had plenty of time, really, but she could stop by the office and do some work before the closing.

He shrugged, scratched his crotch, and took a bite of sandwich. "Sho all right." Chomp, chomp. Swallow. "Lemme finish my lunch and we'll be on the road. Won't take me long to get dressed to work in the warehouse. It ain't like I meet the public. What you gonna do this evening while I'm working?"

"Dance lesson."

"Yeah, it figures."

"It does figure, Jake. If you don't like it that I dance, I'm sorry."

"Hey, it's okay with me, babe, long as it makes you happy and you don't try talking me into dancing with you. I just can't see myself tripping the light fantastic and all that shit, you know?"

"Do I try talking you into it?"

"Not anymore." He grinned to let her know he was kidding, then said, "You still got that same swish instructor?"

"Same one," Mary said. "He's not gay, though."

"Well, maybe not. But I seen some of them dance instructors that night I went out to the studio to pick you up last year. They look like hair stylists with muscles."

"You're a homophobe, Jake."

"Which is what?"

"Never mind."

Mary went into the bedroom and put on a clean skirt and blouse, then combed her hair and inserted her tortoiseshell barrette and clipped it tight. She checked her image in the mirror, turning her head quickly, as if to catch herself off guard and glimpse the true Mary. She decided she looked sufficiently businesslike to deal with real estate attorneys.

She phoned Angie to make sure Fred was at her place, then she drove Jake there. She pulled up to the curb and didn't turn off the motor.

"Sure you ain't got time to come up?" he asked.

"I've used too much time already. Angie understands. She won't be insulted."

He popped open the little car's door, then worked his bulk out and stood on the bright sidewalk. Heat wafted into the car. Before shutting the door, he leaned down and peered in at her. The sun was hitting him square in the face, making him squint. "You sure you're all right, babe? I mean, after last night?"

"You were gentle enough, Jake."

He shot her a wicked smile. "More gentle than you like?"

"Shut the door, Jake. I've just gotta get to work."

Still smiling, he slammed the door hard enough to jolt the car and give her a headache.

Hoping she wouldn't need to buy some Tylenol, she watched him disappear into the sun-washed building before she drove away.

By the time she reached the corner her fingers were manipulating the radio's pushbuttons, searching for dance music. Tango, if possible.

19

When she entered her office she was surprised to see Victor seated behind her desk, gazing up at her like a lonely puppy and smiling as she pushed through the door. His hair lay like a fallen gate over his bald spot, and his wire-rimmed round glasses snagged the sunlight and made his eyes look as human as flashlight lenses.

"Mary, how's your mother?"

She placed her purse on a desk corner. "She'll be all right, thanks. I thought you had floor time out at Suncrest subdivision today."

He stood up out of her chair, tucking in his white shirt, then shrugged. There were yellow crescents beneath his armpits. "When I heard you couldn't be in till noon, I thought you wouldn't mind if I used your desk as a quiet place where I could catch up on my paperwork."

"I mind, Victor." He said nothing, acted as if she'd approved of his presence. She didn't like the idea of Victor at her desk, able to search through the drawers. Not that she had anything to hide, but privacy meant something. It was like rape, having your personal belongings handled by a man you despised. She moved around to sit in her desk chair. It was still warm from Victor. She didn't like that, either.

"You used my desk last month when I was away on vacation," he pointed out.

He was right, but she said nothing. It had been Gordon Summers who'd instructed her to use Victor's desk while her office was being painted.

"Buncha memos for you," he said, pointing to the pink forms on her desk. "Not much important, really. Mr. Summers is still at the seminar in Chicago, and he asked for a copy of the Gratiot contract to be faxed to him. I took care of that."

As he spoke he was staring at her intensely, making her uneasy. Why did she often attract men like Victor? She wished he'd leave her alone, that he wouldn't bother trying to hide his bald spot, that he wouldn't be so ordinary, that he had a chin. Mr. Nice. Mr. Stability. Mr. Monotony. Why wasn't she ever attracted to men like Victor? Maybe because they were almost always *like* Victor.

"Where you going now?" she asked, trying to hurry him along, thinking, Go anywhere, please!

"Out to grab what's left of that Suncrest floor time, I suppose." The sales agents regarded floor time at the subdivisions as gold, where they had a virtual lock on any serious buyer who came along.

"Good luck out there," Mary told him, with all her might willing him to leave.

"Thanks. I've got a couple of prospects from last time I was there. Gave them my card. Oh, by the way, I told Mr. Summers about your mother being sick."

"What? Why'd you do that?"

"He asked why you didn't answer the phone. Asked where you were. I mean, I'd of never brought up the subject at all if he hadn't asked. Boss man asks, we gotta answer. You know that."

"Yeah, I do know." She also knew this was no time in her life to change jobs.

"You don't mind if I said something about your mother, do

you? I mean, worst can happen is Summers'll send her flowers."

"No, I don't mind, Victor." *Leave! Leave!*

"Was that your mother I saw you with at Uncle Bill's Pancake House?"

My God, was he following her? "Probably," Mary said.

"I go there sometimes after church. You a religious person, Mary?"

"No, but I'm a spiritual one."

"What's that mean?"

"I guess that I believe in something, but I'm not sure what it is."

"Well, that's better'n having no god at all."

Mary bowed her head and pretended to study something on her desk. In the periphery of her vision she could see Victor's stomach paunch and his gray suitpants. He hadn't budged, and the front of his pants was twisted in a way that made her wonder if he had an erection.

He cleared his throat. "You need any kinda help with your mother, Mary, you know you can call on me."

She stared harder at the papers on her desk, not even knowing or caring what they were. "Thanks, Victor, but everything'll be fine, I'm sure."

She said nothing more, letting the silence expand and fill the room with pressure that might force him out the door.

Victor deflated the silence. "Anytime."

"Huh?"

"I said, you can call me anytime."

"All right." She still refused to look up at him.

Finally she heard him walk away.

A few minutes later his bland blue Chevrolet nosed from the parking lot onto Kingshighway. He glanced over and saw her watching him through the window. That seemed to please him. The Chevy's tires *eeped,* and he waved to her as he drove away.

Are you a religious person?

What an asshole question. How many people stopped to think their religion gave them convenient parent substitutes? Our Father which art in heaven, and the Virgin Mother, provided the unconditional love and infinite capacity for forgiveness we all yearned for from infancy. It was all such an obvious sham that Mary couldn't sustain faith. It was beyond her how anyone could.

After running up the closing figures on her adding machine to double-check them, she left for the title company. She didn't return to her office until four o'clock, still seething from dealing with the purchaser's unreasonable attorney, and worked until six.

Before driving home to change clothes and pick up her dance shoes, she stopped at a Denny's restaurant and had a club sandwich and glass of iced tea for supper. She'd had a cup of soup from the vending machine at work and wasn't all that hungry, but she wanted time for her food to settle before she stepped onto the dance floor at the studio.

Helen and Nick were practicing tango, working on a routine. Ray Huggins spotted Mary from his office and smiled and waved to her, but she didn't see Mel anywhere.

She sat down on the vinyl bench and started changing shoes, hoping he'd appear; he'd stood her up for lessons a few times, been sick or had car trouble, and she'd taken her instruction from Nick or Stan. Sometimes it was good to switch instructors briefly, to get accustomed to different styles at high levels of skill, but Mary preferred Mel. He was the one she'd be dancing with in Ohio, and right now that was what was important.

As soon as she'd fastened the strap on her right shoe, she looked up and there he was, padding across the floor toward her from the storage room in back where the instructors kept their competition costumes. He had on a totally black dance outfit with shoulder pads and a sash around his narrow waist; he looked like a cat burglar out to steal love.

"I was practicing a bolero routine with Maureen," he explained, holding out his hand for Mary. "We're gonna do it in Miami."

"Bet it's great," Mary said. Maureen, who was the tallest female instructor, looked good dancing with Mel.

"So how do you like my Latin outfit?" Mel asked. He did a quick spin. "I bought it from a shop in Kansas City. There's a kerchief and a red vest that goes with it."

Mary told him he looked dashing, and wondered if the costume was what he'd wear when they danced tango in Ohio. She also wondered how it would look with the dress she was having made. A seamstress named Denise Jones, who specialized in dance competition dresses, had already taken her measurements and down payment on a dress to be worn during the rhythm dances. More than a few women danced competitively for little reason other than to wear the sometimes spectacular dresses, and the flashy and stylish all-important shoes.

Mel walked over and made sure the tango tape had a while to run, then returned and said, "Let's work on head motion tonight. When I lead you into promenade position, you need to put a little more snap into it when you turn your head."

"I'll try."

"I know you will, Mary. That's why you're one of the best students here." He was grinning as he stepped into dance position, moving tight against her and flexing his knees.

"Did you teach Danielle Verlane to tango in New Orleans?" she asked.

He kept position. "How come you wanna know?"

"I'm just curious because she was your student, I guess."

"I taught her some tango."

"Ever teach a woman named Martha Roundner?"

"I dunno. Maybe. You ready?"

"Sure."

"Don't smile during tango," Mel said. "Look sexy. Think candlelight and condoms. It's a dance of male domination."

The one beat arrived and they were dancing.

"Good, Mary! Great! You really are improving."

She couldn't answer, and she realized she was dancing holding her breath. Bad habit. She forced herself to breathe as she remembered to whip her head around in the direction of the promenade step.

Then she quit thinking altogether and simply danced, fell into a kind of trance where everything seemed to happen automatically. Even the music seemed to lose melody and only the sensual tango rhythm remained, beating through her heart and veins.

Time rushed like dark water, and Mel was stepping away from her.

The music had stopped.

"Wow! What happened, Mary? That was terrific!" She knew he often tried to lift her confidence with exaggerated praise, but this time there was something in his eyes, an enthusiasm and a genuine surprise.

"I don't know," she said honestly. "Just catching on, I guess."

"Eee-yow! Catching on is right! Hey, you're breathing hard. You wanna take a break?"

"No, no, I'm okay. Let's work on the *cortes,* tracing a smooth line."

"You got it, Mary! Practice, practice, practice. That's dancing—do it a hundred times and you know it." He rewound the tape and moved back into dance position.

They waited for the one beat and began again.

Mary had wanted to talk to Helen, to ask her if she'd heard about the Seattle murder, but a mambo group lesson had begun during the lesson with Mel, so Mary changed shoes, caught Helen's eye and waved to her, then left the studio.

She'd driven straight home and snacked on microwave popcorn and diet soda, but now she couldn't relax. For about an hour she lay on the sofa with her eyes closed, going over in her mind the tango lesson with Mel. In this version he was wearing the kerchief around his neck, and the red vest. She was enthused over the way it had felt tonight, the oneness with the rhythm and the ease with which she'd followed his lead.

She was so much more comfortable on the dance floor. For the first time, she was not only sure she'd compete in the Ohio Star Ball, she thought she had a chance to win.

Mary stood up out of the couch and picked up her dance shoes. The pair of shoes she'd mailed away for had been in a package by her door. They hadn't fit, and the style was horrendous and nothing like the illustration in the brochure. She'd sent away to Chicago for a new pair of Latin shoes from one of the catalogues at the studio. Good ballroom dance shoes had to be bought by mail and often had to be returned or exchanged several times until a comfortable fit arrived. These shoes were marked in British sizes and ran narrow, so guesswork was involved.

She brushed the suede soles of her old dance shoes with her wire brush. She started to slip her feet into them but then she stopped. She decided to change into something looser and less inhibiting than the Levi's she'd put on when she'd come home. Her robe would be okay.

But when she'd stripped to her underwear and picked up the robe, for some reason she dropped it back on the bed. No one could see her in the spare bedroom where she practiced, so why wear it? In fact, why wear anything at all?

She peeled off her panties and removed her bra, leaving on only her well-worn Latin shoes with their two-and-a-half-inch high heels. Then she shoved aside what furniture there was in the spare bedroom, switched on her portable tape player, and fed it a tango cassette.

She assumed dance position and began a tango with an imaginary partner. He led her beautifully through one flawless step after another, her nakedness taut and elegant.

A soft scraping sound at the window made her freeze in mid-step, made her heart pause in mid-beat. She stared at the curtains and was sure there was no gap; no one could see in. No one could be outside the window anyway, here on the second floor.

She put on her robe and forced herself to walk to the window, stood for a moment, then flung open the curtains.

Nothing.

No one and nothing.

Only the dark night. The noise must have been in her mind.

It was almost ten-thirty. Jake would be getting off work soon.

After showering, then slipping again into her robe, she went back into the living room and slumped on the sofa. Her legs were beginning to stiffen, but she felt spent and relaxed. She used the remote to switch on the TV and tune in CNN news.

Within a short while the footage on the Seattle murder was repeated, as she thought it might be. Cable news ran their tapes over and over. First came the second interview with Rene Verlane. Throughout it, Mary stared fixedly at his handsome, brutal features, feeling his odd appeal and wondering why. The man wasn't merely the pitiable widower of a murder victim; he was a prime suspect.

More tape was shown in this extended coverage of the story. This time a high-ranking police officer named Morrisy, a rough-looking man wearing a frown, a white shirt, and a fancy badge, after complaining about leaks to the press, reluctantly admitted to the voracious news media what the secret thread was that possibly connected the Seattle and New Orleans murders. In both cases there was evidence of sexual intercourse with the victims after death. "Necro-file-ya," he said, mispronouncing the word with obvious distaste.

And this time there was a photograph of Martha Roundner, the Seattle victim.

A bullet of ice shot through Mary and she heard herself gasp. Martha Roundner was virtually her double.

20

"I gotta say I see only a vague resemblance," Jake said.

It was almost midnight when he got to Mary's apartment; he'd stopped at Skittles after work and she could smell liquor on his breath, mingled with the faint odor of stale perspiration from his efforts at the warehouse.

"Look closer!" Mary almost shouted, but the TV picture faded and the photograph of Martha Roundner was replaced by a bald man loudly and enthusiastically demonstrating a Chinese wok.

Jake shook his head. "Hey, I didn't have to look closer. That woman's got a rounder face than yours, and her eyes are set closer together. Got kind of a flatter nose, too. Not like yours."

"*Had,* Jake. She's dead. She *had* a rounder face and flatter nose. Somebody in Seattle killed her the same way the dancer in New Orleans was killed."

"What dancer in New Orleans?"

"The one whose photograph I showed you."

"Oh, yeah. Now, that one *did* look something like you, if you care to stretch a point."

"What's that mean—stretch a point?"

"Means she didn't look all that *much* like you, only a little bit. Hell, maybe even not at all, you see her in person. Seems to me you might just be seeing what you wanna see, you know? People do that all the time. How's he keep from cutting off a finger?"

The man with the wok was frenetically slicing vegetables with a wicked-looking chef's knife, the blade snicking dangerously close to his knuckles.

Mary's heart was beating with an odd exhilaration, as if she'd gulped down five cups of coffee. She felt as if she were living a split second ahead of real time. It was hopeless trying to get Jake to stay on a subject or look at things reasonably, especially after he'd been drinking.

She said, "You mean to say you didn't see any resemblance at all between me and Martha Roundner?"

"Bastard's gonna accidentally whack off his whole hand one of these days. Maybe his dick."

"Jake?"

"Martha Roundner had a rounder face," he said, grinning stupidly. Oh-oh. He'd had more to drink than Mary'd originally thought. A familiar tickle of alarm stirred in her.

"So what's your point, anyway?" Jake asked.

"My point is that somebody's murdering dancers who're my physical type, then having sex with them after they're dead."

"Listen, Mar—Whoa! What'd you say?"

Jake had missed that part of the news report. "They were killed by a necrophiliac," Mary said.

"Which is what?"

"Somebody who has sexual intercourse with dead women."

"Well," Jake said, "that happens to us all once in a while." He started to laugh but phlegm cracked in his throat and he bent over in a brief coughing fit. The scent of liquor on his breath wafted strongly over to Mary.

"Jesus, Jake! These women were murdered, violated, then mutilated with a knife. Don't you have any compassion?"

He wiped the back of his hand across his mouth and swallowed. "They were out fucking around on their husbands at the time, weren't they? Least that bitch in New Orleans was."

"No, she was simply out dancing."

"Same fucking thing." An irritated, dangerous edge had crept into his voice. "Tell you what, Mary, I had a shitty day at work, what with the supervisor riding my ass all day. Let's you and me go to bed and talk about this tomorrow."

"I'm not tired, Jake."

"Not tired? 'S damn near one in the morning. Even the little birds are asleep." His voice was casual, but there was a feverish earnestness in his eyes. And a look she'd seen in the eyes of predators in *National Geographic* TV specials. She knew for sure now what was in his mind.

"You go ahead, you wanna go to bed. I'll be in later."

"Mary, Mary . . . you'll be in now, and it won't be to sleep, huh?"

"Not tonight, Jake."

He moved toward her. She tried to spin away—a dance step— but he caught her elbow. Then he bent down and kissed her on the lips, holding her head tight to his with his free hand on the nape of her neck, biting her lower lip. Then he kissed her gently, for a long time.

Mary felt her resistance break loose and begin its downward spiral, like a leaf spinning to earth in autumn. Jake's commanding bulk was near and overpowering; she could feel the heat of him. She let herself be led toward the bedroom.

The next morning, while Jake was still asleep, Mary walked softly into the living room. The sun angling low through the window was warm on her bare feet. She sat down by the phone and asked Long Distance Information for Rene Verlane's number in New Orleans.

She'd thought Verlane probably had an unlisted number, and she was surprised when the operator read it out for her to write down.

She didn't let herself hesitate before punching out the New Orleans area code and the phone number. What she was doing was insane and compulsive, she knew. But she'd lain a long time in bed thinking about it, and she was determined. She had to call Verlane, had to tell him he was right, the same man killed his wife and the Seattle woman; they looked so much alike, and they were murdered and molested in the same manner, so it just had to be. Mary understood and sympathized with Rene Verlane, because she looked enough like the victims to be a sister. And, like them, she danced.

A woman answered the phone on the third ring and said she was the maid. Mr. Verlane wasn't available to come to the phone and might not be for several days, did Mary care to leave a message?

Mary said no and hung up.

Of course! Verlane was traveling in search of his wife's murderer. He'd be in Seattle, where he said he was going on yesterday's TV interview. He'd seemed vehement about that, a man with a mission.

She thought about calling back and trying to get the name of his hotel, then she decided the domestic help wouldn't give it to her, wouldn't necessarily believe her when she said who and what she was, and why she was calling. Rene Verlane was probably wary of the devious news media. And the police, suspecting him of murder, might not be above trying to trick him. One deadly game led to another.

A horn honked down in the street, a driver signaling to pick up a car-pooler. An intrusion from the outside world. Mary pictured herself sitting there holding the phone. Such a foolish figure. She shouldn't have called. What exactly would she have said if Verlane *had* come to the phone? The fact that she resembled the two dead woman, and that she danced, might have interested him, but where would the conversation have gone from there?

Probably, Mary thought, to someplace where she'd have made a total ass of herself.

Her body jerked when the phone rasped to indicate the receiver had been out of its cradle too long.

She hung up and pressed down hard on the phone, as if trying to anchor it to the table with glue. Verlane might not be in Seattle long; a wealthy man like that probably took planes as casually as others rode buses, brief journeys from this city to that. Maybe she'd call another time, when she could be sure he was home. Or maybe she was only telling herself that, knowing she wouldn't call but not wanting to slam the door on that option. She knew she did that kind of thing at times, clinging to choices as if they were life preservers on a storm-tossed ship. It was a trait she couldn't change. Sometimes finality terrified her.

Glad now that Verlane hadn't been able to come to his phone, she went into the kitchen, where she poked a fresh filter into Mr. Coffee and spooned in grounds, then poured in water to the four-cup level. A cup for her, three for Jake whenever he got up and ate breakfast.

Jake was a man of unpredictable movements and appetites. Mary idly wondered where he'd been the past year during the times he'd been away from her. Had he stayed in the city? His job seniority allowed him to take vacation or sick days almost at will.

He'd probably never mention where he'd stayed, and she wouldn't ask. He might consider it prying, and there might be consequences.

She examined her left wrist, hoping the marks would fade before she left for work. Then she glanced at the clock and hurried to the bathroom, where she showered and dressed quietly. So she wouldn't disturb Jake.

21

On the way to work, Mary stopped at a corner lineup of newspaper vending machines and bought a *Post-Dispatch* and a *USA Today*. On page six of the *Post* she found the news item she was searching for, and the photograph of Martha Roundner that had been shown on TV last night. She folded the paper in quarters so the photo showed, then drove the rest of the way to Angie's apartment to check on her before going to the office.

"The woman looks a little like you, maybe," Angie said, after prompting. She held the paper at arm's length and peered blearily at the photo, as if it were something that might cause her trouble. "Around the mouth mostly. She and you ain't dead ringers, but I can see what you mean." Her voice was still flat, an instrument badly out of tune.

Mary gave up trying to convince her. "You feeling any better this morning?"

"Sure. Some."

The apartment smelled stale and musty, and there was dust thick as peach-fuzz over everything. It was getting uncomfortably warm, too, and Angie hadn't switched on the air-conditioner. The potted plant from her hospital room was on the windowsill and had a parched, brownish look to it, and there was an ashtray on the carpet, littered with the snubbed-out butts that were making the place smell stale. Mary looked at the two glasses on the coffee table. There was an amber residue in each of them, layers of bright color in motionless liquid. Morning-after melted ice made the stillest water in the world.

"That's Pepsi-Cola," Angie said defensively, pulling her terry-cloth robe tighter around her thin body.

"Two glasses?"

"Yeah. Fred and me sat around and talked last night. Straightened out some things."

"Such as?"

"Who and what we are to each other. It was that kinda conversation. You've had them, I'm sure."

"You know more now?"

Angie shrugged. "No, not really, but talking it out till my throat was sore helped somehow." Her mouth still had that withered look above the upper lip, and the faint tracing of a mustache. Time to apply a depilatory, Angie. Time to push your age back where it isn't a worry, for either of us.

"Where's Fred now?" Mary asked.

Her mother gestured weakly with a limp hand that still bore a purple-red bruise from the IV needle. "Other room."

"Bedroom, you mean?"

Angie sighed. "Don't interrogate your old mom, Mary. You ain't the police and you ain't got the right."

Mary thought about last night with Jake. She laughed coldly. "Yeah, I guess I see your point. Anyway, I gotta get to work. You sure you're gonna be okay?"

"Oh yeah. One day at a time, like the AA people say. I can make it through this. I have before, you know."

"Yeah, you have." Mary started toward the door.

"If you're done with them papers," Angie said, "leave 'em here. I could use something to read."

"Sure," Mary said, surprised and glad her mother was interested enough in the world to want to find out more about it. Age and alcohol hadn't quite won yet. Angie continued the struggle, probably not in any real hope of victory, but more out of the realization that all there was to life, ultimately, was a losing battle.

"I heard on the news them murdered women was violated after they were dead," Angie said. "It's awful, but that's better'n if they was raped and then killed."

There was no arguing that. "I guess so," Mary said.

"There's a lotta sick and evil people out there in the world, Mary. Best you remember that, what with your own dancing and all."

"I never forget it, Angie."

"You been bothered again, after what happened to your door?" Angie asked. Mary still hadn't told her about the dead bird incident.

"Whoever did it isn't likely to come back. The police were right, it was just a fluke thing. Kids, maybe."

"Let's hope you're right."

Mary tore out the photograph of Martha Roundner and slipped it into her purse. She laid the folded newspaper on the arm of the sofa before walking out.

In the interest of fair play and employee moral, Hal Bauer, Summers Realty sales manager, had given Victor another day of floor time at Suncrest. At least Mary wouldn't have to cope with Victor today.

It was, in fact, a slow day at Summers Realty. Gordon Summers was still in Chicago. Most of the salespeople were out showing property, and Hal and the administrative help were cubbyholed in the conference room with a CPA. Something about new tax legislation. There were no closings scheduled for the day, so she spent her time readying the paperwork for two residential closings to be made later in the week.

In one of the offices was a cabinet containing telephone directories for most major cities. Mary watched the intermittent traffic roll past, glittering in the sunlight, for a while, then glanced at her watch and saw she had forty-five minutes till lunch time. She stood up, walked into the back office, and found a Seattle directory.

She had nothing important to do at the moment, so why not do this?

She didn't examine the question too closely.

Back at her desk, she opened the yellow pages to the listings for hotels, then dragged the phone closer. She began with the large chains, calling them one by one and asking if there was a Rene Verlane registered.

It was well past noon, and she hadn't eaten lunch or even left the phone, when she reached the *M*'s and was told by a desk clerk at a Seattle Marriott hotel that Rene Verlane had checked in yesterday. The clerk asked if Mary wanted him to ring Mr. Verlane's room, but Mary said she'd call back, then hung up.

Her face felt flushed and her knees were rubbery. She left her hand resting on the receiver, running her fingertips lightly over the warm plastic. The phone had suddenly become something intimate and dangerous.

"Mary?"

She withdrew the hand and jerked her head around.

Victor was standing in front of the desk, smiling down at her. He was wearing gray slacks, blue blazer, white shirt, red tie. Original. If he were a car he'd be a station wagon.

She said, "I thought you were out at Suncrest."

"I was." He tapped his brown vinyl Samsonite attaché case with an air of extreme importance, as if it contained the code for nuclear war, and his grin widened. "I need to get a contract okayed, then I'm driving back out." He peered at her through his round glasses; sunlight shot off the lenses as if they were cubic zirconia. "Listen, you okay?"

"Sure. Why?"

"You had a funny look on your face when I looked in your office."

She put on a nonchalant expression and shrugged. "Just daydreaming, I guess."

"About what?"

Wouldn't *you* be surprised? "Personal." Her voice was clipped and angry, surprising *her*.

Victor backed up a step, his smile wavering. "All right. Sorry. Sure didn't mean to pry."

Mary knew she'd gone too far, for Victor and for herself. Victor was such a wimp, but at times he could elicit a primitive kind of pity. That was the fulcrum of his life, manipulating and surviving by getting others to feel sorry for him. Even though people knew this, it was effective. She made herself smile. "Sorry, Victor. I snapped, didn't I?"

He immediately appeared reassured. "Well, I understand. What with the problems with your mother and all. By the way, how is she?"

"Much better."

"That's good." He advanced on the desk, and for a moment she thought he was going to lean forward and pat her hand. But he stopped and said, "Well, I better see if I can clear this deal with Hal." He opened his attaché case and straightened some papers. Mary noticed a red-handled pocket knife tucked in a compartment next to his calculator. He saw her staring. "It's a Swiss Army knife," he said. "I carry it 'cause it's got a screwdriver, leather punch, even a scissors on it. Comes in handy for everything from opening packages to fastening 'sold' signs." He quickly closed the case. "Speaking of 'sold' signs . . ."

"Hal's in a meeting with the CPA right now."

"I know. We talked this morning and he told me to call him out of it if this contract was signed. It's for one of the display houses, and there's a lotta extras involved." He took a stride toward the back offices.

"Wait a minute," Mary was surprised to hear herself say. She reached into her purse and drew out the photograph of Martha Roundner, then spread it flat on her desk. "Who's this look like?"

Victor rested his palms on the desk, leaned close, and studied the photo for a long time. His face took on a strained expression Mary had never seen before.

"I'll be damned," he said, standing up straight and using a forefinger to tap his glasses back up on the bridge of his nose. "She looks a lot like my sister in Phoenix. You wouldn't believe how much. Who is she?"

"Never mind," Mary said, returning the photo to her purse. "I don't think you know her."

Victor looked puzzled for a moment, then gave her another of his tentative smiles and walked away to drag Hal out of conference as instructed.

Long ago Mary had read a story about a man who thought his double was maliciously ruining his life, and followed and killed the man. At the story's end, it was revealed that there was no resemblance at all, except in the mind of the killer. Mary wondered for a moment if she might be reversing the story, projecting her own image on the photographs of victims because she identifed with them so strongly. Because she wanted—

She decided that was absurd. Cast it from her mind with an internal violence that tightened her stomach.

She didn't have a lesson scheduled for that evening, and Angie had said she was going out with Fred. So after work Mary spent half an hour cleaning up the mess Jake had left in the apartment: dirty dishes from his late breakfast, wadded underwear and socks on the floor, a glut of dark hair in the shower drain. He could leave a bathroom looking as if a freshman track team had used it after a meet. She lowered the seat and flushed the toilet, trying not to inhale. What, if anything, did your mother teach you, Jake?

When the apartment was reasonably neat, and she'd finished her frozen sirloin tips dinner, she put on her flat-soled training shoes and practiced dancing in the spare bedroom. For over an hour she did tango steps in front of the full-length mirror, gliding and swirling gracefully, perfecting her head movements during fans and promenade turns. She looked good. She knew she'd improved dramatically in only the past few weeks. It was like that with dancing; you'd hit a sticking point and think you'd never make progress, then suddenly it was as if a dam gave and you were surprised to stride out on the floor a much better dancer. Moments that made life worthwhile.

When her legs were tired and her feet began to ache, she switched off the light and walked into the living room. She sat on the sofa and removed her shoes, stretched out her legs and crossed them at the ankles.

But she couldn't relax. She wondered again if there really *was* a resemblance between her and the two murder victims. Other people didn't seem to see it. Was the reason for her fascination with Rene Verlane really the fact that he was suspected of murder? She'd heard about eager victims flirting with death, but she certainly wasn't one of them. Was this a lucid moment, or was her imagination running wild now?

You're being ridiculous, she admonished herself. Facts are facts, and talk show psychology won't change them.

Feeling, even hearing, the pounding of her heart, she found her gaze drawn to the phone.

Weary but restless, she stood up and carried her shoes into the bedroom. She sat on the edge of the bed and slipped a pair of white cotton tube socks onto her feet, then her comfortable old Reebok jogging shoes.

She left the apartment and walked for blocks, all the way over to Arsenal Street. The air was so humid it seemed to press like velvet against her flesh. She was perspiring. Tower Grove Park lay to her right like a dark and dangerous void. She knew she shouldn't be walking at night after what had happened to her recently, but something in her compelled her to press on, striding parallel to the edge of the park.

It was a few minutes before ten when she got home. Coincidence? Or had she hurried to reach the apartment in time to settle back down on the sofa and watch the ten o'clock news?

There was nothing on the news about the Verlane or Roundner murders. Mary used the remote to mute the "Tonight" show and watched Jay Leno, nimble for such a big man, dance slowly about and clasp and unclasp his hands during his monologue.

It was two hours earlier on the West Coast. As she stood up and moved to the phone, she realized she'd memorized the number of the Mariott Hotel in Seattle.

Rene Verlane was in his room. He answered the phone on the second ring. She recognized his voice from the television interviews, and she had a vision of him speaking to her from one of the news tapes shot in his New Orleans home, a conversation real yet unreal.

He said hello again, puzzled, and Mary cleared her throat.

This was madness, but she was determined not to panic and hang up.

22

She cleared her throat again, swallowed, and said, "I want you to know first off I'm not some kind of weirdo calling for kicks because your wife was murdered." Oh, God, should she have said *that?*

For a long time he didn't say anything. Silence hummed and crackled on the connection that stretched more than a thousand miles. Was he ever going to speak, or would he simply hang up?

Then: "All right, but what and who are you?"

Relief rushed through Mary. "I'm a serious ballroom dancer, like your wife was. My name's Mary Arlington."

Again a pause. "So why're you calling, Mary?" His voice was calm but tight with wariness.

"To let you know I understand why you think dancing has some connection to the murder. And because I dance. I guess you could say I'm offering my sympathy and moral support. I don't want anything in return."

She could hear the thermostat click and the air-conditioner take on a throatier tone. Her fingers squeezing the receiver were starting to stiffen and ache; she loosened them one by one, flexing them.

"Okay, Mary, I appreciate that." He still sounded dubious, not quite sure he should be talking to her. "However'd you find me?"

"I saw on the news you went to Seattle, so I phoned some of the hotels. Got lucky the second call. I agree with you about how maybe the same person killed your wife and Martha Roundner. I knew it the moment I saw—" She stopped herself; she didn't want to go too far and have him think she was one of those crank callers, the kind played by wild-eyed actresses in movies and on TV slasher films.

"Saw what?"

"Well, I can't deny that your wife, Martha Roundner, and I, we're all more or less the same type. I mean, same shape face, same color hair, probably the same complexion, though that's hard to tell on TV or in photographs. There's a real similarity in our features, too, the sorta general look we have. Everybody who's seen the photos remarks on it."

"I see." She could hear him breathing. "You think you're in some kind of danger, Mary?" He still sounded puzzled.

"Oh, no! What I mean is, because of the similarity, and the dancing, I suppose I feel personally involved in some way with what happened." Hearing herself say it, she wondered again if it made sense. "Listen, if you think that's crazy, I don't blame you."

"No, no, not crazy. Crazy's what's been happening to me lately."

Mary pressed the receiver harder to her ear. "Have you found out anything yet? In Seattle, I mean?"

It was a very long time before he answered, then there was a change in his voice, a weary disillusionment. "You're not from the press, are you?"

"Me? God, no! I absolutely despise what the press is doing to you!"

"What are they doing to me?"

"Not taking you seriously when you say your wife's murder had something to do with dancing. And they keep badgering you; at least that's the impression I get from the news." *And they see you as a suspect.*

"They really haven't been all that bad," Verlane said. "It's the police I can't stomach." His southern accent made them *poh-lice.* "They play their little mind games, keep their secrets. You can't imagine what they can be like till you actually get involved with them the way I have. Sweet Lord, they've even suggested . . . Well, never mind."

"When Martha Roundner was murdered, was there a ballroom dance competition about that time in Seattle?"

"That's one of the things I'm going to find out. I only got here last night and haven't had a chance to do much. The Roundner murder was three months ago; do you recall any kind of competition then *anywhere at all* in this part of the country?"

"No, but that doesn't mean there wasn't any. Ballroom dancing's really getting popular, and there's almost always a competition going on somewhere. If there was a competition in or around Seattle at that time, it oughta be easy enough to find out about it."

"Should be," he agreed. "Do you enter dance competitions?"

"Sometimes," Mary lied. "My next one's the Ohio Star Ball in November."

"That's an important one, isn't it? I remember Danielle talking about it, but she never danced there." A catch in his throat. "Never had the chance."

Pity swelled like a balloon in Mary. "You danced sometimes, too, didn't you?"

"Never in competition," Verlane said. "I only got good enough so I could keep up with Danielle at social dancing."

"She was beautiful. I mean, I don't say that because we look something alike—It's just such a shame, what happened."

"Did you and Danielle ever dance in the same competitions? Do you remember her?" Something sad and eager in his tone now, as if he yearned for more memory to hold onto.

"No, but some of the dancers at my studio recognized her

photograph and remembered her dancing. They said she was terrific, especially in the smooth dances."

"What studio do you dance at?"

"Romance Studio. Part of the chain."

"It just occurred to me I don't even know what city you're calling from."

"St. Louis."

"Ah, I was there about three years ago. A bond fund convention. I'm a stockbroker."

"I know you are. It was mentioned more than once on the news."

"You must watch the news a lot."

"I do. And I read a lot." She decided to take a chance. Her heart double-clutched and began to race. "Listen, if you ever need to know anything about ballroom dancing, I mean how things work with competition or anything, you can give me a call anytime and I'll try to help." She realized her words to Verlane were almost exactly those of Victor offering to help her with Angie.

"All right, I might well do that. Thanks, Mary."

She suddenly didn't know what to say. Several slow seconds passed. Thick silence built in the line, clogging it like cholesterol in a vital artery.

"I guess I'll hang up now," she finally managed to stammer. "I'm sorry."

"Sorry?"

"About your wife and all."

"I see. Thanks for that, too."

She told him her phone number. He didn't ask her to repeat it, or excuse himself to find a pen or pencil. She hoped he was really writing it down. Well, hotels usually had stationery and pens handy by the phone, didn't they?

He thanked her again for calling, then told her good-bye.

"Good luck," she said, and hung up.

She sat with her fingers lingering on the phone, her blood racing. Her mind was whirling somewhere above her and seemed to circle back to where and who she was with infinite slowness. What a thing to have done—to call the husband of a murdered woman!

Now that she'd spoken with Rene Verlane and he was real and not simply another image on TV, it bore down on her with new and unexpected weight that he was not only the widower of a homicide victim, he was suspected of committing the crime. She'd actually talked to a murder suspect. How many people ever did that?

How many people were crazy or desperate enough to try?

She considered phoning Helen and telling her what had happened. She even started to lift the receiver. Then Mary decided she didn't want to share any part of her and Rene Verlane's phone conversation.

Why should she? It was private. It was intimate.

23

Seattle had changed things.

Morrisy sat before his half-finished eggs Benedict at Brennan's and stared at the fax sheets he'd been carrying around in his pocket. The similarities in the Roundner and Verlane homicides couldn't be discounted, and it did seem that ballroom dancing figured into whatever psychosis the killer carried in his sick mind. Morrisy had seen Schutz about it, and Schutz had agreed, but he'd said there wasn't enough data or insight to determine just how the dancing fit in, or even if it did for sure.

Fingering the smooth meerschaum pipe in his shirt pocket, Morrisy thought about how he hated to dance. Bonita had dragged him out on the floor a few times, forcing him to do his awkward box step. Finally he'd deliberately stomped on her toe and she'd believed he was no dancer. It took something like that with a woman like Bonita.

The waiter wandered by and refilled his coffee. At the next table another waiter had touched flame to liqueur and some kind of fancy breakfast dish blazed. It had always struck Morrisy as ridiculous to set food on fire. He enjoyed eating at a place like Brennan's, though, with its high-toned atmosphere and its lush garden; it was one of the perks of his position and if he continued to put on weight the hell with it.

He stared into the flames until the waiter extinguished the fire. Then he gazed into the dark depths of his coffee cup, thinking. The Roundner woman's body had been decomposed to the point where determining time of death was difficult, but she was probably killed on a weekend. Rene Verlane claimed to have spent that time at home, but it was possible he could have taken a flight to Seattle under an alias, committed the murder, and returned home. Only his wife, Danielle, would know for sure, and Danielle was dead. Maybe that was *why* she was dead.

And Verlane was in Seattle now, had even announced on TV he was going there. Snooping around, as if an amateur could uncover something the police had overlooked. Like goddamn Rockford or something. It was all an act, anyway, Morrisy thought. Verlane was playing the bereaved husband to the hilt, trying to get the media on his side and divert suspicion away from him. The guy did have brass nuts, Morrisy would give him that. But that's all he'd give him other than a shitpot full of trouble.

Morrisy sipped coffee, wondering about the dance connection. Maybe there really wasn't any except for the fact the killer figured women wrapped up in ballroom dancing were kind of natural victims from the beginning. They literally yearned to be swept off their feet, to give themselves up to music and whoever they were dancing with. Vulnerable romantics of the sort who made work for Morrisy. At least that was how Morrisy saw it. He figured most men regarded that kind of dancing as nothing more than an opportunity to cop a feel, find out where they stood for the rest of the night with their partners when the dancing was over.

Either way, he'd continue to downplay the dance angle with the media. That was the kind of strategy that boosted career chances. Why shoot himself in the foot by looking like a second-guessing fool for maybe no reason?

But women who danced, maybe they did have something meaningful in common. He'd have to ask Schutz about that. And ask him about how Verlane might feel about dancing, the way his dead wife was so hung up on it. Schutz still had the idea the killer might be doing these women and then not remembering any of it afterward. And Morrisy still didn't see how that was possible. How could anyone who'd seen the Danielle Verlane crime scene think whoever'd been responsible could ever forget it?

Schutz had come to believe that Rene Verlane didn't necessarily fit the profile of the guy they were looking for, but Morrisy didn't buy into that notion, either. He was 90 percent sure about Verlane. Instinct, maybe, but it was instinct that had gotten him to where he was in the department, so it wasn't something to be ignored. He only wished he hadn't gone public with his stand against a dance tie-in, because his instincts were sure beginning to whisper something different now, especially since there'd been a dance competition in Seattle around the time of the killing.

He wondered if Waxman would come up with anything on whether Verlane had registered at a hotel in Seattle during the time frame of the Roundner murder. He doubted it. The airlines had no record of him flying out of New Orleans; if he'd used an alias for that, he sure wouldn't register at a hotel under his own name then go out and do the Rounder woman. But then killers could be unpredictable in small ways. They were a quart of oil short to begin with, so who could tell how they might think, especially if they were the compulsive type, which Schutz said this character was. At least Morrisy and Schutz agreed about that.

Morrisy looked up and saw Captain Bill Quirk easing his bulk between the white-clothed tables, nodding to people he knew. Important people.

Quirk had said he'd meet Morrisy here to discuss the Verlane case. Morrisy wasn't crazy about that idea. The news media had been laying it on thick, even national news, so the pressure was on and Morrisy knew he figured to get his ass reamed for not coming up with a suspect that could be brought in and booked. When that happened, the media would briefly go spastic, then they'd calm down and concentrate on something else for a while and things would ease up.

Morrisy smiled. The media thought they knew it all, now that it had been made public the two women were humped after they were dead. But they didn't know it all, only thought they did.

Quirk had assumed Morrisy was smiling at him and smiled back.

The way a shark might smile at a smaller shark.

24

Rising straight up from the bed, Mary gazed down at her sleeping form, then drifted inches from the ceiling, swooped low, and passed through the window pane as if it were a sheet of cold water.

And she was high up into the night. Everything below was in vivid detail in the artificial illumination of the city. The surgical-like seams of tarred roofs, the silver turnscrews on the domed aluminum tops of streetlights, and, as she rose higher, the geometric maze of blocks and then neighborhoods. Beneath her, unaware of her, nighthawks circled, their wings winking like black sequins.

But up here the air was thin, and she was having difficulty breathing. Her lungs pumped desperately, thirsting for oxygen that existed only at lower levels. She could hear herself begin to rasp, shrill and airless screams that trailed away in the void.

She awoke with Jake on top of her, pinning her to the mattress. Her wrists were in his merciless grip, nailed to her wadded pillow. He'd worked her twisted nightgown up above her breasts, and his nude body pressed down on her with monstrous weight. She could move nothing but her head and her legs. She thrashed her legs helplessly in the air, pounding his buttocks with her heels. He laughed, liking that.

"Jake, damn it!"

His only answer was his bellowslike breathing.

"Goddammit, Jake, get *off* me!"

For an instant he raised his sweating body and she could breathe. Then he was tight and hot against her again, and inside her even though she was still dry. She heard herself whine, then bit her lip against the pain.

"Mary likes that, huh?" he asked.

She made no sound.

He began the relentless rhythm.

He'd at least used some kind of lubricant, probably the K-Y jelly, so the pain lessened somewhat. He grunted, probing her particularly deep, seeking soft distances.

"Like that?" he asked again.

He released her wrists; what could she do with her hands now anyway?

After shifting his weight slightly, he began moving faster. Thrusting! Thrusting!

A woman in the room was moaning, her breath catching. Who it was Mary had no idea. What was happening had nothing to do with her. Nothing.

She lay as if crucified with her limp arms spread wide, gazing up into darkness and listening to the perfect rhythm of the headboard beating against the wall, and in her mind she danced.

"The more you feel the music," Mel told her that evening at the studio, "the easier it'll be to move to it."

He took her hand gently and led her across the dance floor to where one of the big Bose speakers was standing on its pedestal. A mambo was pounding out of it, almost loud enough to rattle Mary's fillings.

"Put your haaand on the speaker," Mel said, imitating a televangelist, and pressed her palm to the warm side of the wooden box.

With each drumbeat or deep bass note she could feel the speaker throb. She let the syncopated rhythm pulsate up her arm and into her body, down to the floor.

Mel raised his forefinger and cocked his head to the side, listening for the one beat. "One!" he said, sharply dipping the finger. "One, two, three, four!" His body undulated from side to side as he counted out the beat in time with the throbbing speaker, waving his finger as if it were a conductor's baton. "That's how you need to feel the beat with your entire body so you can dance your best," he said. "You understand what I mean, Mary?"

She told him yes, she thought so, though she wasn't exactly sure.

"You need even more lessons," Mel told her, patting her hand and removing it from the speaker. He grinned. "But not to worry; I'll have you more than ready by the time Ohio rolls around. You're making amazing progress, Mary, really you are."

"By the way," she said, "there was another dancer murdered, this time in Seattle. Martha Roundner. She's the one I asked you about. You sure you didn't know her?"

"Can't say as I did. Hey, they ever catch the creep that killed Danielle Verlane?"

"Not yet."

"So let's mambo!" Mel said, leading her back toward the center of the floor. In the corner of her vision she saw Ray Huggins enter the studio and walk toward his office. He glanced over at her, paused staring for a moment with his fists on his hips, then flashed her a wide smile and clapped his hands. "Way to move, Mary!"

She thought of waving to him, but Mel led her into an arm check and she was whirling so he could pick her up on the one beat.

Finally the music stopped and he stepped away, grinning and wiping the back of his wrist across his forehead. "You got it tonight, hon. Let's do something slower now so you don't wear out the instructor." He trod smoothly toward the stereo to put in another tape. Over his shoulder: "What'll it be, waltz, fox-trot, or tango?"

"Tango."

"Big surprise," Mel said. He studied the cassettes, then drew one from the shelf and slipped it into the stereo. After punching the Play button, he turned back to face her.

"I'd like to work some more on my promenade turns," Mary said, in the silence at the beginning of the tape.

"Anything you want, Mary."

He came back and drew her into dance position, and when the music started they began to tango. She was pleased to learn that the head motion and smoothness she'd achieved practicing by herself in her apartment were still in her dance. Her responses to Mel's lead were automatic.

"Beeeeautiful!" Mel said, taking her through a pivot.

She thought so, too.

When the lesson was over, Mary sat on the vinyl bench to change back into her street shoes.

A warm draft whirled around her ankles as Helen shoved through the door carrying her dance shoes.

"Hi, Mary Mary," she said. "Like these?"

She held out the new shoes for Mary to look at more closely. They were Latin, open-toed models with straps and inch-and-a-half high heels. Made of silky silver material etched with thin dark lines of no discernible pattern, like delicately veined marble.

"They're called 'Cracked Ice' in the catalogue," Helen said, sitting down and slipping off her black leather pumps. "Aren't they just great!"

"Terrific," Mary said, and meant it. If her dress were the right color, she wouldn't mind wearing shoes like them in the Ohio competition.

"I read he had sex with her after she was dead," Helen said.

"Wha—?"

"The guy that killed the dancer down in New Orleans. He was a whatchamacallit."

"Necrophiliac."

"That's it." Helen worked her feet into her new shoes and doubled over to buckle the straps; her voice was momentarily muffled. "Double-yuk! Imagine some sicko wanting to get it on with a corpse." She sat up straight and breathed out huffily. "Had to be the husband."

Mary was surprised. "Why do you say that?"

"Well, the husband's always the prime suspect anyway, because usually he turns out to be the murderer. And I heard of it before, husbands wanting to screw dead wives. It's some kinda total male domination thing."

"That's insane."

"Hey, don't get so upset. It's the weirdo husbands that're insane."

"You must still be bitter about your divorce."

"Better believe it, Mary Mary."

"I mean, you talk like necrophilia's a common domestic problem, like not putting down the toilet seat."

"No, no, it's rare, I admit. Just like somebody killing his wife. And when there's sex after death, odds are it's the husband. I mean, if he was wacky enough to kill her in the first place, why's it so hard to believe he carried things farther?"

"He didn't kill her in the first place."

"Oh? Why not?"

"The woman in Seattle. She was probably killed by the same man."

"Not necessarily. I read where that one was laid after she was dead, too, though." Helen clucked her tongue. "And you said it wasn't common."

"If Rene Verlane killed his wife, how come he traveled to Seattle to try to find her killer?"

"How do you know he did that?"

"I ta—I saw it on the news."

Helen grinned slyly. "It'd be a peachy way to try to avert suspicion, wouldn't it? Pretend the same man killed your wife and the woman in Seattle. Even go to Seattle and act like you're trying to prove it."

"You're only speculating," Mary said, "and pretty wildly at that."

"Oh, I know. Fact is, except for the killing part, a guy like that might make the perfect husband if he was rich; I mean, you'd never have to fake another orgasm."

"God, you're something, Helen."

"Maybe, but I don't murder dancers."

"And you don't know who does, so you oughta be careful what conclusions you jump to."

She looked at Mary curiously. "What the hell, I'm not on a jury, so no harm done."

"But someday somebody just like you might be on Rene Verlane's jury, and send him to the electric chair or whatever they use in Louisiana."

"It's possible, I guess," Helen said, standing up and rocking back and forth in her new shoes. She waved to her instructor, Nick, who'd just emerged from Huggins's office. "It's possible, too, he's guilty as original sin."

"Hey!" Nick said. "Tango time!"

Mary watched Helen, head bowed and studying her feet in their new silver shoes, follow him out onto the dance floor.

Cracked Ice, Mary thought. Cracked Helen.

25

She wanted to call him but knew she shouldn't. At this point there was nothing more for her to say to Rene Verlane. Mary thought that for once she'd handled the situation perfectly; the phone conversation had gone better than she'd thought possible. To try extending their tenuous relationship now, on her initiative, would be like adding too much of an ingredient to a successful recipe. Rene had her number, and if he wanted to talk to her, he'd call.

Mary considered, then denied, that she might simply be afraid to call. He might not *want* to talk to her next time. The balance of credibility might tilt and he'd regard her as a thrill-seeking crackpot using the phone for long-distance kicks. She wasn't that at all, and she didn't want him to see her that way. It was his turn to call; she'd asked him to dance, and now he should lead.

She did call Angie, who said she was feeling better and not drinking and needed to be alone that night. It wasn't that you didn't love your kids when they grew up, she told Mary, but you needed time by yourself.

"With Fred, you mean?" Mary asked.

"No, not with Fred. Not tonight. You okay, Mary? You're the one that doesn't sound quite with the program tonight. Jake there with you?"

"He's at work."

"Good."

Mary wound up assuring Angie that *she* was just fine, then hung up. She didn't mind being alone herself.

There was no mention of either murder on the ten o'clock news. Mary swallowed the last of her chilled white wine and carried the glass into the kitchen. Was Angie right now drinking something stronger than wine? Wine wasn't like gin or scotch or bourbon; wine was a connoisseur's drink and could be controlled. Still, Mary didn't like the thought of Angie trying to exercise that control, so she made it a point never to drink wine in her presence.

She rinsed out the glass, dried it, and admired the rainbowed world of light in it before replacing it stem up in the cabinet. She'd hoped the wine would make her sleepy, but it hadn't. Some source of energy seemed to have infected her blood like a virus.

She walked into the bedroom and got undressed. There was always the possibility Jake might come home early, so she decided against practicing nude. She put on her nightgown and Latin shoes, then went into the spare bedroom to dance.

Though she felt a stiffness in her knees and hips at first, within a few minutes her body was inundated with the rhythm of the taped music, and the steps, the moves, began to flow. She did rumba for a while, concentrating on making her Cuban motion smooth and precise, holding the slow count and shifting weight completely. Then she worked on the smooth dances, fox-trot, waltz, and tango.

In the middle of a series of pivots, she caught slight movement from the corner of her eye and dug in the ball of her foot to stop.

Jake was leaning hipshot against the doorjamb with his arms crossed, grinning at her, like a street-corner lounger eyeing passing skirts.

She caught her breath. Swallowed. "Didn't hear you come in."

"I'd have worked overtime," he said, "only the fucking boss got my job classification mixed up. Everything about that place is exactly what's wrong with American industry."

"So why not talk to *his* boss?"

"Ha! *His* boss is even more fucked up than he is. I mean, that guy is *royally* fucked up."

"What about the union? You talk to the shop steward? Maybe you could file a grievance or something."

He stopped smiling and grunted in disdain, all the while with his gaze nailed to her. She knew suddenly what kind of black mood he was in; apprehension knotted her stomach. "You oughta know the goddamn union's in bed with the company," he told her. "That's how it works these days. They're all of a sudden saying at the warehouse that seniority goes by department instead of for the whole crew. What a crock of shit!"

"Well, they're not laying off, are they?"

With an elaborate, lazy shrug, Jake pushed away from the doorjamb and stepped into the room. He was wearing faded Levi's and a gray T-shirt with SCREW THE WHALES lettered on it. "It ain't like I'm about to get laid off," he snarled. "But this way they

112

can throw my ass into a boxcar and make me unload produce instead of keeping me checking outgoing shipments, where I fucking deserve to be. They got a guy been there five years less than me playing with his pencil on the loading dock. He don't know his ass from a hole in the ground about checking outgoing."

She walked over to him and lightly touched his arm, trying to defuse him with a display of sympathy. The arm was tense, cool yet sticky with sweat. "Listen, Jake, things'll come around. Anyway, it's time-out for a while. There's no need to bring the job home with you. Just forget about it till you go in tomorrow, okay? Let's go in the kitchen and I'll—"

He pushed her hand away and glared at her. She saw the hostility in him, the hungry violence circling like a great bird looking for a deserving victim. She didn't want to be the object of that violence. She backed away.

"Like you don't bring your half-ass obsession home?" he asked. "Like you forget about ballroom dancing when you're not swishing around with your fag instructor at the studio?"

"Jake, for God's sake, Mel's straight as you are."

She knew immediately she shouldn't have said it. In his present mood, Jake might interpret her words as an attack on his manhood. His hooded dark eyes fixed on her and didn't blink. A familiar, dangerous calm settled over him. The cruel thing that lived inside him was taking control.

No, no, no, not again! "Anyway," she said, "you know what I mean. Don't you?"

He moved very close; she could smell onion on his warm, fetid breath. Not liquor, thank God. "No," he said, "how could I know; you got a mind like a goddamn circus. Why don't you tell me what you mean?"

"I mean . . . I guess I mean there's nothing effeminate about Mel Holt."

"Ha! You don't call showing desperate women where to put their feet when they ain't waving 'em in the air a fag occupation?"

"No, I don't. Really, you wouldn't, either, if you understood." Why did she keep saying the wrong thing?

He glided slowly toward her until her back was pressed against the wall. His breath hissed regularly, like great pressure escaping, but not fast enough to prevent more from building. She was beginning to experience the paralysis of fear. Her arms and legs seemed detached, independent creatures with sluggish wills of their own.

"Jake, don't start this! Please!"

"I want you to tell me that Mel asshole's probably a faggot," he said in a gentle voice that didn't fool her. "Go ahead, tell me."

"I can't do that, Jake. Honestly, he's not."

"Oh? How would you know? You sleep with him?"

"Of course not! You know I didn't!"

"How the hell could I know that? I don't just *know* stuff, like you do. Not without any goddamn proof."

She tried to slide between his bulk and the wall, but he blocked her with his arm and she hadn't any strength to resist.

Suddenly she was ten years old, trapped in Duke's grip as he ignored her feeble struggles and unbuckled and removed his belt to administer one of the beatings Angie still maintained Mary deserved. What had she done? Messed up at school? Broken something valuable? Spilled something at the table? What had she done this time?

Nothing, damn it! Nothing! *It wasn't fair!*

"Jake!" She placed her hands on his chest and shoved, whipping her head from side to side and trying to pull free. She was aware of him drawing back his hand, as if to deliver a hammer blow. No way to avoid it. No way to prevent the pain.

She stopped struggling, clenching her eyes shut.

Resigned.

Waiting.

And suddenly he was no longer against her. The warmth of his bulk, the oppressive smells of onion and perspiration, were gone.

She opened her eyes barely in time to see him hurrying out the door, his shoulders bunched as if he were hunkered down and angling into a fierce wind.

"Jake!"

She heard the door to the hall open and close.

Silence then. A cessation of time. Her aloneness seeped into her and lay like a cold slab in her stomach.

For a while she stood hugging herself, cupping her bony elbows in her hands and gently swaying.

Then she walked over to the tape deck, pushed Rewind, and began to dance.

Around midnight she took two Benadryl capsules, hoping they would help her sleep, then went to bed and lay staring into the darkness. It had cooled down outside, so she had the air-conditioner off and the window open. A breeze was playing with the curtains; writhing shadows brought grotesque life to the wall next to the bed. Trying not to think, listening to the night sounds of the city, she fell asleep.

When the bed lurched she awoke. The luminous blue digital numbers on the clock said it was ten minutes past three. The Benadryl capsules hadn't worked to keep her asleep, or maybe she'd developed a resistance to them.

She let her gaze slide sideways through the darkness. Jake was settling down beside her on the mattress. He sighed and she smelled bourbon. He mumbled something that sounded like "Motherfuckers," then he was motionless and quiet. Within a few minutes he began to snore.

Mary lay without moving, barely breathing. It was impossible to know how deeply Jake was sleeping. Or what he might do if he awoke.

She was still and fearful until daylight, dozing only in brief and intermittent stretches, and wakened suddenly by thrills of panic.

Five minutes before the alarm was due to rip the silence, she turned it off. Then she climbed out of bed gingerly, wincing as the springs squealed. Stepping where she knew from experience that the floor wouldn't squeak, she gathered her clothes and carried them into the bathroom to dress. She could go without breakfast, or she might drive through McDonald's and pick up coffee and a Danish to eat at work.

Careful not to disturb Jake, she crept from the apartment and made her way down the creaking wooden stairs to the vestibule. She pushed out into the bright warm morning, hating the fear that walked with her.

Jake had come within a heartbeat of starting in on her last night. When that happened, it usually wasn't long before whatever it was that sometimes stopped up short of violence failed, and he'd be rough on her. Jake the time bomb. When he was this way she could almost bring herself to leave him and to mean it.

Almost.

She was like a ship captive to an undertow. Drifting toward the rocks and unable to do anything about it, because that was what happened sometimes if you were a ship.

The ocean she sailed on terrified her, but the inevitability of its tides was something she had faith in and understood.

26

Two days later he called. Mary was in the kitchen, about to insert a frozen lasagna dinner into the microwave, when the phone rang. She quickly wiped her hands on a paper towel, then lifted the receiver from the extension phone mounted on the wall near the refrigerator. Said hello.

"Mary Arlington?"

She recognized his voice at once, the Southern accent, but for a moment she couldn't answer. She'd been expecting Angie to call.

"Yes, it's, uh, me," she said, feeling awkward, not knowing quite how to respond. She needed time, a few seconds to gather herself. She noticed the front of her blouse was vibrating with her heartbeat.

"You told me it'd be okay if I called," Rene said. "This a bad time?"

"No, not at all. I was just about to defrost something for supper." She forced a laugh, as if she'd made a joke and usually she prepared elaborate meals. Stupid, stupid to mention supper! Now he'd think she was hungry and hurry the conversation.

"You said you might help me, Mary, and I think maybe there's a way you can."

She started to speak but the words lodged painfully in her throat. Everything in the kitchen, the microwave oven with its door hanging open and its light softly glowing, the glistening drop of water poised to plummet from the mouth of the sink faucet, the gleaming chrome toaster smudged with fingerprints, all seemed more vivid than they had before the phone rang. The sharp scent of bacon grease rose from the skillet Jake had used and left on the stove.

"Still feel that way?" he asked.

"Sure. I mean, of course I meant it when I told you I'd help."

"I'm calling from a pay phone," he said, "because I think the police might have my home phone tapped, and I don't want to involve you in this to the point where you might get hurt or embarrassed."

That seemed reasonable to Mary. This was something like a film *noir* movie on late-night cable TV—intrigue and shadows and romance. "Did you find out anything in Seattle?" Barbara Stanwyck asked in black-and-white.

"I visited the studio where Martha Roundner trained. Talked to some of the people in the Seattle dance community. They told me Martha Roundner was a regular at quite a few night spots where there was dancing. Not unusual for somebody as far into ballroom dancing as she was. But I guess you know that. You go out dancing often?"

"Sometimes, not often."

"There's a good chance Martha Roundner went dancing the night of her death, though nobody at any of the dance clubs remembers seeing her."

"They wouldn't, necessarily," Mary told him. "Those places are full of activity and usually very noisy. Sometimes the lighting's low, or tricks are done with it. Strobe lights, colored beams, moving shadows, that sorta thing."

"I know. It doesn't mean much to me, either, that nobody remembers for sure she was out dancing that night. It was her roommate who said she thought that was where Martha mentioned she was going. Said Martha danced three or four nights a week. Her favorites were the Latin dances, especially tango."

"That's my favorite, too," Mary heard herself say.

"They found her car in the airport parking lot, miles from where her body was discovered. Seems obvious the killer drove it there, then flew out of town."

"Maybe that's what he wanted everyone to think," Mary suggested.

"That's what Martha's parents said, despite the fact there are no fingerprints other than their daughter's in the car. Poor old people are getting no more satisfaction outa the police investigation than I am. Sweet Lord, you talk to them and your heart almost tears in half."

"I bet her parents are right, though, and the police are wrong."

"Uh-huh. A certain deviousness accompanies whatever compels somebody so mentally twisted. Which is why the police make no headway; they're looking for the usual criminal type with a penitentiary IQ." He was quiet for a moment, but she could hear his breathing, in counterpoint time with her own. "What I need, Mary, if it's not too much trouble, is some old dance programs from the various competitions in different cities. I want to check the names of the entrants against police homicide records. Maybe Martha Roundner and Danielle aren't the only victims of this psychopath."

Romance Studio subscribed to most of the trade magazines, and competition programs tended not to be thrown away. Mary thought about the stack of magazines and dance programs on a bottom shelf in Ray Huggins's office.

"Don't say yes if you have the slightest reservation," Rene told her. "I probably shouldn't have called."

"I was only trying to think of the best way to go about it," Mary said. "I'm pretty sure I can at least send you copies of the registration lists from some of the competitions."

"That'd be terrific. But, listen, don't mail them to my home. I wouldn't be surprised if the police are watching my mail. I rented a post office box in Baton Rouge. I'll give you the number and zip code. Address the envelope to Roger Lane. Can you remember that?"

"I think so."

"Good. You don't think I'm paranoid, do you? About the police?"

"No. I can understand why you feel the way you do."

"They keep their secrets, play everything so tight. They still probably haven't told the news media everything about the murders."

Mary said, "It's just the way they are, I guess."

"I don't wanna cause you any trouble. Don't want anybody to know you did this."

"Me, either," Mary said. "But really, I don't mind."

"It's kind of you to help me. You've got your own life, your own problems. When something like Danielle's murder happens, it leaves the husband so . . . alone. More alone than I've ever been, or than I'd wish on anybody else."

"Well, nobody's got a corner on loneliness."

"Misery doesn't love company, in this case. Misery just hates misery."

"I know exactly what you mean."

"Why? You're not miserable, I hope."

"Only sometimes."

"Oh? Is there some way I can repay? Some way *I* can help *you*?"

"No, no, it's mainly my mother. She's not in good health."

"What's wrong with her? I can afford the best doctors."

"We don't know exactly what's wrong. Then there's . . ."

"What?"

"Jake."

"A guy named Jake's a problem?"

"Yeah, I'm afraid sometimes he is."

"He somebody you're romantically involved with?"

"He lives with me."

"And it's not going well?"

"No."

"Wanna talk about it?"

"No. Or maybe yes. God, I don't know."

"It can't do any harm if I play Dear Abby. So what's the trouble between you and Jake?"

"He . . . gets physical at times."

"You mean he beats you?" Rene didn't sound surprised.

"Not very often."

"They say men like that don't change," he told her softly. "Abby says it. I say it."

"So's Angie say it."

"Angie?"

"My mother. She's forever trying to talk me into breaking away from Jake."

"Maybe mother knows best."

"Yeah, maybe she does."

"Mary, why *don't* you leave him?"

"I don't wanna face my world without him in it, I guess. It's more than just insecurity, though I admit that's part of it. Maybe only a woman'd understand completely."

"I know some women are that way about some men."

"Was your wife like that?" She immediately wished she hadn't asked. God, what a question!

"Sometimes, but not with me."

Mary wondered what that meant.

"I better let you get to your supper," Rene said. "They can suspect me of murder, but never of bad manners."

"It's okay, really. I'm not even hungry."

But he was insistent. He gave her the Baton Rouge address, and she jotted it down on the flap of the cardboard box that had contained the lasagna.

"It might be a few days," she said.

"That's okay. Honestly, I can't tell you what this means to me, that somebody out there understands and is willing to help."

"Why don't you call again when you get the stuff," Mary said, "so I can be sure it reached you okay."

"I will, Mary. And thanks again."

He hung up.

She immediately phoned Romance and booked a lesson with Mel for the next evening. Ray Huggins wouldn't mind if she took or copied some of the old dance programs in his office. She could say she wanted to look them over in preparation for the Ohio Star Ball. And if he did mind, well, she'd think of some way to copy them on the machine in the corner of his office. To help Rene. That, suddenly, was of supreme importance.

After all, he was battling odds in trying to find his wife's killer, and maybe to prevent similar murders.

A list containing possible victims might be of immense value to him.

27

"So what's with you?" Jake asked, when he came home from work. "You look like you hit the lottery."

Mary shrugged. "I guess I just feel good, is all." She thought about asking him what had happened at the warehouse then decided it was safer not to bring up the subject. Sometimes it didn't take much to trip Jake's detonator.

He peeled off his sweaty T-shirt, stretched elaborately, then flexed his muscles. Was this show of machismo for her? "Usually you're in bed asleep by this time," he said, and swaggered away toward the kitchen.

"Couldn't sleep tonight," she said, loud enough for him to hear. "I feel sorta nervous."

She heard him clattering around in the kitchen. "Thought you said you felt good," he shouted.

"People can feel two ways at the same time."

He'd returned to the living room carrying a can of beer. Some of it had fizzed over the rim when he popped the tab, and the front of his gray workpants was spotted, as if he'd been careless going to the bathroom. He took a sip of beer, licked his lips, and stared down at her where she sat on the sofa with her hands folded in her lap. Looking down at her that way, he made her feel very small. He must know that.

"I'm sorry about last night," he said. "I was, you know, upset with them assholes at work. If you knew what I go through at that place sometimes, you wouldn't blame me."

Surprised by his apology, Mary smiled. It wasn't like Jake to admit he'd been wrong. "No harm done." Maybe he was making progress establishing some self-control. "You want a snack or something?" she asked. "I think we got some microwave popcorn."

"Sounds great. Lemme shower and I'll be right back."

She sat for a moment alone, not getting up until pipes clanked inside the walls like mysterious signals and she heard the hiss of the shower running. Then she went into the kitchen and stuck a bag of Orville Redenbacher's popcorn into the microwave.

After yanking the tab on a cold can of diet Pepsi, she stood staring through the oven's portholelike window, watching the paper sack expand and listening to the muffled explosions of corn kernels. The warm scent of the popcorn filled the kitchen. It was one of her favorite smells, and she knew it would waft through the entire apartment and linger. After a little over a minute, the explosions inside the inflating sack built to a constant chatter; Orville Redenbacher in there with a machine gun.

Handling the bag gingerly so she wouldn't burn her fingers, she divided the popcorn evenly into two bowls. By the time she carried them into the living room, Jake had finished showering. He was sitting on the sofa, barefoot, and wearing a clean pair of khaki pants and a white undershirt. His black hair was tightly curled from the shower's steam, still moist and slicked back so his hairline seemed to have receded to lend him a look of lofty intelligence. He was a handsome man, and not as bad as some; she shouldn't have been thinking . . . what she'd been thinking.

"Want another beer?" she asked.

He shook his head no.

She got her Pepsi can from the kitchen, then sat down next to him on the sofa with her bowl of popcorn, her legs tucked beneath her. As she often did, she seemed to see herself and her surroundings from above. She and Jake side by side on the couch, Mr. and Mrs. Domestic.

Jake had switched on the TV. They sat munching popcorn and watched the end of an old movie starring Edward G. Robinson as a crime kingpin holed up on some sort of island near Florida. A hurricane was involved.

"Know why everyone thought that little kike Robinson was so tough?" Jake asked.

Mary contorted her tongue to work a kernel from beneath it, then said she had no idea.

" 'Cause *he* thought he was tough. Look at him. Don't he look just like somebody's tailor or accountant?"

Mary couldn't remember the CPA at work ever snarling at her the way Robinson did, but she simply nodded.

"Goes to show, it's what *you* know you are that's important," Jake said wisely, slipping his arm around her.

"I guess," Mary said, her breath catching as he gave her a squeeze. She thought it might not be best for some people to really know themselves too well.

After Robinson was dead, Jake switched off the TV and took her into the bedroom.

He made love to her gently that night, not playing rough until near the very end. Through it all she lay quietly and submissively, still tasting popcorn.

And it was morning and the alarm was warbling.

"Jesus!" Jake said groggily. "Turn that fucking thing off!"

Though she was only half awake, Mary groped blindly until her hand closed on the vibrating plastic clock. She pressed the button that quieted the alarm, and the clock suddenly lost life in her hand and silence hummed in the room.

She struggled out of bed and walked stiff-legged into the bathroom, then stood beneath the shower, letting the needles of water wake her all the way.

Jake remained sleeping soundly while she got dressed in the dim bedroom to the lazy rhythm of his breathing. She took time for a breakfast of a piece of toast with strawberry jam on it, and a cup of coffee.

She was about to leave the apartment when Jake appeared in the kitchen doorway, wearing only his Jockey shorts and yawning. "Want me to walk you down to your car?" he asked.

"Why would you want to do that?" She put the jam jar in the refrigerator.

"I mean, after what was done to your front door, and the bird on your car aerial outside Casa Loma, I figured it might be wise."

"Nothing like that's happened lately," Mary said. "Anyway, you're still in your underwear. I better get to work, Jake."

She was almost out of the kitchen when sharp realization made her stop and turn to face him.

She said, "I never told you about the dead bird."

He looked startled and seemed to snap fully awake. "Oh, I guess Angie musta mentioned it."

"When'd you talk to Angie?"

"Hell, I dunno."

"I never told Angie, Jake." And she was sure he hadn't heard about it from any of the dancers; he didn't know any dancers.

Fred? No, before walking to her car that night, she'd seen Fred driving away from Casa Loma with the blond woman.

She watched Jake, reading the guilt on his face, knowing the look so well. "Jesus, Jake—you!"

"Listen, Mary—"

She felt like hurling herself at him, beating him with her fists. Reacting as he would react. But she didn't move. "Why would you do those sick things?"

"Because they *were* sick, don't you see? I wanted you to be scared, think you were threatened by some psycho so you'd feel the need for protection and take me back. Maybe it was wrong, but I did it for us, Mary. And it worked. It *did* work."

"That isn't why we're back together, Jake."

"Think about it before you jump to any conclusions, Mary. You'll understand my point of view."

"I want you gone for good when I come home, Jake. Outa here!"

He took a step toward her. Instead of retreating she moved toward him, surprising both of them.

"I'll go to the police, Jake. I filed a complaint about the door, and I can tell them about the rest. They'll haul you into court, send you to a goddamn mental hospital."

He smiled, but there was more fear than confidence in it. "Are you gonna do that, Mary?"

"Just be here when I come back and find out." She spun around and walked fast out of the apartment, slamming the door behind her.

By the time she reached the street her heart had slowed enough so her pulse wasn't pounding in her ears.

There was an accident involving a school bus on Grand Avenue, stopping traffic for blocks. Mary was twenty minutes late for work. "Tardy," it had been called at Saint Elizabeth's Primary. Probably it was still called that, and in the same accusing tone. She and the students were tardy today.

Her nerves were frayed by the time she nodded hello to Jackie Foxx and Joan the receptionist and walked into her office.

Even before she'd sat down at her desk, she saw the messages in her box. One of them was about a client who was supposed to come in and pick up an amortized loan schedule.

The other message was a request to call Dr. Keshna at Saint Sebastian Hospital.

Mary punched out the scrawled phone number, gave a hospital operator a department code, asked for Dr. Keshna, and waited through two minutes of barely recognizable Beatles music.

Finally Dr. Keshna's lilting, gentle voice came over the phone. "Miss Arlington, I thought I should call you about the results of your mother's tests."

"Are they—Is she all right?"

"For the most part, yes, she is. Please don't worry. I want to tell you, also, that she gave me permission to talk to you about this only after much persuasion on my part."

"What about the tests?"

"There's evidence of heavy damage to her liver and pancreas. Also there's some heart fibrillation, probably due to alcohol ingestion over the years. She's in no immediate danger, but I must stress to you, as I did to her, that it's important for her to stop consuming alcohol."

"Entirely?"

"Entirely and for the rest of her life, Miss Arlington."

"I'm not sure she can do that."

"I'm not, either. I know it's difficult, but the purpose of my call is to convince you that your mother has no choice. I'm afraid irreparable damage has already been done. She's on the threshold of some very grave medical problems. It's my duty to try to see that she, and you, understand this."

"I understand," Mary said. "Does Angie?"

"I'm not sure. That's why I thought I should talk to you."

Mary could imagine the gentle Dr. Keshna trying to reason with Angie, when Angie didn't want to reason. "I see. Thanks, Doctor."

"I'm sorry, Miss Arlington." Dr. Keshna hung up softly.

Mary sat staring at her desk, seeing nothing on it.

"Anything wrong?"

Victor, smiling down at her.

"Nothing!" she almost barked. "Everything's fine. I'd like to be left alone, is all."

Startled but still smiling, he backed away. She was immediately sorry she'd been so sharp with him, but dammit, why didn't he realize she didn't yearn for his company? Why was he always trying to insinuate himself into her life?

Indomitable, he cheerily called good-bye as he left the office. He glanced in at her as he strode past the window, swinging his right arm and attaché case like a pendulum.

Mary remembered her conversation with Jake and pushed it away from her thoughts. She didn't have to think about Jake anymore. Didn't have to, and wouldn't. It was over.

That evening she drove to Romance Studio straight from work and arrived half an hour early for her tango lesson with Mel. She was relieved to see Ray Huggins relaxing in his office with his feet propped on his desk. He was wearing gray leather Latin dance boots.

As she suspected, he didn't object at all to her making copies of programs from past competitions. He assumed she was interested in the ads for dance shoes and various paraphernalia placed by the mail order houses and dealers with booths in the vending areas. Huggins seemed pleased by her interest, and in fact offered to give her the programs.

But Mary said copies would do fine. Becky the receptionist came in to run them off on the Xerox machine, saying she'd give them to Mary after her lesson with Mel.

It wasn't her best lesson. Mary's body discipline broke down and twice she misread Mel's lead. She explained to him that she was simply having an off night, but he was plainly worried. If she could have such an off night here in St. Louis, it was possible in Columbus.

When she got home there was no sign of Jake. She checked the closet, then the dresser drawers he'd used. Nothing. He'd moved out. Probably right now he was shopping for roses. It wouldn't make any difference this time. Finally he'd done the unforgivable.

Mary sat down with the program copies and immediately sorted out the registration pages, containing the names of dancers. She slipped a rubber band around them and placed them in a large envelope she'd addressed to the Baton Rouge post office box.

She pasted a liberal number of stamps on the envelope, then walked to the mailbox at the corner and dropped it in. It landed hard at the bottom of the obviously empty metal box. She peered at the pickup schedule and saw that the mail had been collected an hour ago, but there was another pickup at midnight.

In a few days, Rene should call and tell her he'd received the envelope.

He'd be grateful, she was sure.

28

The weekend crawled past, then Monday, and Rene hadn't called to confirm he'd received the envelope. Mary began to wonder if she'd pasted on enough stamps. She tried to reassure herself by thinking the worst that could happen was that the envelope would be delivered with postage due. But did it work that way if the recipient had a post office box? If it didn't, would the envelope be returned to her with "Insufficient Postage" stamped on it in officious red letters? Was it even now wending its way back toward its origin while Rene nervously awaited its arrival in Baton Rouge?

She found herself thinking too often about the envelope, even to the point where it interfered with dance practice.

"Don't let your feet wander along with your mind," Mel admonished her with a smile, as she stepped sideways in the wrong direction during a tango.

"Sorry," Mary said, embarrassed, "I was doing fox-trot."

"Better not get the two mixed up in Ohio," Mel said, sharply this time. He wasn't smiling now, and there was a hard pinpoint of light in his eyes.

It wasn't like him, or any of the Romance Studio instructors, to be openly critical. Mary felt her blood rush hotly to her cheeks, but before she could stammer an apology he led her through a series of pivots and backward basics.

"Mel—" She gasped, a little breathless from the pivots.

" 'S'okay, Mary. You're doing terrific." Despite his reassuring manner, there was an intensity about him she hadn't seen before. The way he was staring at her . . .

When the music stopped, he wasn't breathing hard. She was.

"I need a break," she gasped, raising a hand palm-out as if to halt something advancing on her.

"Sorry," he said. "Guess I got wound up and needed to wind down. Doesn't happen very often."

"So, are you?"

He backed away and stood with his hands on his slim dancer's hips; the man probably had a waist smaller than Mary's. "Am I what?"

"Wound down."

Mel cocked his head sideways, did a perfect spin, and grinned at her. "Tell you what, Mary, the lesson's about over, and I don't have anyone coming in for another half hour. Let's go next door to the sandwich shop, get a soda or something, and talk about the competition."

She didn't know what to think. "You usually do that with students before they compete?"

"No. But there's some stuff we need to get straight." His eyes slid sideways, then back, like those of a schoolboy plotting a classroom conspiracy. "I suppose we can talk here if you want."

Helen was smooth dancing with Nick, staring curiously at Mary over his perfectly squared shoulder. Helen was a human seismograph able to detect the slightest irregular tremor in any relationship.

"Next door's better," Mary said.

The Hungry Hobo sandwich shop adjoined the studio in the strip shopping center, so there was only a short distance to walk through rain so gentle it was almost mist. Before leaving the studio, Mary and Mel sat on the vinyl bench and changed to their street shoes. Step in a puddle with suede-soled dancing shoes and they were useless for anything other than expensive bedroom slippers.

Helen was still craning her neck to see them as they left the studio together.

When they'd settled into a booth near the window, Mary ordered a diet Pepsi, and Mel absently told the waitress he'd have the same.

Mel sat staring out the window at the damp evening until the drinks were brought, then he looked directly at Mary. She was used to seeing him in the overhead lighting of the studio, but now his lean face was starkly sidelighted and appeared older and more serious, youth with a hint of mortality.

He took a sip of soda through his straw but didn't seem to taste it. He said, "Mary, when I say you're getting better fast, I really mean it."

" 'Course you do." She said nothing more, waiting for him to toss back the conversational ball, wondering where this little impromptu talk was talking them.

"We, uh, speaking in confidence?"

"Sure, if you want it that way, Mel."

" 'Cause I'm gonna run a risk in what I say."

"There's no risk saying anything to me," Mary assured him.

"The way a dance studio like Romance works," he said, "is that we gotta make sure the students walk out feeling good so they wanna sign up for more lessons, or for our night on the town, or some party or other. Maybe the Romance Studios' intercity competition. Long-term contracts, competitions, that kinda thing's gotta be our top priority."

"You have to make money," Mary said. "I'm not naive, Mel; I realize it's a business."

"Some women don't. They get too emotionally involved. That can lead to a kinda gigolo aspect, if you know what I mean."

Mary knew. She was sometimes visited by an image of a middle-aged spinster trying to hold back time, making a fool of herself, and hoped it wasn't her, the Ghost of Mary Future.

"That's a small part of the dance scene," Mel said. "Older women being escorted by their young instructors, each one fawning over the other. Usually there's nothing real intimate going on, but I guess sometimes there must be."

"Sure. People are people."

"Rich divorcées, or widows with their husband's insurance money, that's what keeps a studio like Romance out of the red. Among ourselves, we instructors call those students Cadillacs, and we're told to give them special treatment."

"Cadillacs, really?"

He shook his head, as if frustrated that he wasn't getting

through to her. "The in-house competitions between the Romance Studios in different cities, like the one coming up in Miami, aren't exactly fixed, Mary, but they come close."

She'd noticed how almost everyone who entered came home with some sort of medal or trophy, so it had struck her before that the Romance competitions must not be too critically judged, but still she was surprised to hear Mel admit it. She supposed she was guilty of seeing only what she wanted, and closing her eyes to the rest. But why was Mel opening her eyes?

"What about the Ohio Star Ball?" she asked, already knowing the answer.

"That's a different story. That kinda competition's sanctioned by the National Dance Council of America and is on the up-and-up. If you do well there, you *know* you can compete. Except for a few cases of politics maybe, among the top pros, it's honest and you'll only win what you deserve."

"Then how come you're telling me this?"

" 'Cause I'm not just going up to Ohio with you as part of my job so the studio makes money. Maybe it was mostly work before, but things have changed. You've improved tremendously the past few months. More'n I thought you could, tell you the truth. You can win, Mary. *We* can win." He reached across the table and touched his fingertips to the back of her hand; the contact was electric. "I want to win up there, Mary. Before I commit myself to it completely, I gotta know you feel the same way."

Something in Mary's breast expanded; hope and confidence combining to form a helium swell of exhilaration, of supreme confidence. "I've felt that way for weeks, Mel." She clutched his hand, barely realizing she'd swept her arm across the table.

He withdrew his hand, but he said, "This isn't an act to get you all enthused. Not a standard studio con job to milk more money out of you. I need to know you believe me."

"Con job. Milk more money. Would the studio actually do something like that?"

"Sure. You should be a fly on the wall during one of our staff meetings. It's a rough business, Mary."

She stared at him over her kinked straw. "You'll find out I can be a determined competitor, Mel. Maybe not in other areas of my life, but in this I can fight and win."

The wind blew and peppered the window with rain. "Well,

ballroom dancing's not exactly fighting," Mel said, rotating his cup in its circle of dampness.

"Depends on who's doing the dancing."

Mel looked at her in a way she'd never seen; his studio mask had been removed to reveal who he really was. And now he was seeing who she was.

"I do think you mean it, Mary."

Mary said, "Believe it."

29

Slumping down in the booth, Mary watched Mel stride out the door to return to the studio. She could see him out the window, a graceful figure viewed through a plane dividing inside from outside. It seemed to Mary that always there was a pane of glass between her and the people she tried to love, to really talk to, invisible but solid, keeping her on the outside. But tonight she'd been inside, with Mel. As he hunched his shoulders against the rain and jogged out of sight, lightning illuminated the parking lot like a cosmic flashbulb.

In a daze, Mary slowly sipped the rest of her Pepsi, trying to assess the significance of her conversation with Mel. Her world had changed in a way subtle but profound, a shifting on its axis that altered time and climate.

She continued to think about this as she drove home over rain-slick, iridescent streets, cozy in the car's scaled-down confines, mesmerized by the *thwump! thwump! thwump!* of the windshield wipers. The talk with Mel had pleased her immensely, even inspired her.

And scared her. So much was expected of her now.

She was still replaying the conversation in her mind when she worked her key into her apartment door and heard her phone ringing.

After flinging the door open, she tossed her dance shoes into the wing chair and ran to the phone. She lifted the receiver and breathed a hello.

"Mary?" Rene's faint but rich Southern accent, turning her name to honey.

"Yeah, me."

"It's Rene. You outa breath?"

"A little. Phone was ringing when I walked in the door."

"I drove into Baton Rouge today and got the envelope," he said. "I wanted to thank you." He didn't sound as if he was speaking all the way from New Orleans; he might have been right there in the room with her, his mouth near her ear.

"Is the stuff I sent a help?"

"I think it will be. And the schedule of upcoming competitions is a bonus. There are some names on the dance registration lists I can recall Danielle mentioning from time to time. Friends from the competitions."

"Maybe if you look up those people, talk to them, you can learn something. You know, one of them might know some little piece of information and not realize it's important." She felt slightly foolish, like a character in a crime melodrama urging someone to search for the missing piece of the puzzle. As if in real life it always existed.

But he said, "Could be. Though I'm more interested in finding out if any of these women's names cross-check with the names of murder victims in various cities, especially dance competition cities." He was quiet for a moment. "I'm not sure I want to see any of the same names on both lists," he said. "It'd mean there's a modern-day Jack the Ripper operating in different cities, and the police haven't picked up a pattern. That prospect's beneficial to me in my predicament, but it's still kinda ghastly to think about."

"Have you considered giving the police the names of the dancers Danielle mentioned? Maybe they'd get busy and figure out something. They're supposed to be the experts."

He snorted. "Some experts! I tell you, Mary, the more I have to do with the police the less I trust them. Just the opposite of us; each time we talk I trust you more. There's some humanity there, some real concern."

Flattered, she said, "I feel like we know one another, even

though we never laid eyes on each other. I mean, sometimes you get a sense about people, a certainty in your heart. Like a kinda instinct that's never wrong."

She thought he might reply that he had the same feeling about her, but he said, "You still planning on entering the Ohio competition in November?"

"Still am. I'm getting in all the practice possible. It's hard work, but I love it and it's worth it."

"Dancing meant so much to Danielle." His voice was a wistful sigh. "It means a lot to you, too, doesn't it, Mary?"

"Yes. It didn't start out that way, but now I'm . . . I don't know, it's like I'm only truly me when I'm dancing. You understand something like that?"

He laughed sadly. "Yeah, I've more or less heard it before. Sometimes, Mary, when we talk I feel I'm on the phone with Danielle."

Not knowing what to think of that, she said nothing. For an eerie instant she saw herself as some kind of medium: Danielle using Mary and phone lines to communicate from the grave.

"Mary? I meant that as a compliment."

"Well, we can talk anytime you want."

Again the sigh, weighted with a sad resignation. "No, I'm afraid we shouldn't do that."

Mary wondered what he meant. Did he fear getting involved so soon after the death of his wife? Did Mary frighten him in some deep and tragic manner? But she was being ridiculous; my God, they'd never even met. What would Jake think? She felt a thrust of fear, like a spear deep and cold in her midsection. Jake. He was still in her thoughts, a potent figure lurking in the corridors of her mind.

"I can't let someone innocent like you get involved in this mess," Rene said. "I haven't exactly made it a secret I'm determined to find whoever killed Danielle. The police are watching me, and it'd only be a matter of time before they knew I was contacting you. We've run enough of a risk already."

"I'm not afraid of the police. I haven't done anything wrong, and neither have you."

He laughed, as if admiring her pluckiness. "It's not a question of being unafraid. Or being innocent, for that matter. People don't really know how the police work until something like this happens. A nightmare that spins a web. I know you understand, Mary."

Do I? "Sure. I guess, if you say so, it makes sense."

"You really are empathetic." His gentleman's voice dripped appreciation, admiration, making her think of magnolias and mint juleps, though she had no idea how a mint julep tasted. "You're so very compliant."

"Is that good?" The little girl in her, begging for approval.

"In some women, yes."

Had Danielle been compliant? "If you need help again, you will call me, won't you?"

"Of course. I can trust you, Mary."

"You can, Rene." It was the first time she'd called him by his first name, been that familiar. "Honestly, you can trust me."

"When this is over, Mary . . ."

She waited in the silent stillness of her apartment, her thoughts drifting in the abyss of the long-distance line. Could wait no longer. "What?"

"If we don't talk before then, I'll get in touch with you after Danielle's killer's found."

When she didn't answer, he said, "I promise."

"Good luck," was all she could think of to say, the words choked and heavy.

She was sure he uttered her name once, softly, "Mary," then the phone clicked and droned in her ear. The conversation had gone so quickly she hadn't even told him about what Jake had done, and how she'd evicted him from her apartment and her life. Damn! Rene was the one person she desperately wanted to tell. But now she couldn't. Not yet.

She let the receiver clatter into its cradle and sat staring straight ahead into an uncertain future, afraid.

What's happening? What am I letting happen?

What really frightened her, what thrilled her, was feeling the tug of a dark and powerful current, strange yet familiar, and not knowing where it would carry her.

In the street below he stood in the shadows and watched her windows, waiting for a glimpse of her as she moved about her apartment.

There!

She'd crossed his line of vision, a figure so fleeting it might have been any woman who vaguely resembled her. Yet he could feel the connection between them, so intimate, the thing that linked their fates to a single profound destiny.

That one brief look at her heightened his resolve, and he stood without moving, staring and seldom blinking, until all her windows went dark.

30

Trying not to think about Rene, Mary concentrated with heightened intensity on her dancing. It was safe and predictable, the reassuring and protective pattern in her life.

Mel was more than pleased by her progress, no doubt assuming it was solely their conversation in the Hungry Hobo that had stoked her fire. When they danced Latin steps requiring the smoldering eye contact that would impress judges, Mary was convinced that occassionally something real and vibrant passed between them. He was learning about her; each time they tangoed he'd remind her that this dance was one of male domination, and she must convey that in her interpretation at the Ohio Star Ball. The tango had been born in Argentina, banned by government and church for its sensuality, popularized in France, and here was Mary working to impress judges in Ohio. In that context, her situation with Rene seemed not so remarkable.

A new Mel was emerging, or at least a dimension of him she hadn't expected. The fierceness of his dedication and competitiveness surprised and awed her. She wondered what other Mels might live inside his young skin. What else might she not know about him?

It was odd, she thought, that she was the one who'd finally ended her affair with Jake. He was the only man in her life who'd never deserted *her*. Duke had left her, by drinking and dying. Her high school sweetheart, Wayne, had married his second cousin shortly after graduation. Mel? There was no denying that Mel was being paid for his attention; if she stopped writing checks to Romance Studio, the magic door to the dance floor, and to Mel, would close. Even Rene was now distant from her, though there was good reason. Other men in her life, such as Victor, didn't count because she couldn't care about them, sometimes couldn't stand to be near them.

And her involvement with Jake did seem to be ended, for him as well as for her. There were no roses this time. Not even a phone call.

That was fine. That was the way Mary wanted it. She was sure she was strong enough to turn Jake away if she had to, but she didn't want to be put to the test.

Except for her dancing, and the fact that Angie seemed better but was seeing more of Fred, Mary's life stayed on a satisfactory level into early September.

Too satisfactory to last.

She was in the shower when Jake flung aside the plastic curtain so abruptly it tore. Some of the metal rings fixing it to the rod broke and clattered like bouncing coins over the tile floor.

Her heart jumped with fear and she heard the soap *thump!* on the bottom of the bathtub.

He was smiling at her in a way she recognized, as if she weren't Mary, but merely an object placed on earth for his amusement, an inflatable doll with deluxe features.

Fear squeezing her words, she said, "I'll have you arrested for rape, Jake. This isn't a goddamn movie where the girl always swoons if only she's pushed around enough."

He moved closer, the shower spray splashing on his bare arm. "Isn't it?"

She cowered back into the corner of the shower stall, staring at his hand, noticing it was trembling. *Don't lose control, Jake. God, don't lose control.*

"Turn off the water and get in the bedroom," he commanded in a strained voice. "It isn't going to be flowers and sweetness this time. You've shown you don't deserve it."

And suddenly she was calm when she should have been most

frightened. "You might eventually get your way, Jake, but I'm going to fight you. Then I'll go to the police. Then I'll go to court. I can do that, and I will, I swear. Rape means prison, Jake. I'll sell everything I've got and borrow more, and I'll hire the best lawyer in the city and I'll see to it that rape means prison."

He backed away a few steps, seeming more puzzled than afraid of her threats. She realized it was her lack of fear that was making him hesitate. She was supposed to be programmed to give in and then forgive. That was how he remembered her. That was Mary.

"Damned if I don't think you mean it," he said through a shaky smile. "Did you think I was really gonna rape you, Mary?"

She was aware of the water pounding on her, getting cold. She reached out and twisted the shower handle to Off. "I still think so, Jake." Goose bumps were breaking out on her shoulders and arms; she hoped he wouldn't notice.

"Let's talk about this," Jake said.

"Our talking days are over. Leave now or I go to the phone and call the police." She was amazed that, despite her nudity, she'd managed to summon a degree of dignity to lend weight to the threat.

"But I haven't even done anything."

"You broke in here."

"Oh no, I used my key. That's perfectly legal. And I never even touched you."

"Leave the key on the table on your way out."

He stood poised for a moment, mentally and physically off balance. He'd encountered a new and unexpected strength in her and didn't know how to react. Emotions pulled at his features. His lower lip twitched and for a terrible moment she thought he might begin to sob, beg her to take him back, but he'd merely been trying to find words to speak.

Whatever words he'd found, he couldn't utter them intelligibly.

He backed from the bathroom, looking at her with an odd and decisive detachment, and he was gone almost as suddenly as he'd arrived.

She heard the front door slam.

She stepped from the tub and wrapped her robe around her without bothering to dry herself. Her teeth chattered until she clenched her jaw. She was shaking and cold inside the robe.

In the living room she saw Jake's key lying next to the lamp on the end table by the sofa. She picked it up and squeezed it until its edges hurt her palm. The threat of the police had turned Jake away because he knew she'd meant it. She remembered what he'd told her about Edward G. Robinson being tough because he knew he was tough. Well, she and Jake had both known this time she was tough enough to follow through on her threat.

She wished she could talk to Rene and tell him the police were good for something after all.

Instead she went to the door and fastened the chain lock.

31

After the macabre dance, he wrestled her to the ground. That was when she gave up. Her gaze darted around and found only darkness. He'd been clever, waiting for her here. There was no one to help her, no hope.

She could feel him sense her surrender. Grinning down at her in the dim light, he raised his body slightly, keeping a tight grip on her hair, pressing her head tight against the ground. He held the knife up where she could see it, moving the blade in a lazy circular motion.

"All right," she gasped, still out of breath from her struggle. "All right, whatever you want." And she was sure she knew what he wanted; she'd felt his erection seconds ago as he'd brought his body down on hers.

Or did she know? The knife darted to her throat and she felt the cold kiss of the blade.

When she looked into his eyes and saw a darkness blacker than the night, she knew she was going to die.

Suddenly he moved, pulling the knife away and granting her a reprieve. Through paralyzing fear and a strange gratitude for sparing her momentarily, she felt his free hand groping beneath her skirt, yanking down her panty hose, then her panties. A fingernail scraped the back of her thigh. She was glad he was going to rape her; she'd live that much longer, anyway. And where she was, so near to death, every second of life loomed huge and of monumental importance, the difference between being and not being.

He surprised her once more, though. She realized what he was going to do when he grabbed her hair again, then adjusted his grip and moved well to the side, obviously so he wouldn't get blood on him, and jerked her head back unbelievably far to expose her throat.

He said something she didn't understand, his words floating to her from another universe. It didn't matter what he'd told her. She knew she belonged to the dead, even before she felt the slash of the knife, breathed in but drew no air, and prayed for it to end soon after all.

32

"Way I see it," Helen said, "he's killing his mother."

She was sitting next to Mary on the Romance Studio bench. Mary hadn't understood her because Helen had been bending down to buckle a dance shoe as she'd spoken. When the words did fall into vague meaning in her mind, she asked who was killing whose mother.

Straightening, face still flushed and mottled from being upside down, Helen swiveled on the bench and stared at her. "You okay, Mary Mary?"

"Been a rough day since morning," Mary said, "but I'm all right."

"Killed his mother is what I said."

"Who?"

"The guy that murdered the dancers in New Orleans and Seattle. That's why the two women looked something alike. They find

139

this guy, I betcha dollars to doughnuts it turns out his mother was the same type as his victims. He hates her but he's scared shitless of her, so he murders other women as a sort of symbolic gesture of his contempt. Kills her over and over again. That's the way it works."

"Sounds like talk-show psychology," Mary said. Her gaze shifted to the office door, waiting for Mel to emerge so her lesson could begin. Waltz music was floating from the big Bose speakers, and tall Lisa and her instructor were gliding over the floor. Lisa did an elegant *develope*, holding the count and extending her pointed foot gracefully as she slowly raised and lowered her long, long leg.

"It's a known fact mass murderers do that kinda thing because of their mothers," Helen explained. "Like Ted Bundy and Son of Sam."

"I don't remember reading about them hating their mothers."

"Well, you gotta admit they couldn't have had a healthy relationship with old mom, or they wouldn't have felt the way they did about women."

Trapped, Mary had to agree. But she said, "The police aren't even positive the same man killed both dancers."

"Yeah, they are," Mary said knowledgeably, "they're just not clueing in the public. And can you blame them? You know how the news media is—jackals with microphones and typewriters. They'd make an investigation, then a trial, impossible. Cops are smarter'n a lotta people think, and in a case like this they use something called VICAP. I read about it in a magazine just this morning, part of a list of things where America still leads the rest of the world."

"Vicap? Sounds like a cold medicine."

"Stands for Violent Criminal Apprehension Program," Helen said smugly. "It's a central storehouse of information about crimes and criminals all over the country, so a computer can pick up similarities in them and print them out and the police can know about matching M.O.s—that means Method of Operation. So when those two women were killed, the cops' computer linked up with VICAP and showed they were both humped by the killer after they were dead. See, that's the common denominator in the two crimes, and you can bet there's others they're keeping secret. Other things that were done to those poor gals."

"Why wouldn't the computer point out the fact both women were ballroom dancers? The police don't seem very interested in that."

"Probably they're not interested because that's not the sort of information they'd feed a computer about a murder victim in the first place, that she knew how to dance. Or that she competed. Big deal. To them the only ballroom dancing's the kind that goes on at proms or country clubs. They wouldn't figure it'd matter any-more'n if she played racquetball or liked sour cream on her po-tato. The similarity's not in the main data bank, so the cops disregard it. Cops think like that, you know."

Mary didn't know, but everyone else seemed to have a handle on how the police operated.

Still sitting down, she bent forward and slipped her street high heels into her dance bag. She saw on the carpet the scuffed toes of a man's black leather dance shoes, and looked up at Mel.

He was smiling down at her, so young, gentle, anything but threatening.

"They're playing a waltz," he said. "We might as well do that. Can't work on nothing but tango, or that's all you'll know how to dance in Ohio." He held out a hand for her, palm up, like a beggar imploring for alms. Not a hand that could ever harm anyone.

She followed him onto the dance floor and he led her into some basic box steps to warm her up, then through some balance steps and spiral turns. For a second they swept close to Lisa and her partner. Mary and Lisa glanced at each other, and Lisa suddenly tightened her posture and tilted back her head farther to empha-size a long and graceful dance line. Mary responded, kicking from the hip to follow Mel's lead. A spark. An instant of rivalry and competition that might not have occurred a few months ago, before the two women had begun grooming for Ohio. Lisa had gone to the in-house Romance Studios' competition in Miami and returned with a first in rumba and a second in fox-trot. Buoyed by success, however bogus, she'd been expressing grandiose ideas about Ohio.

Mel guided Mary to the edge of the dance floor and they stood for a second watching Helen and Nick waltz past and swirl into a parallel hesitation step. Helen was improving fast, too, and had plans to compete and succeed in November. A few competitive volts had also passed in her glance at Mary. The bulldog was coming out in the ladies.

"What we're gonna do now," Mel said, "is practice how to get on and off the floor. That's important, 'cause when we walk on, it's the judges' first impression of us. When we're gonna dance rhythm, you take my arm"—he extended his right arm and she wound her left through it—"and you look at me while I lead you out onto the floor. Sometimes I won't be looking at you, 'cause I'm the one watching where we're going. We walk fast, with a sense of purpose. I'll choose our spot, probably toward the center of the floor, where the judges are most likely to pay attention to us. Main thing is, we need to seem confident." He grinned, then bumped her lightly with his hip. "No problem for us, huh? We *are* confident."

And he was right; she was surprised to feel a confidence that matched his own. Why couldn't the competition start tomorrow? Or in five minutes?

He led her onto the floor as he'd described, and she almost pranced with eagerness.

As they were dancing, she watched Helen glide through a series of waltz pivots. She decided she could do them better.

For several measures all three whirling couples swept across the floor, rising and falling in unison on invisible waves of sound. It all clicked into place for Mary, as it had been doing lately, and she felt beautiful, whole, and without care. It was what dancing was about, finding oneself by losing oneself.

When they stopped, Mel told her everything would be fine if she danced that way in Ohio.

He walked over to the drinking fountain, and she followed. She felt so close to him at that moment, and had an overwhelming compulsion to confide in him. Right now, he might understand and be interested in her as a person, a woman as well as a student.

"I broke off my relationship with the guy I was living with," she began. Just making conversation, her tone suggested; how 'bout those Cardinals? Playing great baseball!

"That whatsizname? Jake?"

It encouraged her that he remembered Jake's name. "Yeah, he wasn't treating me the best."

"That so?" Mel leaned down and sucked water from the stainless steel spout's feeble offering. She waited while he straightened up and wiped his forearm across his wet lips.

"It was what I needed to do," she said.

"What *we* need to do," Mel said, "is put our problems aside and practice some more." He grabbed her hand and led her to the center of the studio, looking beyond her.

They assumed dance position.

Later that night, though she was exhausted, Mary practiced tango before the mirror in her apartment. She was beginning to feel as if the image in the glass were someone else, a very real other Mary whose body she controlled, and whose smoothness and precision far surpassed her own.

She was interrupted by the telephone. She seldom used her answering machine to screen callers these days. There was the slim possibility Rene might call. Of course, it might be Jake on the phone, but she was sure now she could handle that.

She quickly lifted the receiver, hoping as always.

Not Rene. Not Jake. Fred.

"I thought you better know Angie's back in Saint Sebastian," he said. Something in his voice. Bitterness? No. Fear?

"Alcohol again?" Mary asked. She knew the answer.

Only thought she knew.

"Cancer," Fred said flatly. "They removed some polyps or something from her cervix that turned out to be malignant."

Mary's insides went cold. This was completely out of left field, the place this kind of news always seemed to come from. "What? Whoa? Are you telling me my mother's got cervical cancer?"

"I'm afraid that's what it is, Mary."

"I'm driving down there," she said, as distant as if the woman in the mirror had spoken, the other Mary who didn't have to feel.

"Now, Mary, there ain't much point in that. Angie might even be asleep by the time you get here. I think they gave her a sedative or something."

"I'm leaving right now, Fred."

He sighed. "Room four-oh-five, Mary."

She hung up, feeling dizzy, and grabbed her blue windbreaker from the closet, hearing the wire hanger ping against the floor.

Then she walked directly out the door without bothering to turn off the lights or the music.

Cancer. The dreadful word. She didn't want to say it, or even to have it unsaid and crawling around in her mind.

With a rush of guilt, she realized her sense of impending doom was for herself, not Angie. Loneliness was gathering around her like a cold fog, affording only glimpses of a terrifying future.

Selfish! she admonished herself.

As she descended the creaking stairs, she repeated Angie's name softly, each utterance rending her heart. "Angie, Angie. Mother."

A terrible apprehension had taken form in her breast, an organic, destructive engine racing and fueled by fear.

She couldn't stop trembling.

33

Though visiting hours were over, the nurse on duty allowed Mary into Angie's room.

Angie wasn't asleep. Her eyes were half closed, but she was propped up in bed, and when Mary entered she smiled at her.

The room was almost exactly like the one Angie had been in for detoxification two months ago—same drab, institutional green walls, same black vinyl chair near the bed, same blood-pressure testing equipment and mysterious, many-dialed gadgetry mounted on the wall. But the other room had smelled of iodine, and this one had a musty scent about it, as if rain had blown in through an open window days ago and nothing had quite dried out.

On the windowsill was a small wilted flower arrangement, probably from the gift shop in the lobby. Fred's scrawled signature was visible on the card, but Fred seemed to be nowhere around.

Mary sat down in the black chair, hearing it sigh as the cushion was compressed. "So. When'd you find out about this, Angie?"

"About a week ago. One of Doctor Keshna's tests picked up something was wrong, then I came in and had more tests. After they removed some polyps from my cervix they did a biopsy and it came up positive. I didn't mention it to you 'cause there was no sense you knowing. Nothing to be done anyways."

"Nothing to be done? What's that mean?" Mary asked, with a mingling of anger and fear.

"Means my blood's spread the cancer and I gotta go through this chemotherapy business."

"So what do the doctors say? Will chemotherapy do it? Will that cure you?"

"They say it might. I'll be in here a few days, to start treatment, then it'll be outpatient stuff till a few weeks pass. They tell me I'll get weak then and probably have to check in and stay for a while. I tell you, Mary, I'm lucky; thank God for Blue Cross–Blue Shield."

Mary stared at her. She'd known people who'd undergone chemotherapy. Sometimes it worked, sometimes not. Cervical cancer. Oh, Christ! *You might be dying, Mother, and your reaction is to thank God for your insurance.*

"Don't take all this too hard," Angie said. "I told you I got great medical coverage, and it might be nothing."

"Nothing? Cancer?"

"Don't say it, Mary. I don't like hearing the word."

"I sure as hell don't like saying it." Mary wiped her eyes, which had welled with tears the second time that evening. These tears stung. "Dr. Keshna taking care of you?"

"No, not her specialty. Brainton's my doctor. Yuppie type, looks about twenty-two. Cervical cancer's his game." Angie shook her head weakly. "You know, this didn't have a damned thing to do with my drinking. Ain't that ironic?"

"That's supposed to be a comfort?"

"Worth drinking to."

"I'm gonna talk to Dr. Brainton."

"Go ahead, Mary. Maybe you can convince him I'm well and they'll tell me to go home."

"Don't be so fucking sarcastic!"

Angie, very tired from whatever they'd given her, sighed long and loud and let her head drop to the side on the fluffed white pillow. She smiled resignedly and not with her eyes. "I was furious, too, when I first found out. Couldn't be happening to me. Just ain't goddamn fair . . ."

"Angie, chemotherapy has a lotta side effects, doesn't it?"

"Yeah, I'll feel like shit for a spell. Hair'll likely fall out, that kinda thing." She was quiet for a while.

Mary heard people pass in the hall, soles shuffling. A woman laughed. *How dare she!*

"Duke went quick, didn't he?" Angie said with an edge of envy and maybe resentment. "Saw the other car coming and suffered about two seconds, if he was sober enough to know what was happening at all. He was always lucky, the bastard."

"Lucky when he married."

"Ha! Tell you, Mary, I was gonna leave your father. Finally gonna take you and go. Then came the accident." Her voice wavered and weakened, like a radio signal fading.

"Sure you were, Angie."

"You don' know . . ."

Mary waited for her to finish what she'd started to say. "Angie?"

Her mother was asleep. An old, old woman whose lips fluttered when she exhaled. Her soul might escape her like a feather.

Mary stood up from the chair. Angie was right; she *was* furious. At cancer, at herself, even at poor Angie. At fate. At the charlatans who assured people there was a reason for things. The parish priest she hadn't seen in years. The nuns who'd taught her in the sweat-and-varnish purgatory of Saint Elizabeth's. She paced from one side of the room to the other, faster and faster, whirling at each end of her short journey to prevent herself from striding into the wall. *Stay mad, you won't be afraid.*

Finally she stood still, staring at Angie and listening to her faint snoring. Then she left the green, musty room and asked at the nurses' station if she could talk to Dr. Brainton.

The doctor, she was told, had left for the day and wouldn't be back until ten o'clock tomorrow morning. Mary thought of asking for his home number, but she knew the nurses would refuse, angels of mercy protecting a god. It wouldn't be right, or informative, to try calling the doctor at home anyway; she'd no doubt get only his answering service.

She rode the elevator down to the lobby, walked through a

maze of halls to Detox, and asked to see Dr. Keshna. Then she waited in one of the molded plastic chairs by the table laden with dog-eared copies of *Time* and *Newsweek*. A newspaper was folded sloppily in one of the chairs; did it contain something on the murdered dancers?

"You always seem to be on duty," Mary said, when Dr. Keshna, in a rumpled green surgical gown, had pushed through the wide swinging doors and was standing calmly before her.

Dr. Keshna nodded solemnly, as if yes indeed she did live at the hospital.

"I've been upstairs visiting my mother."

"How is she?"

"Well, other than a little cancer, she's okay."

Dr. Keshna had obviously dealt with shocked and angry relatives who were themselves stunned by whatever microbe had attacked their loved ones. She said nothing. Her large dark eyes were kind and knowing. Mary wondered if the doctor was what Hindus called an "old soul," one who'd been reincarnated countless times and acquired a residue of wisdom.

In the face of her placidity, Mary realized anger was futile, illogical. It could change nothing.

She slumped down deeper in the hard chair, until the base of her spine ached. "Okay, I'm sorry. None of this is your fault."

"It's something that happens," Dr. Keshna said.

"How much do you know about her condition?"

"Some. Not as much as Dr. Brainton."

"He's not here to ask. You are."

"Yes."

"Will she live?"

"Possibly."

"What are the chances? The odds?"

"That I couldn't say."

"Did what happened to her have anything to do with her alcoholism?"

"Maybe yes, maybe no. Human organisms work dependent upon each other. I don't mean to be flippant, but nothing to do with cancer, or alcoholism, is perfectly predictable."

"So, is a medical prognosis just an exercise in unpredictability?"

"Always, I'm afraid."

"You don't talk like most doctors."

"Your mother's not my patient now, and I couldn't predict the outcome of her illness with any accuracy."

"I'm only asking for your guess."

"After she completes chemotherapy, then we'll see." The sad, wise smile. Old smile. "Until then, try to be patient."

Mary felt her sorrow, her rage, rise up in her. And something else—hopelessness. She bowed her head and began to cry silently. The tears tracking down her cheeks felt hot, as if she were fevered. She wanted to pray but resisted. At least she had the courage of her nonconvictions.

Dr. Keshna's fingertips touched her quaking shoulder. "I'm sorry. Do you want me to give you something to help you sleep?"

She nodded, and the doctor disappeared, then returned in a few minutes with a small brown plastic vial. "Take only one pill, just before bedtime," she said.

Mary thanked her and accepted the pills. Then she stood up. Her right hip was partly numb and her legs felt as heavy and unresponsive as if she'd been dancing for hours. Dr. Keshna was gazing at her again with her very wise eyes, understanding and unfathomable pity in them; she seemed to know something about Angie and Mary but there was no way to impart the knowledge. She touched Mary lightly again, this time on the back of her arm, as if she might ease anguish with the laying on of her tiny, gentle hands.

Neither woman spoke as Mary trudged from the hospital into the night.

34

He'd followed her home from the hospital and watched her park her car, then walk with her head bowed to her apartment and disappear inside. Lights came on, but she didn't move around and he didn't glimpse her through a window. She was no doubt tired, after her busy day and busy night.

He smiled. He knew about what she did, almost everything she did. She wouldn't like that if she found out, but wasn't that the delicious part?

She'd still be awake. He could walk up to her door and knock, and she'd answer.

And it would be as simple as that. Inside. He'd be inside, and there'd be nothing she could do about it. He absently ran his hand over his tumescent penis, thinking about that. It was always this way. A measure of time would pass, then he'd have to act. Something made him act, often when it wasn't wise, and he simply had to make the best of the way things turned out. Sometimes that was difficult. It was a good thing he was smart.

Suddenly he stepped down off the curb and started across the street toward her apartment, repeating her name in his mind: *Mary, Mary, Mary.* She could probably feel that upstairs, but she wouldn't quite know what the feeling meant. Not yet.

Light washed over him as a car rounded the corner, but he didn't pay much attention.

Until he saw the dull red and blue bar of lights on the roof, and the official lettering on the door.

A police car!

The patrol car slowed as it approached him. He continued to cross the street without speeding up. He could hear the car's engine slowly laboring near him. When he glanced to the side he saw there were two men in the dusty blue cruiser. As he stepped up on the sidewalk it almost braked to a halt and he thought for sure the one on the passenger side would say something to him, stop him and question him. Why were they so interested in him, anyway? Did he look suspicious? Could they somehow know his thoughts?

He stopped near a parked car, a big expensive gray Buick, and pretended to be fishing in his pocket for a key, taking his time, waiting for the patrol car cops to lose interest in him and travel on. A big luxury boat like the Buick, he must be an important man with influence; they better have a good reason for treating him like a criminal. A citizen could sue!

Great! Now the police car was sitting still in the middle of the street. And he had no key. What now? What would they think if he walked away from the Buick? That he forgot his briefcase?

No, not the way he was dressed.

More headlights!

A pickup truck had turned the corner onto Utah and stopped behind the patrol car, its driver waiting for the car to drive on.

Desperately, he fumbled with the door handle and found the Buick was unlocked. Much better! Luck going his way. He climbed in and slid across the seat until he was behind the steering wheel. Acted as if he were bending forward to fit the key in the ignition.

That must have done it. The pickup truck eased closer to the cruiser's rear bumper as its driver became impatient, and the cops gave up their curiosity. The police car edged forward, then picked up speed. The truck followed at a deferential distance.

He sat behind the steering wheel and watched through the windshield until both vehicles had disappeared down the street.

Then he got out of the Buick and ran in the opposite direction until a pain beneath his heart made him stop.

As soon as she awakened the next morning, Mary reached out a hand and passed it over the smooth, cool expanse of the sheet, as if to reassure herself she was safe in her own bed.

Daylight was exploding silently through the spaces in the venetian blinds, shooting needles into her eyes. She closed them again and thought for a moment that Angie's cancer was a nightmare remembered. But it wasn't. The undeniable fact of it settled over her like a pall.

She hadn't been able to get to sleep right away last night, sitting up and watching TV, the end of the Letterman show, people whose pets did amazing things on cue.

Later, in bed, she'd lain awake for a long time staring into darkness, her thoughts as aimless as stringless kites, dipping and soaring anywhere they wouldn't have to settle on Angie.

She opened one eye and peered painfully at the clock whose alarm she'd forgotten to set. Seven-thirty. If she hurried, she could still get to work on time. She assured herself of that as she struggled out of bed. The angled beams of sunlight were warm where they struck her bare legs.

After using a quick, cool shower to bring herself fully awake, she got dressed and walked into the kitchen. She needed coffee badly.

She added a little water to yesterday's leftover brew in Mr. Coffee's glass pot, poured some into a cup and put it in the microwave. She walked around the apartment while the coffee was getting hot, pacing, relieving some kind of pressure she didn't understand.

Finally she walked back into the kitchen. She decided to drink her coffee black, maybe clear her head by using caffeine as a substitute for a good night's sleep.

Still not hungry, but knowing she should eat, she stuck a piece of bread in the toaster, and when it popped up she spread strawberry jam on it.

As soon as she'd sat down with her toast and cup at the table there was a knock on her door. Hurried footsteps descended the steps to the foyer, and she barely heard the street door open and close.

Lowering her toast from where she'd lifted it halfway to her mouth, she set it next to her steaming cup, then she walked into the living room and crossed the carpet to the door.

She looked through the fisheye peephole and saw no one in the hall. Leaving the door on the chain, she opened it a few inches and saw the package on the mat. It was wrapped in brown paper and had a UPS sticker on it.

She closed the door briefly to unfasten the chainlock, then quickly brought the package inside. There was the return address in blue felt-tip pen: Spangle Soul Shoe Co., Chicago.

The Latin dance shoes she'd ordered! She wanted to look at them now. Though she didn't have a lot of time to spare, she'd open the package before leaving for work. Life had its priorities.

She carried the package into the kitchen, got a steak knife from

151

a drawer, and sat down at the table. After a sip of coffee, she used the knife to cut the tape on the package and peeled away the wrapping paper. Then she opened the box and lifted out one of the shoes from its cushion of crinkled tissue paper.

It was white satin, with what appeared to be two-and-a-half-inch heels. Mary was pleased. The shoes looked much like their catalogue illustration, and they'd do just fine for her rhythm dances in Ohio after she had them dyed black to make them appear more Latin, as Mel had advised.

Now came the big question: would they fit? It was difficult getting anything through the mail that actually fit. And there was no selection of ballroom dance shoes in St. Louis, which was why she'd sent away to Chicago. This would be the third pair she'd tried, and she didn't want to send them back as she had the others.

A folded paper in the shoebox caught her eye. A brief handwritten note in with the shoes, expressing the hope that Mary would be satisfied. Personal service was important in the small world of mail order dance supplies, which was why it was so easy to return merchandise to the seller. Returns and exchanges were almost expected.

She took off her street shoe and slipped one of the dance shoes onto her foot.

As she stood up and put weight on the foot, she felt it spread in the new shoe. Maybe this pair would be too tight. She couldn't be sure; she needed to put on both shoes and go through a few dance steps, on the carpet so she wouldn't mar the suede soles in case she decided to return them. Had to find out if they pinched.

But there really was no time for that now, she cautioned herself; she'd better get to work and shuffle the necessary papers for this afternoon's closing at the title company.

She returned the shoe to the box with its mate, then worked her street shoe back on her foot. Hurried a few bites of toast and a long sip of scalding coffee. Ready for the day. Sure.

As she took the stairs to the street, she brushed crumbs from her hands, then from the front of her coat.

It was eight-twenty when she got to work. There was one phone message for her, abbreviated in the receptionist's precise handwriting, red ink like blood on the memo sheet:

"Man/8:10/wdnt lve nme/wil cal bk."

35

But he didn't call. Not by lunch time anyway. The hours were getting heavy.

Probably, Mary told herself, it hadn't been Rene who'd called the office that morning. How could he know the phone number? She didn't recall telling him where she worked, but of course she might have mentioned it and forgotten. If so, what else might she have said and not remembered? If Rene knew where she worked, what else might he know about her?

By two-thirty she was almost worn out from praying each time the phone rang, feeling the emptiness in her when each call resulted in an ordinary business conversation. Instead of humming with passion, the line buzzed with talk of closing costs and adjustable rate mortgages.

At three o'clock, just after she'd worked up some figures with Victor on what it would take to finance a four-family, the phone didn't disappoint her.

"Mary? This is Rene."

"I know your voice." She saw herself as if through the window, a conservatively dressed real estate employee talking on the phone, her hammering heart not visible. The closing woman. Amazing what went on beneath the calm surface of normality.

"Sorry about calling you at work, but I needed to talk."

"It's okay, really."

"I tried your apartment last night, but you weren't home. No one was."

"Rene, the guy we talked about—Jake—he's moved out for good."

"It was your idea?"

"Yeah. Things weren't good between us. They never were good, actually."

"It sounds like you did the right thing."

"I'm sure I did." He didn't say anything, but she could hear him breathing. "Rene, did I mention to you where I worked?"

"No. Why?"

"The phone number here. How'd you get it?"

"Oh! I figured you'd left for work this morning, and I didn't wanna call again at your apartment. Then I remembered you said you worked at a real estate company, so I got a St. Louis phone directory at the library and started going down the list. Called each one till I got to Summers and asked for you, and a woman said you hadn't come in yet, so I knew I had the right place. Is it okay? I mean, can you talk?"

"Sure, no problem."

"Another woman's died, Mary. Here in Kansas City."

Whoa! She mashed the receiver harder into her ear, as if to press in the realization of what she'd just heard. "You're in Kansas City?"

"Yeah, but not for long. The police don't know I'm here yet, and I'm catching a flight back to New Orleans in a few hours."

"The woman who was killed? . . ."

"She was a dancer, in her thirties, with dark hair. Like Danielle."

Like me. "And you were in Kansas City when it happened."

"I'm afraid I was. For the dance competition. Checking up on some of the names you gave me. I talked to a reporter with one of the papers, a man I met about five years ago at a convention here. Name's Pete Joller. I told him about my theory of a sort of intercity Jack the Ripper who kills ballroom dancers. He thinks it makes sense, and he agreed to help me cross-check the names with a list of Kansas City female homicide victims the past five years. He called last night about midnight, and I expected him to let me know the results. Instead he told me he'd gotten word a woman had just been discovered with her throat slashed. He checked and found out she was a ballroom dancer—local, though, not part of the competition."

"Had she?—"

"That's all I know about it," Rene interrupted, his voice tight. "But just the fact I was in town when it happened'll get the police all over me again."

Mary barely saw, barely heard, the cars swishing past outside the window on Kingshighway. The people in the cars were engrossed in their own problems, their own universe, and had no idea what kind of conversation was taking place so close to them;

a different world behind every windshield. "You got any kind of alibi?"

"No. I was at the dance competition, but nobody'll remember me. Then I went back to my hotel. The murder occurred about ten o'clock, when I was in my room alone."

"What can I do?" Mary asked. She was beginning to grasp the dimensions of this, how it would look for Rene when the New Orleans police found out. And they would find out, especially if the woman had been violated after death. "Where were you?" they'd ask their prime suspect. The answer could prove fatal.

"I don't want you to do anything," Rene told her. "I'll have to tell the police I was in Kansas City for the dance competition, hoping to learn something about Danielle's murder."

"That's the truth."

"You and I know it, anyway. The police'll be skeptical. I won't tell them about you giving me information."

If you have to, go ahead. She thought it, heard it in her mind, but she didn't say it. She was afraid of the police, of authority. Fear had been with her all her life, like a parasite in her bowels, sapping her of resolve and independence. The frustration, the curse, was that she knew it and could do nothing about it. That was the nature of fear.

"I just wanted to talk to you before you saw or heard about the murder on the news," Rene said. "Wanted to assure you, no matter what you hear about me, no matter what anybody says, I never so much as laid eyes on that woman."

" 'Course you didn't."

"I'm afraid the police'll buy into the importance of the dancing connection now, after three murders. After all, it's what I've been trying to convince them of all along. I should stay away from dance competitions. I've been hanging myself and didn't know it; it never occurred to me a woman'd be murdered while I was in the same city. The police'll think I have some mental problem about dancers who look like Danielle. I don't, of course. Sweet Lord, I do some dancing myself. My mother was a ballroom dancer. A dancer's the very last person I'd hurt."

"Maybe this murder's not even connected. Maybe the dead woman *did* just happen to take dancing lessons."

"And get her throat slit the way Danielle did?"

"It could have happened that way. People get murdered all the time, ten times more often than they win the lottery. Almost one every day here in St. Louis."

"I hope that's the way it is, despite the fact this murder fits with my theory. I haven't seen the victim's photo yet. Pete didn't even know her name when he called. I hope she's black or Oriental and her husband's already confessed. But I doubt it; I've got a feeling I was right about this, and the killer came to the competition to scout a victim. It builds up in someone like that, someone mentally tortured. The pressure gets worse and worse. It was time for him to kill again, and I happened to be in the same city when he acted out his sickness. It's not really that much of a coincidence, you stop to think about it. Christ, it's something I should've taken into account."

Mary gathered her courage until it encased her heart like cold, hard armor. "Rene, if you have to, go ahead and tell the police about why you went to Kansas City, about the information I sent you. Honest, I don't care."

"I *do* care. I promised I'd keep you clear, and I meant it. Your name stays out of this. Which is another reason I called, to tell you I won't talk with you again till this is over. If I try to contact you, the police'll almost certainly know. If they were watching me before, they'll be hiding in every shadow now, using every kind of electronic eavesdropping gadgetry. They're merciless and relentless, and they'd close in on you like wolves."

"Rene, it doesn't matter—"

"It does to me, Mary. I won't have you dragged through this kinda crap."

"Don't worry, any problems it causes can be worked out."

"But it doesn't *need* to be that way. Not on my account, anyway. It was never my intention to mess up your life, Mary. I won't let it happen."

"Rene—"

"Bye, Mary. I'll talk to you again when this is over. A promise."

"But—"

The receiver clicked in her ear.

"Mary?"

She hung up the phone and stared at Victor, standing before her desk and frowning down at her. The bright light from outside was behind him, creating a blinding aura around him, making him seem slim and tall and making her squint.

"Something wrong, Mary? I hope not your mother?"

"Nothing," she said. "Nothing, Victor. Please!"

"Please what?" He looked perplexed.

She sighed. What could she tell him? What could you ever tell someone like Victor? "You call that four-family buyer about closing figures?"

"Sure did. I'm leaving now to meet him at the Maplewood property. I just thought I'd stop by your desk and let you know."

"Good, Victor. Fine."

Still looking puzzled, he shrugged into his coat, shot her a quizzical smile, and went outside.

Mary immediately switched on the small portable radio she kept in her desk drawer.

The rest of the afternoon she played with the radio dial, jumping from station to station. She heard mostly music, a smattering of news, a few minutes of a heartfelt debate about cellulite, but nothing about a murder in Kansas City. Maybe the police were keeping it secret for now. No, that couldn't be—that reporter, Pete something, had phoned Rene, so the press must know. Probably it simply wasn't a big enough story to make the national news. It wouldn't become big enough until the police realized Rene had been in town, or until they made the connection between the Kansas City victim and the women murdered in New Orleans and Seattle.

Assuming there actually was a connection.

Rene had learned about the murder around midnight, so the story might be in the papers. Newspapers reported crime more thoroughly than radio or television; crime seemed to get more complex, unlike how it sounded or looked, the longer it was covered.

As soon as five o'clock arrived, Mary hurried from work and drove to a drugstore, where she bought a *Chicago Tribune* and a *St. Louis Post-Dispatch.*

In her car, with the lowering sun beating through the windshield and giving her a headache, she examined the papers and finally found the news item on page four in the *Post.*

She sucked in her breath. The victim's photograph accompanied the story, and her name, Vivian Ferris. The story had made the St. Louis paper because of the relative nearness of Kansas City and the viciousness of the crime. The victim's throat had been deeply slashed, her breasts and genitalia mutilated, and the speculation was that she'd been raped.

Mary was sure the autopsy would reveal intercourse had occurred after death.

She felt dizzy. Death and sex, sex and death. Marriages and funerals. Lady-killers and lovers' leaps. Was death so much a part of the danger and allure of sex?

Despite the grainy black-and-white newspaper photograph, she was positive she and Vivian Ferris could have passed for sisters.

36

As she was driving to try on her dress at Denise's before work the next morning, Mary heard on KMOX news that Rene had been questioned by the police, then released. Two people at the Kansas City dance competition were sure they'd seen him there at the time of the murder, a tall man with dark hair and a deeply cleft chin, avidly watching the dancers.

Though she'd planned on waiting until she'd picked up the dress, Mary stopped at a vending machine and bought a newspaper. She leafed through the front section until she found the story.

The information was the same as the report she'd heard on her car radio, only it confirmed that Vivian Ferris had been sexually molested after death. A newer, more sharply focused photograph of the victim was in this edition; Mary was struck even more by the resemblance to her own image in the mirror. Dark hair, lean features, even something about the tilt of the head. And beyond that, some *essence*.

Helen had laughed and told her it was her imagination, that she and Vivian Ferris looked nothing alike. She'd argued with Helen about that.

Occasionally Mary would answer her phone and no one would speak, though she was sure someone was on the other end of the connection. Crank phone calls? Or Jake?

Despite, or maybe because of, the day she'd resisted him and forced him from her apartment, Jake still concerned her. Though no longer in her life, she suspected he'd reappear in a way she wouldn't like. He was a problem looming like a specter in her near future, one of those dilemmas the mind shied away from, like an impending war too terrible to contemplate.

Denise, chunky and energetic, met her at the door, holding the black dress high on a hanger so she could be impressed. She said, "Duh-*duh!*" A drum roll was conspicuous by its absence.

But Mary *was* impressed. The skirt draped in graceful folds where Denise had raised the hem above the knee on one side, the filmy shoulder sleeves appeared perfect, and the sequins caught and gave back morning light like black stars winking at midnight.

"So whad'ya think?" Denise asked, grinning and obviously proud of herself.

"I hope I do it justice," Mary said, reaching out and touching the dress as if it were alive and might snap at her.

"Quit doin' a number on yourself, Mary, just try it on." Denise stepped away from the door to let her in. Her own stocky body was clad in baggy slacks and a sweater with a hunting scene on it, knitted men aiming their rifles at a V-formation of knitted ducks. One of the ducks had tumbled from the sky to beneath her left breast. Her taste and talent were reserved for her clients.

As soon as Mary zipped up the dress in the changing room, she knew it was perfect. It *fit* perfectly, anyway. How it looked might be another matter.

Avoiding stepping on the many pins lying in ambush on the carpet, she slipped into her Latin shoes, now dyed black, and apprehensively stepped outside the privacy curtain.

She stood in front of the full-length mirror and stared at herself, adjusting the diaphanous sleeves. Denise was gazing at her in the mirror, forefinger to lips, as if warning her to be silent in this moment of truth. She cocked her head to the side and moved the finger in a whirling motion, signaling Mary to turn around.

Mary spun as if doing a walk-around dance turn, gazing at her reflection over her shoulder, automatically putting on the flirtatious expression Mel wanted during the maneuver in the competition. She shocked herself; she looked saucy and put together. Damned sexy, in fact.

"I love it on you," Denise pronounced. "Absolutely!"

Mary still wasn't sure. She stood in a deliberately awkward posture and studied the dress in the mirror. "Not too much leg showing when I dance?"

"Hell, Mary, you'll be one of the more conservative ones out there. You oughta see some of the stuff I been making lately. More skin than material showing, I can tell you."

"It seems to fit all right." She switched her hips, making the gathered skirt flare. Hey, she liked the way that looked!

"No way anybody can fit it to you better," Denise said, sounding slightly miffed by Mary's lack of enthusiasm.

Mary smiled at her via the mirror. "Okay, I think it's great!"

"Really?"

"Really."

Mary changed back into her working-woman clothes and wrote the mollified Denise a check. She was spending plenty for the dress, but Denise was worth it, and the price was exactly the amount agreed upon and allotted by Mary. And though the Ohio competition would be expensive, she'd set money aside for it. Frugality was about to reward her, exactly as Angie and the nuns at Saint Elizabeth's had preached. What else might they have been right about? If they'd known the score about frugality, why not eternity?

She couldn't stop thinking about the dress as she drove to work, glancing at it now and then in the rearview mirror, where it was draped in a plastic bag on a hanger in the back of the car. The more she thought about it, the more she liked it. And she could wear her simple cocktail dress for the smooth dance competition; that's what most dancers wore in the Newcomer category.

Tapping her fingers on the steering wheel in cha-cha rhythm, she smiled as she drove. She'd danced experimentally on carpet with the new Latin shoes, and finally she was sure she'd found a pair that fit. And they were great with the dress. She was set now with what she needed to wear in Ohio. An important and worrisome hurdle had been cleared.

She was still pleased as she parked in the lot behind Summers Realty. A chill fall wind gusted in off Kingshighway, scattering dust and scraps of paper before it, but she didn't feel cold.

As she was locking the car, she realized she'd momentarily forgotten about Rene. About Angie. About Jake. Just the anticipation of dancing had filled her mind with movement and music and left no room for pain.

Three weeks now, she thought, still smiling but feeling a nervous knot forming in her stomach.

Three weeks until Ohio.

She was sure she was ready. She repeated to herself that she was sure.

Rene, as he'd told her, didn't call her during those three weeks. Mary thought of him every day, and doubt crept into her mind and spread like a malignancy. Would he ever call? Did any man ever really carry through on the important promises?

As the time of the competition drew nearer, she thought less about Rene and more about Ohio, battling her nerves. She began waking up in the early morning hours and not falling back asleep until almost dawn, her mind spinning to music. Other nights she'd lie awake thinking about Rene, until she slept and saw herself or women she resembled, their throats slit and grinning and their pale bodies locked in sexual embrace with a man whose features were blurred. Her nervous state began to show on her face, the strain dragging at her eyelids and the corners of her lips.

After Ohio things might be different. She would have passed through the fire, emerging annealed, and free.

One day the hospital called and informed her that Angie had been placed in intensive care. It wasn't unusual during chemotherapy, Dr. Brainton told Mary. Something about the white corpuscle count and anemia. Angie could have visitors, but they must only view her through a window, couldn't even send flowers; the intensive care unit had to be kept sterile.

Mary dutifully went to Saint Sebastian every day and stood for a while outside Angie's room. She'd waved to her through the window the first few times. Then Angie became too weak or disinterested to wave back. Sometimes she didn't seem to know anyone was there, and simply lay with her eyes closed or staring up at the ceiling. She was thinner and seemed much older now, and her eyebrows and most of her hair had fallen out. Yet ancient as she'd come to appear, there was something infantile about her, as if she'd aged full circle and returned to the newborn stage of her life cycle. The lack of hair and eyebrows, maybe. Mary had become the strong one and the caretaker. Daughter had become mother, and mother daughter. Time and death having their joke.

Dr. Brainton assured Mary that while Angie's condition was delicate, she was in no immediate mortal danger. But he didn't sound sure. Whatever his reputation, a doctor who looked like a bond salesman two years out of college didn't inspire confidence.

Mary suspected Angie might die soon. Suspected yet didn't admit it. To accept the impending death of a parent, you had to bend your mind around your own mortality. There was an undeniable progression there, the dark plainly visible at the end of the tunnel. She kept such thoughts to herself and placed them in an isolated part of her mind where she could almost ignore them.

A few days before Ohio, she answered her phone and a man's voice said, "I just called to wish you luck."

Not Rene or Jake. When she didn't reply, the caller said, "This is Jim, Mary."

At first she didn't know which Jim, and stood silently shuffling through her memory.

He laughed. "The Jim that danced with you at Casa Loma."

"Oh, God, I'm sorry. My mind's been whirling lately."

"I'm not surprised, with the big competition coming up. That's why I called. I remembered you telling me you were gonna compete in Ohio, and I ran into somebody from Romance who told me you'd really meant it. I figured I'd wish you the best up there."

"I appreciate it, Jim, honestly."

"Anybody else from Romance gonna compete?"

She told him the other dancers' names, and they talked about dancing and nothing else for another ten minutes.

"Call me when you get back," he said, "let me know how you did. I'm interested, because I'm interested in everything about you."

She didn't want to encourage him along those lines; she'd never thought of him in any romantic way. "I'll call," she said. "I promise." Being kind, but not *too* responsive.

"I'll be waiting for you," he said, and hung up.

Mary wondered about the conversation, about how much Jim expected from her. She'd tried to be diplomatic, but what had he assumed from what she'd said?

She gave up trying to get inside his mind. It was impossible to know how some men thought.

*   *   *

She'd had no trouble getting off work for an extended weekend for the competition. Even Mr. Summers stopped by her desk and wished her luck. She felt rather like a celebrity as she drove home from work the evening before she was to fly with Mel and the other Romance Studio contestants on a TWA flight to Columbus.

As she was carefully packing the black Latin dress in a garment bag, her apartment door slammed. Then a familiar footfall.

She knew it was him even before he spoke. Shouldn't be, couldn't be, but it was.

"Mary? Where the fuck are you?"

He sounded drunk, at seven o'clock in the evening.

Not good.

She swallowed a lump of fear and tried to zip up the garment bag. But the zipper stuck and she snagged a fingernail on it. She ignored the pain.

She recalled the way Rene had talked about pressure building and building in violent people. Then the inevitable happened.

"Mary?" His footsteps sounded in the hall, heavy and ominous, from a land of giants in a child's nightmare.

She'd feared something like this. Though they were no longer together, he'd never be able to let her leave without at least trying to destroy the beauty and possibility in her life. She was about to fly, and he had to crush the wings he so resented. Everyone struggled to grow wings, or had given up. It annoyed him that she wouldn't make that capitulation. It was, somehow, a threat to him.

Then he loomed in the doorway, his face a mask of rage. The liquor on his breath tainted the air. The way Duke had smelled when she was a little girl.

"How did you get in, Jake?"

He smiled. "Had an extra key made a long time ago." He was drunk, all right. It was in his voice, his eyes. He was probably here straight from Skittles, boozing it up with his warehouse buddies.

"Get out, Jake. Now!"

She might as well not have spoken. "Guess what that fuckin' supervisor at the warehouse did?" he asked, so furious his spittle tattooed Mary's arm.

She shrank away from him. She knew it didn't matter what anyone had done.

Whatever or whoever had wounded Jake, the price was hers to pay.

37

"Jesus!" Mel said at the airport, "what happened to you?"

Mary didn't think the results of last night were that obvious, with her oversize dark glasses on. Mel must have noticed the bruise on the bridge of her nose, a small, blood-plum stain underlined by a moon-shaped cut where Jake's thumbnail had gouged her when he'd swung and only grazed his target. No way to hide that one.

A dozen dancers and instructors were lounging around the waiting area of Gate 43, carry-ons and garment bags bunched like obedience-trained pets at their feet, waiting to board the flight to Columbus.

Mel moved around in front of Mary and turned her body slightly, toward the wide windows overlooking the runway, so none of her fellow passengers could see her face. He gently removed her glasses and stared at her. Then his handsome young face got ugly. "Oh, fuck, Mary! How you gonna compete with bruises like that?"

She'd never seen him this upset. "They should be better by tomorrow, and I can cover them with makeup. There's nothing on them now, Mel, honest!" Which was true, because she was afraid to risk infection by putting on makeup too soon.

"So what happened to you?"

"Accident."

"Like those other times?"

"What's that mean?"

He shook his head sadly. "Mary, Mary . . . With your face marked up like that, it'll be impossible. Nobody'll be looking at us from the neck down when we dance. At either of us."

"I can cover the bruises so they won't be noticeable. You'll see tomorrow, Mel!"

He did a quick complete turn, snapping his body around in an outburst of frustration. "We might as well go home," he said.

"Who mize well do what?" Ray Huggins asked. He'd walked up behind them from where he'd been leaning, smoking a cigarette near an ashtray. He was wearing pleated gray slacks, fancy two-tone brown leather loafers, and a butter-colored leather jacket. He was grinning.

But when he saw Mary's face he was suddenly shocked and serious, like a man who'd walked in on a burglar. "Yeow! What happened, Mary?"

"An accident."

"Perfect goddamn timing, isn't it?" Mel said.

Mary understood his bitterness. He wanted to compete, and finally he had a student who gave him a chance at a win in the most prestigious competition of all, and look what she'd done. Look what Mary had done.

"My fault," Mary said. After all the time and work they'd put in. She felt so sorry for him, for herself. Her eyes burned and she didn't want to cry. It hurt badly when she cried; she couldn't wipe her eyes without igniting the pain in the bruises.

"Take it easy, Mel," Huggins said. He laid both hands gently on Mary's shoulders; she heard his leather jacket creak. "What do *you* think, Mary?"

"I think I can make myself look presentable tomorrow morning. The bruises'll fade. I want to dance. You know how much I want to."

He gave her shoulders a quick squeeze, then dropped his hands to his sides and shrugged. "Good enough for me."

"But, Ray—"

"Can it, Mel. The lady says she can compete. Mary, you don't hurt anywhere else, do you? I mean, any part of your body that'd keep you from moving okay?"

She was glad she'd decided not to mention the pain in her side, the breath-catching stitch of agony when she inhaled too deeply.

Cracked rib? If so, it would have to wait. The world beyond the competition would have to be put on hold, like an annoying caller at work. "Everything else is fine."

"What the hell kinda accident were you in?" Huggins asked.

"The kind that happens with fists," Mel told him.

Anger flared in Mary. "How would you know?"

Mel touched her arm. "Mary, everybody knows. This isn't the first time you turned up battered and bruised. It's that guy you live with, Helen said. I thought you and him parted company."

"We did, but he had a duplicate key made and let himself into my apartment. And Helen oughta mind her own business."

"You should consider filing charges," Huggins said. "A bastard who'd do something like that to somebody like you belongs in jail."

"He's outa my life," Mary said. "Out for good."

"I don't blame you," Huggins said. He glanced at Mel. "Mel, you take extra special care of this lady."

"You know I will, boss."

Mary put her dark glasses back on and picked up her garment bag that held her dance dresses. She'd checked her old red suitcase containing the rest of her clothes at the TWA luggage service outside the terminal doors.

"Here, lemme take that," Mel said, and pried her fingers from around the handle of the garment bag. He slung it over his shoulder, using his forefinger as a hook. He was so slender the bag curled around him like a cocoon.

"You still mad?" she asked.

"Naw. Check with me tomorrow morning first thing, though. Jesus, we gotta do something about those bruises. You bring some chemical suntan for your legs and shoulders?"

"Sure, just like you said."

"The judges love bare skin in Latin competition, preferably tan. Maybe you can apply some extra to your face, blend it with the bruises. That might work."

They were standing in front of Helen and her instructor Nick, who were slumped in two of the waiting area's side-by-side brown vinyl chairs. Helen's folded garment bag lay in the chair next to her. She was wearing a bulky gray sweater and slacks with a flower design on them, and looked more like a pudgy middle-aged house-wife than a dancer.

"Ready for the big one, Mary Mary?" she asked, then did a double-take and frowned. "You get hurt or something?"

" 'Fraid so."

"Well, dumb question. It's obvious you got hurt."

Jet engines roared outside the windows as a red and white TWA airliner lifted off the runway, trailing dark wisps of uncombusted fuel that lingered like scratches on the pure blue sky. Comprehension, then anger, washed through Helen's eyes. "He came back, huh?"

Mel gave Mary a protective hug that made her side throb with pain. "She had an accident, okay? 'Nuff said."

Mary didn't want to do any more explaining. "I better get my boarding pass," she mumbled, and hurried to where a uniformed attendant standing behind a counter was examining tickets and resolutely pecking at a computer with a long forefinger. The other dancers and the instructors were talking about her, she was sure, but she told herself she didn't care. Damned if she'd care! She was going to Ohio to compete. That was a certainty. Whatever needed doing to make it happen, she'd do it.

She asked the attendant to assign her a seat near the rear of the plane, on the side of the aisle where there were only pairs of seats.

"No problem," said the attendant, a haggard, graying man. He studiously avoided staring at Mary's face. Or was that Mary's imagination?

No one spoke to her during boarding.

She sat alone in a window seat on the flight to Columbus. Mel sat near the front of the plane, walking back once to check on her when he got up to use the lavatory. In the seat in front of her was a boy about two years old who had a bad cold and sniffled and cried steadily until he fell asleep over Indiana.

Riding the hotel limo, which was actually a Dodge van, in from the airport, she stared straight ahead and said nothing.

Everyone was uncharacteristically quiet. Finally they were here, mere city blocks away from music and dance floor and spectators and judges. And the blunt white nose of the Hyatt Regency van was forging through traffic along those blocks, ticking them off like time.

What Mary and the rest of the dancers had been thinking about and sweating about all these months was suddenly becoming very real.

Was actually about to happen.

Miserable and apprehensive, Mary swallowed hard. Her throat was parched and she realized her fists were clenched. The knot in her stomach drew tighter and made her want to double over on the firm vinyl seat.

This, she thought, must be what astronauts feel in the last stages of countdown, when liftoff and critical risk become a virtual certainty.

The van lurched to the outside lane, then bumped and veered into the driveway of the hotel. Its brakes squealed, causing the cluster of businessmen standing outside the hotel entrance to turn for a moment and stare.

"Anybody got the jitters?" Huggins asked, laughter flitting an inch beneath the surface of his voice.

"Naw, I always got bats in my stomach," Nick said.

"Belfry, too," Mel told him. Everybody laughed harder than they should have.

Helen pointed a glitter-enameled fingernail out the side window. "Our home for the next three days," she said.

Mary thought, Only hours to Blast-off.

He sat deep and unnoticed in a warm leather sofa and watched them enter the hotel. They'd been arriving in groups and checking in all day. There was a look about women who danced, something in their posture and precise movement that flaunted and excited.

The heat and rage expanded in him as he watched them line up at the desk to register, talking and smiling, so at ease and unknowing. They even stood motionless like dancers, weight on one leg, hip thrust out, tempting, tantalizing. Where their flesh didn't show, they glittered, or their strong bodies stretched fabric as tight as his skin was stretched by his desire. He thought about the knife and had to lower the magazine he'd been pretending to read, so it covered his lap.

Even the older women who danced kept their attitude of allure despite the fact that they'd become pathetic parodies of their younger selves. Once a whore . . .

But he barely glanced at the old ones hanging on the arms of instructors the ages of their sons. And it was only with the greatest effort that he didn't stare at the young ones.

He formed a perfect image of the knife in his mind and waited confidently for the voice.

A perfect image.

38

The elevator zoomed to the tenth floor with a speed that made her stomach lurch.

To save on expenses, Mary was sharing a room with Helen. The bellhop, a pimply youth with a remarkably crooked nose, led them to 1011, a luxurious but oddly shaped corner room with an angular row of windows looking over downtown Columbus. Mary stood near the bed and stared at her unfamiliar surroundings on both sides of the glass. The reality of what was truly happening was still something of a shock.

The bellhop laboriously carried in their suitcases and garment bags from his luggage cart parked in the hall, then he showed Mary and Helen the room, demonstrating that the TV worked and doors did indeed open onto closet and bathroom.

As he handed Helen the perforated plastic cards that were used for room keys at the Hyatt Regency, the young bellhop wished them both luck in the dance competition.

"How'd you guess that's what we're here for?" Helen asked.

He grinned. "Easy. You both got the look of dancers. Real graceful-like."

Helen tipped him five dollars.

"Anything else you need, ladies, let me know. Name's Howard."

"Thanks, Howard, we'll do that" Helen said, and stood waiting while he bustled out and closed the door behind him.

"Howard knows the way to a dancer's heart," Mary said.

"Or wherever he wants to go." Helen sat on the nearest bed and bounced up and down a few times to test the mattress. For a moment she looked like a twelve-year-old lost in play. Maybe that was really why they were here, Mary thought, to lose themselves in the maypole motion of childhood.

An adult again, Helen rested her hands on the edge of the bed and stared up at Mary, frowning as if she shared Mary's pain. "Your friend Jake did that to you, right?"

"You know he did," Mary said. "Everybody else seems to know, too, so there's no sense talking about it."

"Talking can help sometimes. Relieves the pressure."

"Sometimes not."

"I thought you threw the guy out again."

Mary walked to the windows and looked out at the sun-streaked haze of pollution that lay over Columbus. Unhealthy, she told herself, but undeniably beautiful. Too much in the world was that way.

"Don't let him come back this time, Mary. Be smart and don't let him back in."

Mary turned to face her. "He's out for good, Helen. I know it this time. He knows it, too. I guess that's maybe why he did this to me, because he knew it was finally over." She raised her arms and did a slow rumba box. "Let's concentrate on the competition, huh?"

"You got it," Helen said. "First thing's to see what we can do with makeup so your black-and-blue marks don't show too much tomorrow."

"I think that'll have to wait till morning, when we know how much the bruises have faded."

Helen stood up, making the bed creak. "Okay, then let's unpack and go downstairs and register, find out when we're scheduled to compete."

Mary removed her two dresses from the garment bag and hung them carefully in the closet.

"You got a couple of great outfits," Helen said, holding up her own competition dresses on their hangers, a pink and white gown for smooth dancing, a low-cut red dress for rhythm. She was apparently waiting for Mary's comment. A little confidence boosting was in order here.

"You, too." Mary actually thought the red dress was a bad choice; it would showcase Helen's gelatinous upper arms.

"I got real long gloves to go with the Latin dress," Helen said.

Mary hoped they were long enough. She hoisted her suitcase onto the bed and began unpacking.

When she unzipped her shoe bag and withdrew the new black Latin shoes, she saw that both heels had been reduced to stumps less than an inch long, their truncated ends shredded as if they'd been sawed or whittled with a dull knife.

Jake! Jake with a parting gesture of disdain, a final slash at hope before her flight took off.

Her stomach tightened and blood rushed from her face. For an instant she thought she might have to dash into the bathroom and vomit.

"Whazza matter, Mary?"

She held up the shoes.

"Oh, Christ!" Helen said. "God*damn* him!"

Mary sat slumped on the edge of the bed, suddenly very tired. Weary of fighting Jake and circumstances and the world. And herself.

"What now?" she heard herself ask. "What in God's name am I gonna do now?"

Helen's hand was on her shoulder. "I front you the money for a new pair, that's all. It's no major deal."

Mary looked up at her. "It took me four months to find *that* pair, Helen. I've got feet like an extraterrestrial."

"Don't sweat it," Helen said. "Probably the places you sent away to for shoes have all got booths downstairs. There's supposed to be a whole room full of merchandise down there, every kinda dance paraphernalia you can imagine. That's what Nick told me. I'm planning on looking for a different pair of shoes myself."

Maybe Helen was right! Maybe it *was* possible to replace the black shoes. And if the new shoes weren't perfect, the hell with it, she'd dance anyway. She wouldn't let Jake do this to her. She was finished with that.

At least her stomach had calmed down; it wasn't tightened and drawing her body forward like a tautly strung bow. No way to dance feeling like that. "Helen, it's great of you—"

Helen waved a hand as if swirling water. "You'd do the same, blah, blah, blah. C'mon, Mary Mary, let's head down to the lobby and find out where we register. Then we'll hit the vendors' room and romp through those acres of shoes Nick told me about." She was already striding toward the door.

Mary left her suitcase and cosmetic kit on the bed and hurriedly followed. There'd be plenty of time to unpack later.

On the way out, she hurled the mangled dance shoes into the wastebasket by the desk, listened with satisfaction as they *thunked* against the metal bottom. There was a solid finality to the sound.

Jake! she thought. So long, Jake.

A pair of wide escalators serviced the Hyatt Regency's ballroom on the third floor. They'd taken the elevator to lobby level. Now Mary stood behind Helen as they ascended. Behind them was a spacious atrium with encircling marble steps that also served as benches. A few people were sitting on the steps talking. A man with a ponytail was strumming a guitar so softly Mary couldn't hear it.

Mary and Helen turned left at the top of the escalator and saw a carpeted area outside the ballroom doors where rows of dance supply vendors had set up tables or booths. There were racks of colorful feathered and sequined ball gowns; displays of gaudy costume jewelry to complement dance outfits; stacks of instructional VCR tapes; rows of tuxedos on hangers.

And tables lined with new dance shoes.

Mary immediately felt relieved. If Helen would lend her the money, finding replacement shoes here was certainly possible.

They told one of the women behind the registration table they were signed up for competition, and she located their information packets containing program books and tickets to the various events.

Mary and Helen immediately stepped aside and leafed through the program books. The pages were stiff and slick, and they crackled when they turned. Mary experienced a thrust of near panic when she saw her name printed among the contestants for the first dance in the Newcomer category, a cha-cha at ten the next morning.

"The lower categories like ours compete earliest each day," Helen observed. "A fine way to lose your breakfast."

"We compete nose to nose in three dances," Helen said.

Mary said, "Good luck, but not too much of it." Which was exactly how she felt about tomorrow.

Helen apparently understood and didn't seem to mind the remark. Probably she felt the same way. They slipped their registration packets into their purses and returned to the vendors' area.

More people were browsing among the merchandise, many of them wearing jackets or shirts that advertised dance studios from different parts of the country. A trim, blond couple was wearing matching sweatshirts that bore the logo of a studio in Britain. Off to the side, a woman in jeans and a man in a tuxedo were practicing a fox-trot step. An elderly woman had tried on a low-cut yellow gown and was twirling in front of a full-length mirror to see how the yards of pleated skirt material flowed.

"She couldn't have worn that dress even twenty years ago," Helen said.

Something made Mary stop and stand staring at the closed double doors to the Regency Ballroom. In every life were doors of critical importance; sometimes they were recognizable.

"Let's peek," Helen suggested, and led Mary to the doors.

She pushed one of them open and edged aside so Mary could see beyond her.

A cool draft eddied from the ballroom, and Mary was instantly struck with fear. In this place she was committed to something she yearned to do but that terrified her. The gleaming parquet floor was vast, surrounded by pink-clothed round tables. A mile away, toward the front of the ballroom, was a long dais where judges and various dignitaries of the dance world sat. On the right, a row of video cameras was being set up on tripods on a raised platform. There were more cameras on the balcony that ran along the left side of the ballroom. OHIO STAR BALL was spelled out with pink, white, and red ballons on the balcony facade; strands of tiny lights were wound among the balloons, illuminating them. Workmen were stringing cables. More were setting up balloon decorations that would form a soaring arch above the dance floor. Behind the judges' dais was draped a massive purple curtain lettered OHIO STAR BALL in silver, with a glittering silver star for the "A" in "Star." Tiny bright lights were strung down the curtain's folds, like evenly spaced drops of water frozen and glimmering in suspension.

I don't belong here, Mary thought, intimidated by the size and glitter of the ballroom. I'm not nearly good enough. She was furious with Mel and Huggins for suggesting she come here so she could make a fool of herself. Everything was larger and glitzier than she'd imagined. It was for the pros, the talented, not for a thirty-five-year-old closing woman from South St. Louis.

"We gonna be able to cut this?" Helen asked. Even she sounded uneasy.

"We can do it," Mary said. But she knew she hadn't fooled herself with the empty words, and probably hadn't fooled Helen.

"Say it often enough and maybe we'll believe it," Helen told her, letting the ballroom door swing shut.

As Mary turned around, she saw a man in a white shirt perched on a tall stepladder. He was hanging a rectangular banner above a display of shoes. As he lifted a corner of the banner, the lettering—SPANGLE SOUL SHOES—became visible.

"That's where I sent away for my shoes," Mary said. "C'mon, Helen, maybe I can get a replacement pair just like them!"

"I wanna check out one of those gowns," Helen told her, motioning with her head toward a rack of dance costumes. She dug in her purse and handed Mary her MasterCard. "Use that if you need it, then come on over by that second rack of dresses, okay?"

Mary tapped the plastic card with a fingernail. "Listen, you sure about this, Helen?"

"Just buy the shoes, Mary Mary, then meet me by those dresses and lie about how well one looks on me."

Mary squeezed her hand, then whirled and hurried toward the Spangle Soul display, as if someone might beat her to the last pair of Latin dance shoes.

Actually the display wasn't completely set up; only a few dozen shoes sat in a row on the long table. Their toes were pointed forward in precisely the same direction, like compass needles indicating north. Half of them were men's shoes.

The man on the top step of the ladder noticed her, shifted his body awkwardly, and stared down at her. His white shirt had perspiration stains under the arms. Mary saw that his spine was misshapen, and one of his own shoes had a built-up sole. "Sorry, we ain't quite open," he said from on high with a nervous smile. It was a long way down from where he was, and he couldn't abide further disability.

"I just need to know if you have a certain shoe," Mary said.

He knotted a length of twine to fasten the last corner of the banner. Now he began placing sparkling silver stars on the material; they appeared to be fastened with Velcro. "Be about twenty minutes," he said. "I gotta get these stars in place."

"I bought a pair of shoes from you by mail," Mary persisted, "and the heels are broken. I need to replace them. Tell you the truth, I'm desperate."

He stared down at her again. "You mean they was broken when you got them?" He sounded incredulous, as if she'd just confirmed that the moon was made of cheese.

"No, no. Someone—they got broken later."

"Well, we can't exchange—"

"But I don't wanna exchange them, I'll buy another pair."

The profit motive prevailed. The man wiped his hands on his thighs, then carefully worked his way down the wooden ladder, balancing his box of stars. She noticed that what she'd thought was a wallet jutting from his back pocket was actually a small Bible; maybe he had a conscience and a charitable heart, and finally religion was coming to Mary's rescue. All those hours of mandatory youthful prayer might not have been wasted. He limped over to stand behind the table and face her. She was surprised by how short he was. Whatever was wrong with his spine or his leg caused him to list to his left like a sinking ship even when he stood still.

Mary picked up one of his business cards from the stack on the table. His name actually was Spangle. Albert Spangle. Be a good Christian, Albert Spangle.

"I'm Mary Arlington," she said.

He smiled, transforming his pockmarked, fiftyish face into a mask of rough beauty, the face of a simple and solid man. His eyes were kind and bright blue beneath craggy, graying brows. "Ah, I remember now. Them white open-toed ones with straps and two-and-a-half-inch heels."

"Those are the ones," Mary said, pleased. "But I dyed them black. What I really need's a black pair."

He raised a gnarled forefinger. There was a speck of glitter on its tip, from one of the stars. "Lemme look, Mary. Size . . . six, am I right?"

"You've got a good memory."

"Got to, when you sell most of your merchandise by mail."

"I'll be praying you find them," Mary said. Well, why not a little schmaltz?

She watched silently as he limped over to a jumble of large cardboard cartons, each of them apparently containing shoe boxes.

Spangle crouched down clumsily and rummaged through the boxes for such a long time Mary began feeling guilty. He really did want to help her now, and she was taking advantage of his kind nature. After all, there was no reason she had to have shoes identical to the ruined ones.

She was about to tell him she'd come back later when he said, "Bingo!" and straightened up holding a pair of black shoes. "Only difference is, these here are leather," he told her, limping back toward the display table. He handed them to her with the toes pointed down, as if they were weapons that might discharge.

Mary studied the shoes and decided she liked them even better in leather. She worked her right shoe off her foot. Standing on her left leg and leaning on the table for balance, she bent over and tried on one of the dance shoes.

It seemed to fit. She put on the other and shifted her weight, swiveled her feet. The shoes were definitely more comfortable than the pair Jake had ruined. What luck! Was fate finally swinging over to her side?

Mary reached into her purse and closed her hand around Helen's MasterCard. "How much are they?"

"Eighty dollars," Spangle said. "But since you had bad luck with the last pair, for you they're sixty." He was beaming at her, his blue eyes alive with light. "Fair enough?"

"More than fair. Really. Thank you." She removed the shoes from her feet and slipped back into her street shoes. Spangle took the new shoes from her and inserted them noisily back among crinkled white tissue in their box. "You take credit cards?" Mary asked.

He laughed. "Who don't?"

She handed him Helen's card, then realized Spangle knew her

name and might notice it wasn't on the card. "This actually belongs to my friend over there. If you want, I can go get her and she'll sign for the shoes."

"Naw, that's okay. You can sign for her. I already dealt with you and know you're really who you say."

Mary wondered how he could know, since she hadn't shown him any identification, but she didn't argue.

"I mean," Spangle said, "unless you're making up a pretty good story, you gotta be the Mary that bought the white Latins. You're from Detroit, right?"

"St. Louis!" Mary said, surprised.

"See." Spangle seemed unfazed. "That's how I run an instant credit check. If you'd have said Detroit, no shoes. Anyway, in this business you gotta have a certain amount of faith. And the years have taught me that ballroom dancers are by and large honest folks." He chuckled. "Well, maybe not some of the instructors."

He bent down and got a credit-card machine from beneath the table and ran Helen's MasterCard through it, then filled out the charge form and handed it to Mary to sign. "Tell your friend if she needs a pair of shoes, this here's the place. No special deals for her, though, unless she buys two pairs like you did."

Mary signed Helen's name. "I'll tell her. I'll tell lots of people this is the table if they need shoes."

Spangle laughed, gave her the customer's copy and carbons, then limped back toward the stepladder. "No substitute for good will, no matter what you're selling," he said. "Thanks for the business, Mary, and I hope you knock 'em dead in the competition."

As she walked away carrying the shoes, he was again lurching up the ladder, his box of Velcro stars tucked beneath his arm. He seemed unaware that he'd salvaged her dreams.

She waved the shoe box above her head when she caught sight of Helen. Oh-oh! Helen was wearing a green gown with a feathered bodice and hem. It made her look twenty pounds heavier.

"Great!" Helen said. "You got your shoes!"

"Not only that, the man over there remembered my name and gave me a discount."

Helen hoisted the bodice of the green dress, but it still showed an alarming amount of cleavage. Helen, Helen. "Hey, this is used, but how's it look?" She raised her arms in dance position and did a few tight waltz steps. The flab on her upper arms jiggled, but the dress was gauzy and stiff. "It's marked down," Helen said, not seeing in the mirror the image that Mary saw. She had her own dreams.

Mary said, "It looks terrific," and handed her the MasterCard.

39

He watched her walk up to a heavyset woman in a green dress and hand her a credit card. They talked for a while, but he wasn't close enough to know what they were saying. The vending area was crowded and voices he didn't know clashed and merged and ran over each other.

One voice, however, was familiar and clear, and though he was sure no one else could be aware of it, he heard it with his entire body.

"She's the one," it pronounced with the calm certainty he knew so well. His expression didn't change, but he closed his eyes for a moment as the warm anticipation spiraled through his center. "She's the one."

Mary was awake at five o'clock, lying rigidly in bed and staring at the ceiling. Eventually morning sun filtered through the drapes and washed the darkness from the pale white plaster. Her eyes focused on a sprinkler system head that seemed to cling like a huge spider near a corner. She lay motionless until the alarm sounded at seven o'clock, then she immediately climbed out of bed.

In the opposite bed, Helen stirred.

"You awake?" Mary asked.

"Halfway," Helen moaned sleepily.

"I gotta turn on the light and start getting dressed. Mel wants me down in the ballroom two hours before the competition so we can go through our steps."

Sheets rustled as Helen propped herself up on one elbow and stared at the luminous numerals of the clock on the table between the beds. "You got lotsa time, Mary."

"Well, I'll shower first, so I can be outa your way when you get up. Afterwards I'll turn on the light out here. It's almost full daylight anyway."

"Sure, fine," Helen groaned, and settled back down in bed. Her breathing got louder and evened out. Now and then a hint of a snore. Mary wished she could sleep so soundly.

She rubbed a hand over her eyes and winced from the pain, suddenly remembering how her face looked. Then she saw again the overwhelming vastness of the glittering ballroom. Oh, God! She hurried into the bathroom, switched on the light, and stood before the mirror with her eyes closed.

Gradually she opened them, like a newborn testing a strange world.

No, no! Horrible bruises, and bags beneath her eyes from lack of sleep. She staggered back to the bed and slumped on the edge of the mattress, sobbing quietly.

But not so quietly she didn't wake Helen, who sat up in bed and switched on the lamp. "Wha, Mary? Whazza matter?"

"My bruises are worse."

Helen scooted around and sat facing her. "Couldn't be." She stood up and stretched, then bent over with her hands on her knees and unblinkingly studied Mary's face. "Naw, you don't look any worse to me. Look better. C'mon in where there's more light." She gripped Mary's elbow and led her back into the bathroom. The tiles were cold on Mary's bare feet; she'd been too upset to notice before.

She and Helen stood side by side before the mirror. Two middle-aged women, never beauties, in a strange city to dance against people who really knew how to dance, who were almost professionals. What in heaven's name had they been thinking? What was a tango and how was it done?

And those glaring Technicolor bruises!

"We got fluorescent lighting in here that'd make anybody look a hundred and ten," Helen said. "Notice I look like I been dead five days."

Mary had to admit the pale light glaring harshly down from above the mirror cruelly exposed every flaw. Fine veins just beneath the surface of the skin on her forehead had a greenish tint, like the bruises around her eyes and on the bridge of her nose.

"Bruises are definitely fainter," Helen said. "Believe me, the right makeup job and you'll be better'n just passable. How's the rest of you feel?"

"Nervous."

"Well, so'm I. I mean, physically how do you feel?"

Mary knew she hadn't convinced Helen yesterday. "There's a little pain in my side, but I can move okay."

"You go see a doctor after Jake beat you?"

"No."

"Why not?"

"I'm not hurt that bad. I know. I've got experience. Just bruises, nothing busted."

"Sure?"

"Honest. Anyway, Jake knows how to hit so he doesn't break anything."

Helen's jaw muscles flexed. "So take your shower while I go back to bed, and we'll both feel better. Then we can help each other get made up and fit ourselves into those dresses."

Mary did feel much better after her shower. She toweled dry, peeled off the hotel's complimentary plastic shower cap, and stood nude before the mirror. Yes, not too bad. And the bruises *did* seem fainter. Or maybe she was getting used to them. A nasty purple bruise had developed on her left side, but that wouldn't be visible when she was dressed. She raised her arms and tried a rumba step with plenty of Cuban motion. The ribs ached as her hips swayed, but not enough to bother her in competition if she didn't let the pain show on her face. And she wouldn't let it show. Everything was on the line here; a little pain wasn't going to stop her from dancing with destiny.

She woke Helen again, then stood before the dresser mirror and applied her makeup while Helen showered. She dabbed foundation over the bruises and blended it with a brush. Then she applied flesh-colored cover makeup, carefully blending that with a tongue-moistened fingertip. She sat back and tried to decide how successful she'd been.

She looked like a woman with two black eyes.

"I bought some stuff at the pharmacy downstairs that might

work," Helen said, suddenly standing behind her in a pink robe.

She went to her cosmetic kit on the dresser and got out several small tubes and jars, then returned and showed them to Mary. They were expensive brands of makeup.

"When'd you buy these?"

"Yesterday. Bought them for me, but you can use them. That is, if you wanna give this stuff a try."

"Well, there's nothing to lose, with the way I look now."

Helen dragged the desk chair over and told Mary to sit facing the mirror. She tilted the lampshade, then opened the various containers and stood over her, working gently on her face with the practiced skill of a professional. "I used to have a job at one of those department store counters that give free makeovers," she explained. "Years ago, but I still got the knack. You're no problem, after some of the disasters I've made presentable. Be sure'n let me know if I hurt you."

"You're doing fine," Mary said, and sat perfectly still, trying not to think or to feel the relentless hammering of her heart.

Twenty minutes later, they studied her reflection in the mirror. The other Mary stared back at them wonderingly, then smiled.

"Hardly be noticeable from a distance," Helen said, grinning.

She was right. "It's amazing," Mary said. "*You're* amazing!" She gave Helen a hug. "What you are is an artist!"

"Oh, no, just a miracle worker. You can put on that fake tan stuff you brought so Mel'll be happy, then let's finish getting dressed." Helen began replacing lids on jars, caps on tubes and bottles. "And for God's sake don't look at yourself in that bathroom mirror. The damned thing belongs in a carnival fun house."

Helen was such a good friend. For a moment Mary considered telling her about Rene, but this wasn't the time to talk or even think about Rene and the murders. Or about Angie. Important as they were, right now they represented distractions, and Mary had come too far to defeat herself by agonizing over what she was helpless to change. She was finished wandering into that sort of trap. She hoped.

The competition was scheduled to begin with American-style rhythm. Mary would dance in the first heat, a cha-cha. She struggled into tan panty hose, then got her black Latin dress down from its hanger and worked it over her head without mussing her hair.

She adjusted it and extended her elbows awkwardly to zip it halfway up the back, causing a stitch of pain in her side that for a few seconds left her breathless and light-headed.

"Terrific!" Helen said, looking at her with approval. "With that dress, put on your glitzy earrings and barrette and nobody'd notice your face if you were Frankenstein's bride."

She zipped Mary's dress the rest of the way and fastened the clasp. Then she wriggled into her own Latin outfit, a red dress with a ruffled skirt.

"With or without the gloves?" she asked, and worked her hands and arms into elbow-length red satin gloves. She did some arm styling, then peeled off the gloves and extended a bare arm gracefully in an identical gesture.

"Looks great either way," Mary said, "really." Seeing the dress on Helen instead of on the hanger was a startling improvement.

"Then I'll go with the gloves," Helen said decisively.

Mary arranged and sprayed her hair, then she fastened it in back with her curved silver-glitter barrette and put on her dangling silver earrings.

She stepped into her new Latin shoes and snapped the straps, then stood up straight and appraised herself in the full-length mirror.

She looked put together and professional, she really did. Helen, too, all of a sudden *looked* like a dancer. Maybe Howard the bellhop hadn't simply been bucking for a bigger tip with his compliment. Maybe he'd actually seen something in 1011's new occupants. Well, what the hell, they *were* dancers. Hadn't they taken lessons for years?

"Satisfied with how you look?" Helen asked.

"With how we both look."

"So, it's finally crunch time."

"I guess it is."

"Ready to go after 'em?" Helen swiveled on a high heel before the mirror, jutting out a hip and sneaking a glance over her shoulder like a wary coquette.

"Right now, yeah. But I can't swear how I'll feel down in the ballroom."

Helen said, "Let's find out." She started toward the door, skirt rustling. "Don't forget your key. In these dresses, we might wanna dash back upstairs and use the bathroom."

Mary said, "I'm sure I will." She felt to make sure her perforated-card room key was in her purse, then followed.

As the door clicked shut behind her, her mouth went dry and her heart took flight like a bird.

40

The ballroom seemed even more vast and intimidating this morning. Towering arches of red, pink, and white balloons had been constructed to soar from each corner and intersect over the center of the dance floor. Mary felt small, clumsy, and out of place. Her body forgot how to dance and wanted only to bolt and run for miles. And it was possible. She didn't *have* to stay here. There was no law.

Suddenly Mel was there, in his black slacks and baggy-sleeved white shirt for rhythm dances, not the all-black outfit he'd worn at the studio and in Mary's dream dances.

"Romance Studio's over at table number twelve," he told her, pointing. "C'mon so we can talk, then we'll get in a little practice."

Mary nodded numbly.

She followed Mel to one of the many pink-clothed tables surrounding the dance floor. There was a square of white cloth fastened with safety pins to the back of his shirt, on which *199* was printed in black. On the other side of the floor was a raised platform on some sort of scissorslike jack mechanism with a professional-looking, bulky TV camera mounted on it. It was the sort of camera that might zoom in on David Letterman, but that Mary didn't want aimed her way. Juliet Prowse would be here to hostess the Saturday night professional competition and showcase dances, for later viewing on television. Mary assured herself the TV camera was for Juliet, and for the ballroom dance world's top performers, not for her. Anything to make the knot in her stomach less painful. She felt as if she'd gulped down a baseball.

Mel dropped into a chair and she sat down next to him, her body trembling. He peered at her face and smiled. "The bruises might just be okay," he said. "And the dress is perfect, Mary."

Was he sincere? Or simply trying to buoy her confidence? Mustn't her fear show in her face? She passed her fingertips over the tablecloth; the rough texture of the material made them tingle.

"Now, remember how we get on and off the floor," Mel told her. "Once the music starts, don't get in a rush. And concentrate on the basics. Now and then, when I know the judges aren't watching, I might say something to you or straighten something out in your dancing; don't let that throw you."

"Anything else?" Mary asked.

"Oh, yeah. We're number one-ninety-nine. When you hear the announcer say it, listen close for instructions."

"Anything else?" She knew she was repeating herself like an idiot.

"Yeah. Have fun." He stood up and extended his hand for her to take. "Let's do some tango to get you warmed up and accustomed to the floor."

Despite the fact that there were at least a dozen couples practicing on the desert of a dance floor, Mary was sure everyone in the ballroom was watching her through binoculars.

Mel stepped close and raised her hands to dance position. As they began to dance, a measure of confidence took root in her. Mel's right hand was almost on the bruise, causing occasional flashes of agony, but she said nothing and maintained her posture. They were moving well and must look good together. She drew comfort from his lithe body, absorbing his youth like a vampire. As they practiced pivots she arched her spine and tilted back her head to look up and to her left. Above her the glittering chandeliers and colorful arches of balloons whirled dizzyingly as she floated with Mel's lead, leaning away from the pivot and using centrifugal force to gain velocity. She knew she was doing everything right; it was like flying. She and Mel were cutting through the air like a single aerodynamic creature, something out of mythology.

"Aw*right!*" he said, stopping and twirling her with a flourish. "Dance like that during competition and we got it made!"

Hundreds of people had filtered into the ballroom while they'd been talking and practicing, and were milling around or sitting at the tables. The balcony was lined with spectators, and the platform with the rows of video cameras was being tended by a man and four women. Mary had used her extra money to pay to have her performances taped so she could study them later. Now, staring out at all the bright movement and pale faces in the ballroom, her confidence ebbed again and she regretted paying to have her embarrassment recorded.

"So how you feel?" Mel asked.

"Scared."

"That's okay. Convert that to energy when we dance. And try to relax. The crowd here doesn't use live ammunition."

Dance officials were seated on the judges' dais now. An announcer with silver hair spoke into a microphone and asked that the floor be cleared for competition.

When the floor was vacant and the ballroom hushed, the announcer said, "American Rhythm will be first, Ladies' A Newcomer. Dancers please line up at the far end, down by Mrs. Kellerman." A woman in a blue dress raised her hand, smiling. Mrs. Kellerman, drawing scattered applause. Well, the audience was friendly; Mrs. Kellerman hadn't even danced.

Mary's heart skipped and pounded as she took Mel's arm and he led her toward the far corner of the ballroom, where dancers in glittering, feathered outfits were queuing up with their partners. The announcer introduced the judges, some of whom were now standing at the corners of the dance floor, then he called the numbers of the dancers for the first heat.

When she heard "One-ninety-nine," Mary stopped breathing for a moment.

She felt Mel tug at her arm. Her mind was somewhere up there with the arches of balloons and the glittering chandeliers. Her legs were numb but she knew she was walking. She swallowed and moved like an automaton, letting instinct and training take over.

And found herself in the center of the dance floor.

The music began.

41

Morrisy slumped down heavily behind his desk and sighed. He didn't like the way things were shaping up. He could smell trouble the way a sailor smelled a storm.

Three dead dancers were one—and in retrospect, two—too many to be coincidental. He'd had the wrong idea about how large dancing had loomed in the lives of the dead women. He'd thought they'd simply learned how to dance, taken goddamn lessons, maybe even entered contests sometimes. But mainly he'd assumed they went out dancing the way millions of women did, the way his former wife Bonita had. He wondered if maybe his personal view of Bonita had anything to do with the way he'd been blindsided on this one.

To the media, Morrisy was still playing down the importance of the ballroom dance connection, but he knew it might very well become the crux of the case, the angle that tied the victims to the weirdo who'd killed them.

Waxman wandered in and stood near the window, stared out at hazy blue sky for a moment, then said, "We got Verlane possibly in New Orleans when his wife died, possibly in Seattle when the Roundner woman was killed, definitely in Kansas City for the Vivian Ferris murder."

Tell me something I don't know, Morrisy thought. He said, "Quirk's been on my ass like bargain underwear."

Waxman moved away from the window and stood close to the desk. He'd left the door open and sounds from out in the squad room drifted in. A dot matrix printer going *Gzzzzzzing!* over and over at irregular intervals. Nyak the desk sergeant patiently arguing with a drunk. "I *never* walk a shtraight line!" the drunk was protesting.

Gzzzzzzing! Gzzzzzzzing!

Irritating sound, Morrisy thought. Japanese-made piece of crap sitting out there spitting paper like they'd won the fucking war or something. Well, maybe they had.

"We collar Verlane and search the house," Waxman said, "we might come up with what we need to nail him down tight."

"Might," Morrisy said, actually doubting it. Verlane had proved out tough and smart. Too smart to leave incriminating evidence lying around like ashtrays. Still, to have done what he'd done a man had to be in and out mentally. And Morrisy had seen plenty of tough ones all of a sudden cave in when the cuffs were clicked on their wrists, when they were finally grabbed by the balls. The desire to purge guilt and confess could be as overwhelming as the need for sex. Or the need to kill. Morrisy knew that.

"Verlane home now?" he asked.

Gzzzzzing!

"Jansen's on him and called in a few minutes ago. Says Verlane hasn't left his house."

Gzzzzzzzing!

Morrisy stood up behind the desk and tucked in his shirt. Twisted his bulky body and snatched his suitcoat from its hook. "Time to move on the bastard," he said. "Let's stuff him in the bag."

Verlane didn't answer when they rang his doorbell. And when they forced the door and went inside they found the large, quiet house unoccupied. A couple of lamps were switched on, even though sunlight streamed through the sheer drapes. The air smelled stale, and everything was neat but looked dusty. It had been some time since the maid had been there. The maid or anyone else.

They had their legal ducks in a row, so Morrisy ordered a search of the premises. He wasn't surprised that Verlane had slipped away on Jensen. Verlane, too, must have sensed the weight of the evidence settling on him and figured arrest was imminent.

Morrisy nosed around the place himself for a while, finding nothing of interest. Verlane had expensive tastes, expensive clothes, furniture, jewelry. On a fancy dresser in the French Provincial bedroom was a framed photograph of the dead wife. Danielle Verlane was smiling, wearing a midnight blue dress and standing before some kind of white latticework, her head tilted to the side so her hair was highlighted. The dress was cut low, and the light that made her hair glow lent a three-dimensional roundness to the eager swell of her breasts. She'd been a beautiful piece, all right. Wasted now. In her grave. Morrisy found himself disliking Verlane even more, working up to the curious rage he'd felt before in the course of this investigation.

In one of the closets were half a dozen fancy ballgowns and sexy Latin dance outfits. Morrisy stared at the array of silky bright fabric and feathers. He could imagine how Danielle must have looked in the skimpy Latin costumes.

"Bastard musta been nuts, killing a woman like that," Waxman said. He was standing next to Morrisy and gazing at the dance outfits. "And now he's rabbited out on us when we weren't looking."

Morrisy extended a powerful hand and ran rough, tentative fingers along a red silk dress sleeve.

He said, "Could be I know where to find him."

42

Once she began dancing, it was easier than she'd imagined. The syncopated beat carried her as if she were an electrically charged marionette, her body automatically following Mel's lead. They did basic steps, then cross-overs and an underarm turn. In the corners of her vision, the other dancers moving in unison were blurred and unreal. Or maybe *she* was unreal.

Before she fully realized what had happened, the music stopped and applause thundered into the silence. The dance was over.

The announcer's voice was echoing like God's around the ballroom as Mary laced her arm through Mel's and he led her off the floor.

"Good," he said, when they'd reached the staging area. "You did good, Mary." She couldn't tell from his tone of voice if he really meant it.

The mambo competition passed the same way, everything like an illusion set to music.

During her next dance, a rumba, the reality of where she was, what she was doing, how she was being watched and judged, caught hold in her. Cold panic hit and she rushed an underarm turn. Her bruised ribs ached as she stretched her stride to catch up with the beat.

"You okay?" Mel asked without moving his lips.

She had to stop herself from nodding and losing head position. Instead of answering, she concentrated on her dancing. Spectators were screaming contestants' numbers. Mel danced her close to the Romance Studio table and several voices she recognized shouted, "One-nine-nine!" Okay, *everyone* out there wasn't being critical of her. Mary felt a rush of energy and bore down with the inner edges of her feet on each step, pressuring the floor to emphasize hip roll, doing arm styling in perfect synchronization with Mel's.

Practice had paid; it was all happening almost on its own.

Then it was over.

At least for Mary, for the Friday competition.

About twenty couples danced swing, and it was time to bestow awards in the Ladies' A Newcomer division.

Mary stood next to Mel in the semicircle of dancers who were waiting for their names and numbers to be called, so they could walk forward, accept their prize medallions, and pose proudly for photographs. Time to reap whatever had been sown.

Her name wasn't called, but she wasn't disappointed. The purpose of today's competition was to get her used to dancing under competitive stress. Tomorrow was to be her day, the smooth dance competition in Newcomer and Bronze divisions, including tango. Tango was her dance. Tango was her hope. Everything she did today was to build toward tomorrow, and in that respect, today had been a success.

The rest of the morning she sat at the table and rooted for the other Romance Studio contestants, shouting out entry numbers, sipping diet Pepsi through a straw, and discussing other dancers. She was having a grand time, feeling a part of all this. Why had she ever considered *not* coming here?

Helen didn't place in any of her heats, either, but lean Lisa surprised everyone by dancing a near-perfect mambo and finishing third.

After changing out of her Latin dress, Mary had a lunch of salad and pasta in the hotel restaurant with Helen and an ecstatic

Lisa. Then they returned to the ballroom and watched with increasing awe as the higher divisions competed.

That night, after dinner with the other Romance Studio people, Mary watched the professionals do their routines. It was an impressive show, though nothing like what was scheduled for tomorrow night. That was when television crews would be taping and all the stops would be pulled.

Between performances there was general dancing. A blond man Mary remembered doing a stylish rumba in Bronze competition walked over to the Romance table and asked her to waltz.

After a few sweeping change steps and a pivot, as if he were trying to impress her with his expertise, they settled into lazy box steps and he smiled down at her. It was a smile that went well with his regular features and razor-styled hair. He might have been a TV news anchor. Would he do bad comedy and speak in sound bites?

"My name's Benson," he said.

"First or last?"

"First, I'm afraid. Amberbrake's my last name. Sounds like a butler, doesn't it?"

Benson Amberbrake. "It does," Mary said honestly. "Or maybe somebody who'd hire a butler. I'm Mary Arlington."

"I know. I was watching you dance rhythm this morning. You looked great."

"Not great enough to win anything."

"Listen, don't feel bad. This is some of the best competition in the world. Where you from?"

"St. Louis."

"I'm Minneapolis. This is the third time I've competed, but I've never won anything either." He led her through a hesitation step, grinning down at her. Her hand resting on his shoulder felt hard muscle beneath the smooth material of his suitcoat. He really did dance beautifully. "Competing tomorrow?" he asked.

"Yes, in American smooth. My best chance is the tango."

"I'll be pulling for you." He moved back slightly and peered down at her face. She knew he wanted to ask about her blackened eyes, much more visible close up, but he restrained himself. Maybe they lived in the same world, where a gentleman never inquired about a lady's bruises.

190

The music stopped. "Thanks for the dance, Mary." He crooked his arm for her to take, then escorted her back to her table. "And incidentally, I don't have one."

"One what?"

"A butler."

"Me, either."

"I hope we can dance again."

"Me, too," she told him.

He patted her shoulder almost paternally before walking away.

"See," Helen said, as Mary settled back down in her chair, "that dress of yours was worth the money. That blond guy's a hunk, and he knows how to put one foot in front of the other without falling down."

Suzanne and David Nyemchek, a professional couple from St. Louis, were taking the floor to do a *paso doble* routine. Mary had seen them once before, at an exhibition, and she ignored Helen and watched them, lost in admiration.

That night she fell asleep immediately and slept dreamlessly, and was surprised when the alarm sounded.

He didn't sleep a total of an hour that night. Several times he got up and went into the bathroom. He'd watched her dance and she still danced in his mind and he wanted desperately to masturbate but the voice told him not to because there was a reason so he got out the knife and stared and stared at it and then pressed the cold flat of its blade against his forehead and felt calmer. "Soon," the voice said, speaking to him through the knife.

He lowered the knife and ran his thumb along the blade's edge, cutting it deliberately very slightly. Raised the thumb to his mouth and tasted the blood.

"Soon now."

Saturday morning she was as scared as she'd been the day before. It was as if she'd never danced in competition. Her first heats, fox-trot and waltz, passed in a blur, and she knew she hadn't done well.

"Jesus," Mel said under his breath, leading her back to the staging area, "we gotta get it on, Mary."

We? She knew *she* was the problem. She was moving too stiffly, not quite on the beat. Her bruised ribs still ached, and she seemed to have lost some mobility. Messages from brain to feet were taking too long and arriving garbled.

Concentrate, she urged herself. You're who and what you are and the people watching and judging are no better than you. If you can do it in the studio, you can do it here.

She breathed deeply, willing herself to be calm, and felt better.

Thank God fox-trot and waltz had been scheduled first, leaving time to atone for sin.

When the dancers took the floor for the tango, Mary was surprised to find herself firmly in control despite her nervousness. She could do this—she knew it! Confidence smoldered like an ember in her stomach, then, when the music began, it flared brightly through every inch of her.

Mel led her through a basic, a promenade turn. *Nose follows toes.* She snapped her head around to give the dance definition, shadowing his lead perfectly.

The music took her, and he was a part of it. She could read his mind and body, knew what he was going to do an instant before he did it. And somehow this didn't surprise her. Primal rhythms of communication were older than speech, linked to life and emotion in ways not understood. Dance itself must have preceded speech. Far away, people were applauding and shouting out numbers. It didn't matter to Mary. She and Mel and the music were all that the ballroom and the moment held. Mary was flying.

Then the moment ended, and she was standing still and the applause was now and near.

"Oh, Christ, Mary!" Mel whispered in her ear as he led her off the floor. "That was perfect! That was what we wanted."

If that tango was perfect, so was the one they danced in the Bronze division. They added flares and *cortes* to their steps, drawing applause from the audience.

Mary was sorry when the music ended.

She was nervous again standing in the dancers' semicircle, listening to the names and numbers for the waltz and fox-trot awards, watching the other contestants rush joyfully forward to receive their medallions and applause. The ceremony for those dances seemed to last half an hour, though she knew it actually took less than five minutes.

Then it was time for the tango awards.

"Third place, number one-seven-seven, Lee and Brockman."

Mary watched the couple stride forward smiling and receive their award. Applause. Humble time. Camera flashes like indoor lightning.

"Second place, one-twenty, Frazee and Nyemchek."

Okay, they were competing against the best, even though Nyemchek was only the instructor half of the team. Mary was trembling again. Either she and Mel had won, which seemed highly unlikely now, or they hadn't even finished in the top three.

Time dragged to a halt, as if the earth had paused ponderously on its axis. Mel gripped her elbow, squeezing so hard it hurt her. More bruises?

"First place, number one-ninety-nine, Arlington and Holt!"

Reality spiraled away. Mary floated up to the judge, watched her hand reach out and accept the shiny gold medallion with the numeral *1* engraved on it. She was barely aware of shouting and applause. Mel had to stop her and hold her still while photographs were taken. He didn't have to tell her to smile.

Then they were back at the table. Everyone was standing, shaking Mel's hand, patting Mary's back and shoulders. Helen and Lisa pecked her on the cheek. Nick hugged her. *Ouch!* She let him hug her again.

Finally Mary slumped down in a chair. Ray Huggins was leaning over her from behind. "One for Romance Studio!" he was saying. "Terrific, Mary! Just terrific!"

When he placed his hand on her shoulder she reached up and squeezed it. Released it and felt him move away.

Suddenly she was tired and her legs were numb. So what'd you think, Duke? What can you say now, Jake? Bastards!

She shook thoughts of the two men from her mind. What did Jake, or her dead alcoholic father Duke, have to do with any of this? Thinking of them now would only spoil things. Men like Jake, Duke, Fred, had nothing to do with this world.

She should call Angie and let her know what had happened. Duke.

Why had she thought of Duke?

Helen sat down next to her, unable to stop grinning. "Well, Mary Mary?"

Mary said, "I need a drink."

43

After the professional competition that night, Helen talked Mary into going with her to the hotel bar for a victory celebration. Or was it Mary who'd talked Helen into going? Mary wasn't sure. Of that or anything else right now. Ordinarily she drank only limited amounts of wine, but this wasn't an ordinary night. Wasn't an ordinary time in her life. But she'd had only three martinis and didn't understand why they should be affecting her this way. Alcohol and the flush of triumph were an unexpectedly heady combination.

Where was Mel? Why wasn't he celebrating with her? Mary remembered him hugging her again in the hall outside her room, just after she'd changed into slacks and a sweater, then he'd hurried away toward the elevators. Was he meeting someone? Should Mary feel jealous? She didn't feel jealous right now. Triumph left little room for other emotions.

A man was suggesting they go somewhere else. Mary felt a tingle of hesitation. She liked it here in the hotel bar, though she had to admit the drinks were expensive. But there was no dancing. That was the problem, there was no dancing.

She saw then that the man who'd made the suggestion was Benson, good old Benson Amberson . . . Ambersomething, who'd waltzed with her last night. Blond, handsome Benson, of Minneapolis.

Helen decided she'd rather go to bed and went up to the room, after pecking Mary on the cheek and urging her to have fun, she deserved it. Then half a dozen dancers, two of them instructors, piled out of the bar and went with Benson and Mary to Spectrum, a lounge on Meter Street not far from the hotel. They had to travel in two cabs, and Mary wound up sitting on someone's lap. Well, she didn't mind; it was a night for that kind of thing.

Spectrum had a five-piece band and a tiny dance floor flooded with colored strobe lights that flashed in time with the music. But at least there was dancing, despite what was happening out on the floor right now. Disco. People twitching and jerking around by themselves. Not dancing, from Mary's point of view, more like a kind of whole-body masturbation.

She did swing and rumba with all three of the men, and she had several more drinks. But she wasn't drunk. Of that she was sure. If she'd had too much to drink, how could she be dancing with such grace and precision?

And her ribs no longer ached. Winning had relieved the pain. Winning was sweet medicine. Her life was well now. Mary was complete and well.

Amazingly, time had rushed to one in the morning. Spectrum remained loud and crowded, but Benson and Mary were the only ones from the Hyatt Regency group still on the dance floor. Dancing with Benson, occasionally getting jostled by the spastic fanatics who thought they were dancing, Mary peered over his shoulder through the hued and hazy lighting and saw no one she knew.

Well, that was all right; she knew Benson, didn't she? And after another few dances she'd suggest they return to the hotel. Her legs were getting heavy and unresponsive. She was finally tired and wouldn't mind going to bed. Benson might have the idea he could include himself in those plans, but she was sure he'd discourage easily enough. Benson the gentleman butler, or the gentleman who employed a butler. Gentleman, anyway.

When they returned to their table and she suggested it was time to leave, he was immediately agreeable. Maybe he was tired, too. She wondered again about Mel. Where was he at this moment? Doing his own kind of celebrating? Maybe there was more promiscuity at dance competitions than she imagined. So many healthy, attractive people in top physical condition, under so much stress, maybe it was inevitable.

Benson had overridden Mary's protests at being treated, and he settled with the waitress, leaving an obvious and generous tip to demonstrate to Mary that he wasn't cheap. Now he was striding ahead of her, projecting machismo so he could forge a path along the perimeter of the packed dance floor toward the door. She followed in the vacuum of his wake, avoiding the writhing bodies closing in behind them.

And suddenly they were out in the cool night, standing on damp pavement made iridescent red by the glow of the overhead sign. Benson's handsome face, the backs of Mary's wrists and hands, had the same red cast to them.

"We in hell?" Mary asked.

"Huh?"

"Never mind, just a thought."

The music from inside was barely discernible, only the deep beat of the bass throbbing like a heartbeat through the thickness of walls and door.

Mary shivered and clutched her coat tighter around her. Her stomach did a couple of loops and dives. Maybe she *had* drunk too much. After all, she wasn't used to alcohol any more than she was to victory. "Whew! I hope we can get a cab."

"No problem," Benson said. "We don't need a cab. My car's parked in a lot just down the street. I had to leave it there yesterday because the hotel lot was full."

"There's some luck," Mary said.

"Sure. I'll have us back in our rooms and tucked in within a few minutes."

"Our *separate* rooms." She smiled when she said it, not wanting to wound him.

" 'Course. I wouldn't wanna spoil your big night by trying to hit on you." Now he was smiling, confident and aware of his charm in the way of one who used it often. "Unless of course I can help make your big night even bigger."

She shook her head and touched his arm, partly for support. "If it's all the same to you, I'm ready for my night to end."

"Well, it's not all the same, but it's totally up to the lady."

"Very gal*lant.*"

"That's *moi,* all right." He took her arm and began leading her along the sidewalk, away from the brightness outside Spectrum.

She noticed the neighborhood was mainly industrial. The block was lined with drab office buildings, all of them closed and desolate in the faint orange glow of sodium streetlights. Far down the street, perhaps three blocks away, was the flashing green and blue neon sign of what might have been a bar or restaurant. Now and then traffic hissed unseen on a nearby street, an oddly reptilian sound, like that of monsters stalking in an old Japanese horror movie.

Mary put her weight down crookedly on a high heel and stumbled. Benson helped her regain her balance. Wouldn't do to sprain an ankle now. What would Mel think of her if she managed that bit of clumsiness?

"You okay?" Benson asked.

"Sure. Where'd you say you were parked?"

"Right here."

They'd come to a small parking lot surrounded by a tall chain-link fence topped with barbed wire. The attendant's booth was dark, but the driveway gate was open and there were half a dozen cars on the dimly lighted lot. The nearest streetlight appeared to be burning out, casting a wavering, sickly orange glow over the angled cars. A wind gusted through the lot, seeming to make the streetlight flicker, sending debris and crumpled newspaper skittering in tight circular patterns. Miniature young cyclones full of bluff and bluster, as if boasting they might grow and destroy the city.

"Which car?" Mary asked.

"The dark one near the back." Still gripping her elbow, he led her toward a black or midnight blue compact parked near the alley and back driveway of the lot. He'd simply described it as dark. Funny he wouldn't know the exact color of his own car.

She was about to ask about that when he said, "Why'd you choose tango as your main dance?"

"It's the one that seems to come most naturally to me."

"I can see why. It's a sexy dance. There was a time not so long ago when it was banned by the Catholic church."

"I know."

"But then the church has had its head up its ass all through history. Hey, you're not Catholic, are you?"

"Not as good a one as I oughta be."

"You and so many others." He threw back his head and she thought he was going to laugh, but he simply stared straight up at the night sky, as if searching for some meaning in the stars. What now, Mary wondered? Would he ask for her astrological sign?

"Tango comes natural to me, too," he told her, looking at her again. "But I guess you think I'm feeding you a line, like I'm one of those human vipers that hang around places where there're vulnerable women dancing."

"No, why shouldn't I believe you?"

" 'Cause you're a beautiful woman and I got you alone at last, and, in case you hadn't noticed, we're opposite sexes." He broke stride and grinned down at her. "Pretty good reasons, huh?"

"Not good enough, though." Keep it light, a joke. It wasn't so bad being called a beautiful woman. "Anyway, I thought we'd settled that one."

He didn't answer.

She felt the chill of the wind skimming over the blacktop, heard the rustle of stirring dust and paper. Lonely sounds. The glow of victory and alcohol receded, and for the first time that night she was slightly afraid. All alone, opposite sex . . . what kind of talk was that from Benson?

But she knew what kind.

They stopped walking near the car, and his arms snaked around her, pulling her to him and pressing her tight against his body. Pain raged through her side. "Lemme show you a new tango step," he whispered in her ear. He sounded amused, and that frightened her badly.

"Not this," she pleaded. "Please! I wanna go back to the hotel."

"Aw, why not make your big night complete?" he asked, his lips brushing her cheek. She smelled the alcohol on his warm breath and struggled desperately to get free, but he squeezed her tighter and made a clucking sound in her ear, as if chastising her for being a naughty girl. "You know you wanna do this, Mary. We've both known it all evening, so why make things difficult? Why make trouble?"

Jake! Duke! Christ, she hated Duke!

"Some things are destined to be, Mary. People can't help themselves."

He was right. She knew he was right!

Then she noticed the black car's license plate. Iowa. Benson had said he was from Minnesota. It wasn't his car at all. He'd tricked her to get her alone!

The world began to darken and collapse in on Mary, crushing every part of her.

"Mary, Mary . . ." Benson was crooning.

"You!"

Another man's voice. From the direction of the street.

Benson released her and stepped back, staring toward the driveway.

In the shadows near the attendant's booth, a darker shadow moved.

Benson wiped his arm across his mouth and glared down at Mary, weighing his options. His bared teeth flashed his fear, and perhaps hatred.

He said, "Fuck it!" and backed away from her. "You can goddamn walk back to the hotel."

"Hey, buddy! Hey, you!"

"Screw you, pal!" Benson screamed, and he wheeled and ran out the back of the lot and down the dark alley. She heard his desperate footfalls long after the night had swallowed him.

The shadowy figure melted away from the wall and was moving toward her. "You okay?"

"Yes, I think so. Thanks! Thank you!"

Then she realized there was something familiar about the way the man walked.

44

"You just relax now, Miss Arlington."

She was sure he couldn't see her plainly in the darkness, yet he knew who she was. He must have been watching her and followed her from the hotel, then Spectrum. She knew, but she didn't want to admit, what that meant.

His built-up shoe dragged like sandpaper as he stopped and stood crookedly in front of her. "I was watching you dance earlier," he said. "Thought you was a sight to see. If anybody deserved a pair of my shoes, you did."

She almost thanked him, but said nothing. She couldn't have spoken if she'd tried. Fear had taken root in her throat and threatened to cut off her air. There were only half a dozen places that offered an adequate selection of ballroom dance shoes for sale, and they did most of their business by mail. Albert Spangle would know the names and addresses of almost every ballroom competitor in the country, and he had an obviously innocent reason for attending various competitions, setting up his vending booth and selling dance shoes. He could research and select his victims at his leisure, and the only known connection between him and them would be the legitimate one of merchant and customer, the same connection he had with hundreds of dancers. If he was a murder suspect, so were the many other merchants who sold shoes, gowns, tuxedos, and a wide range of other dance accessories. It was perfect camouflage for a killer. Something in Mary turned cold and shriveled.

"That man do harm to you?" Spangle was asking.

"No," she managed to breathe.

"He sure tried, though." He was grinning knowingly. "You can't trust nobody, Miss Arlington. 'Course, you did lead him on. I seen you."

She willed herself to back away, but fear held her fast. Her feet were embedded in the blacktop. "Lead him on? How? I only had a few drinks with him, danced a few times."

"I mean at the competition. I seen you in your black dress, the skirt slit up the side, shaking your hips."

"Dancing. I was only dancing."

"Sure was. I watched you tango, how you had your cunt right up against that fella's leg."

Dear God, it was beginning in earnest, the verbal dance she knew would end in her death. "But that's the way it's done in tango." Even as she spoke, she knew he wanted her to protest. "The other dancers were doing it, too."

"That ain't much of an excuse now, is it? Other people doin' it? Hear that one all the time. Even Jesus wasn't the only one crucified, now, was he? And them wayward of Sodom and Gomorrah thought the same, like all of them that done the devil's dance. Delilah and witches and warlocks. Ain't history fulla such excuses by the worst people?"

"I . . . guess so." He wasn't making sense, but could she have expected him to be rational?

"It's the way of the wicked, to wrap themselves in the deeds of others. Sin and abortion and abomination. But the godless reap the whirlwind." He moved closer, his grin widening and going lewd, his teeth yellow in the flickering dimness. "It comes to that, always."

This time her legs found strength. She spun on her heel and began to run. But his arm, surprisingly strong, wound about her waist, jerking her back around to face him. Pain jolted through her bruised ribs and she gasped.

"Guess you'd dance with most anybody," he said, still grinning, feeding on her pain. "Even somebody like me." His body was up against hers, his breath fetid and reeking of garlic. "The wages of sin's about to be paid."

Something stung the base of her neck, just above her breastbone. She tucked in her chin and stared down in terror at the long knife he held to her throat. A black worm writhed across the back of his hand. Blood! Her blood! "You . . ."

"I what?" He sounded amused, as Benson had. Benson, where are you now?

"You killed those women!" she spat out, wishing immediately she hadn't spoken. But it wouldn't matter. If he was going to kill her, his mind had been made up when he'd begun following her, stalking her as he must have stalked the others.

"And you don't think they deserved it?" he asked. "Flaunters of cunt, carriers of sin and disease that twist bodies and rot souls?"

"I—I don't know."

"Well, they deserved it, just like you. Unsaved and unclean, moving the way they did, displaying their bodies and inflaming men's blood." He shuffled forward, shoving her back, the knife still against her, his other arm clamped around her waist. A strangely dreamy expression passed over his features and he began swaying in an obscene parody of dance. He jammed his leg painfully between her thighs and up against her pelvis. A tango. God, he thought he was doing a tango. "We don't even need no music, do we?" She was aware he had an erection. He began grinding himself against her, and they staggered like a pair of desperate, grappling drunks.

For a second he loosened his grip, and she placed her palms against his chest and tore herself free from the macabre dance.

He'd been expecting it.

Tricked her.

He laughed as she felt his hand clutch her hair and jerk her head back. Without realizing she'd fallen, she was kneeling. She felt burning pain in her knees and inanely worried about having skinned them, as when she was a small girl. Torn pantyhose this time, though. Duke would be furious.

"End of the dance, Miss Arlington. Judgment be yours in the next world! Godless slut!"

"Please!" she begged. "Do it! Do it!"

She heard her shrieking intake of air, almost a scream, then the cartilage in her throat crackled as her head was yanked back even farther, straining her neck. Above her stretched the dark blanket of night sky, a distant and uncaring universe.

The knife point bit, then the pain faded and she felt the blade slicing into her throat.

An amazing calm came over her, a detachment from what was happening, like the paralysis of jungle prey in the jaws of a predator.

Then there was shouting.

Soles shuffling on blacktop.

Grunting and ragged breathing.

She was lying flat on her stomach, feeling the warm spread of blood beneath her cheek. Still there was no pain.

And Spangle was lying beside her, also on his stomach, his arms twisted awkwardly behind him. Someone was tying his wrists together, twisting what looked like a leather belt around and around them. He was ranting incoherently and glaring madly at her, blood bubbling from his mouth.

"Had to stab him!" a faraway voice said. "Bastard's crazy strong!"

Men's large black shoes next to her face. Wing-tips.

"Better call the cops!"

Running footsteps. "You're *looking* at the cops, goddammit!"

"How'd you?—"

"It doesn't matter!"

A hand touching her shoulder, gently laying back her hair.

"Ah, Christ, Pete, look what he did! Get an ambulance. Dial nine-one-one. Sweet Lord, look what he did!"

Rene's voice? She tried to speak but made only a hissing, gurgling sound, like the old steam radiator in her childhood bedroom. She was so weak. In slow motion she moved a hand to feel her neck. Probed with her fingers. Wet, warm, a flap of something. Skin.

Nausea and terror rose in her. A hand gently gripped her wrist and pulled *her* hand away. She waited for Mother Superior's voice to say, "Mustn't touch."

No voice, though. Something soft was pressed against her neck. Someone was sobbing.

She fell away from the sad, sad sound.

Into velvet blackness.

45

It was Albert Spangle who died in his hospital bed from knife wounds, at the moment Chicago police were searching his flat and discovering gruesome souvenirs of his crimes. He'd murdered six women. In his freezer they found his diary, and the wrapped and frozen uterus of each of his victims.

Spangle had cheated justice, but his capture and death had liberated Rene from suspicion and police harassment.

It was, after all, Rene who'd tracked him down, though Morrisy had caught up with Rene, and along with Columbus police had closed on the struggle in the parking lot and made the arrest.

Rene's projection of the killer's pattern suggested the Ohio competition might be the next place he'd murder. Worried about Mary fitting the victims' profile, Rene had traveled to Columbus with reporter Pete Joller as his constant companion and alibi. Surreptitiously the two had watched Mary and the other dancers, and followed her the night after her victory in the tango. They'd been about to interrupt Benson's zealous advances when Spangle had beaten them to it. They'd then observed Spangle from a distance, assuming at first he was only talking with Mary. When they'd realized they were mistaken, they'd been able to stop him just in time as he'd attacked with the knife.

For the rest of her life Mary would bear a long scar on the left side of her throat. She affected colorful neck scarves to conceal it, and in time thought they lent her a distinctive and dashing style.

Rene devoted full time and tender attention to her; he was nothing like Jake. She was sure it was because he was sorry for her, and he felt guilty about her injury. But it was a happy time in Mary's life. Angie's cancer went into remission and she was released from Saint Sebastian. Jake had become a memory kept at bay. And in early summer Mary married Rene and moved in with him in his house in the New Orleans Garden District.

She wasn't sure if she'd ever feel at home in New Orleans, where the hours flowed slowly and magnolias perfumed the air, and the deceased were interred above ground as if their mortal remains hadn't made the final surrender to death. But Rene truly loved her, or seemed to. And she loved him and was secure in their marriage. The prayed-for miracle had occurred, beginning with her tango win in Ohio. Her life had turned around.

At least once a week she'd talk for hours with Angie on the phone. Angie, who'd contemplated death and understood, and who'd seen her daughter finally escape the deadly cycle of abuse at the hands of Jake. New hope and life vibrated in Angie's voice. And why not? The family curse was broken.

Mary never for a moment missed Jake. Her world was far better than it had ever been, even when Rene began giving presentations at financial seminars around the country, traveling frequently.

Mary had no trouble passing time alone. During the long, warm days, she'd sometimes ride a streetcar to the French Quarter and sit watching the great river sliding muddily toward the Gulf. Evenings she'd spend by herself in the big stucco house, or walking the garish streets of the Quarter and listening to music drifting from inside the old buildings with their open shutters.

Occasionally she'd go dancing.

Glossary

American: One of the two widely recognized dance styles, officially sanctioned for competition by the National Dance Council of America.

Arm check: Dance lead in which the man checks his partner's momentum by placing his palm against her shoulder or upper arm.

Back leading: Occurs when the partner ostensibly being led, and usually moving backward, is actually doing the leading.

Balance step: Sometimes called a hesitation, in which dancers pause for a beat or more either for effect, or to regain balance or timing.

Basic step: The simple step which serves as the foundation for a dance, often the starting point for more complex steps.

Bolero: Latin dance variation of the rumba, done to slower beat.

Box step: Basic step for several dances, in which dancers move between the corners of an imaginary square or rectangle on the floor.

Bronze category: The division of competitive dancing above Newcomer and below Silver.

Cha-cha: Latin dance with a doubling of dance rhythm on every fourth beat.

Check: A break and reversal in a dance's momentum.

Contrabody: The twisting of a dancer's torso to place opposite hip and shoulder over moving foot.

Corte: A tango maneuver in which the man, moving backward one step, dips the woman, then raises her.

Count: Repetitive numerical patterns a dancer uses to maintain rhythm.

Cross-over: Dance maneuver in which partners turn away from each other until they are standing side by side, stepping through with the inside foot. Done often in cha-cha and mambo.

Cuban motion: A technique for exaggerated rhythmic shifting of weight and settling of the hip that emphasizes the Latin beat and is essential in most rhythm dances.

Dance frame: The basic posture that will be maintained throughout the dance, regardless of position in relation to the dancer's partner.

Dance position: The starting position assumed by partners in relation to each other before they begin to dance. It varies at least slightly for most dances.

Dance shoes: Ballroom shoes with suede soles. Women's high-heeled shoes have the heel set in more toward the center of the foot than do street shoes. There are specialized shoes for some dances.

Develope: A hesitation step during which the woman slowly raises and lowers one leg, calf extended and toe pointed.

Fan: (also called flare) A step in which the dancer swivels on one foot with the free foot extended to the rear.

Flick: A quick backward kick from the knee.

Fox-trot: One of the smooth dances, done gracefully to a relatively slow beat.

Gold category: The highly skilled competition division directly above Silver.

Hesitation: Dancer pauses for a beat, sometimes longer.

International: One of the two dance styles sanctioned for official competition.

Jive: Faster, more animated version of swing.

Latin shoes: Any dance shoes constructed and styled for Latin competition.

Line of dance: The counterclockwise direction, or flow, of the general dance, even while the rotation of various dancing couples might be clockwise within that flow. Also a term of reference for dancers indicating a position on the dance floor (facing line of dance, facing away from line of dance, etc.).

Lead: The physical signaling that determines dance direction or maneuver.

Mambo: Rhythm dance during which dancers pause and hold each number one beat.

Merengue: Latin dance done to rapid beat without syncopation.

Newcomer: The lowest category of competition dancing. Newcomers, however, are, like other dancers, allowed to compete in higher categories.

One beat: The beat marking the beginning of a unit of music.

Parallel hesitation: Smooth dance step in which both partners pause for a beat or more while parallel to each other.

Paso doble: Latin dance in which the male emulates the movements of a bullfighter, the woman the motion of his cape. Danced only to the music traditionally played as a prelude to bullfights.

Promenade position: Slightly open dance posture, heads turned in the direction of partners' clasped hands, that allows both partners to move simultaneously at a sideways angle.

Promenade turn: An abrupt turn at the end of a step in promenade position, used to change direction in tango.

Pivot: A swivel on the ball of one foot, free foot forward or back, in which the dancer rotates half a turn on a fixed vertical axis.

Rhythm dances: Dances done to fastest beat or in syncopation, most commonly the Latin dances (other than tango), swing, and jive.

Rise-and-fall motion: The rhythmic rising and lowering of dancers during smooth dances, the waltz in particular, that lends flow and elegance to their progress across the floor.

Rock step: A simple forward or backward step in place, accompanied by a weight shift that suggests a rocking motion.

Rumba: A slow and graceful Cuban dance done to syncopated rhythm.

Rumba breaks: A step in which the partners angle away from each other briefly in unison, to side-by-side position, while maintaining arm or hand contact.

Samba: An African dance modified in Brazil, done to fast, syncopated rhythm.

Silver: Dance competition category between Bronze and Gold.

Smooth dances: Dances that travel along line of dance, usually to slower rhythm, in which grace and precision are emphasized. Includes waltz, fox-trot, tango, Viennese waltz, and quickstep.

207

Spin turn: A turn in which the dancer rotates in fixed position on a vertical axis.

Swing: Rhythm dance, done in single, double, or triple time, featuring spins, underarm turns, and sometimes acrobatic steps.

Tango: Slow, romantic Latin dance originated in Argentina.

Triple-time swing: Swing dance in which two beats are divided into three steps.

Underarm turn: Turn in which one partner revolves beneath the raised arm of the other, maintaining hand contact.

Walk-around turn: Turn in which the dancer uses foot movement to rotate rather than spinning on an axis.

Waltz: Smooth dance in 3/4 time which turning and rise-and-fall motion are important.